"Are you always this adversarial or is this about me?" Levi asked. **"If I've offended you in some way, I'm sorry."**

Sayeh chuckled. "Don't flatter yourself. I'm always like this."

"How's that working out for you?"

"Depends on the metrics you're using to determine success. If you're asking if I have friends, not many. If you're asking how many cases I've closed, quite a few. Look, I know I'm not easy to get along with, but I have a good nose for cases. There's something about Echo's case that has my nose tingling. I'm going to go after what I know needs chasing."

"How are you still alive?" Levi asked. "You worked in the most dangerous division in the Bureau and somehow you weren't killed by your reckless attitude? Your guardian angels must've been working overtime."

"I've always walked to the beat of my own drum. I like it that way."

"I'm starting to see that. You don't find that can get a little lonely?" he asked.

"Too busy to be focused on anything else."

"So, not married?"

She cast a short look his way. "Are you hitting on me?"

Dear Reader,

As a woman with Indigenous heritage, I find the current statistics regarding violence against Indigenous women hurt my heart.

According to several nonprofit agencies working to shed light on this terrible situation, the murder rate of Indigenous women is three times higher than non-Native women. It is the third leading cause of death for Indigenous women; over 84 percent of them have experienced violence.

The time is now to end the cycle of violence.

As always, "See something, say something," and you might just save a life.

Hearing from readers is a special joy. Please feel free to find me on social media or email me at authorkvanmeter@gmail.com.

Kimberly Van Meter

COLD CASE SECRETS

KIMBERLY VAN METER

Harlequin

ROMANTIC SUSPENSE

Harlequin®
ROMANTIC SUSPENSE™

Recycling programs for this product may not exist in your area.

ISBN-13: 978-1-335-50243-8

Cold Case Secrets

Copyright © 2024 by Kimberly Sheetz

For questions and comments about the quality of this book, please contact us at CustomerService@Harlequin.com.

TM and ® are trademarks of Harlequin Enterprises ULC.

Harlequin Enterprises ULC
22 Adelaide St. West, 41st Floor
Toronto, Ontario M5H 4E3, Canada
www.Harlequin.com

Printed in Lithuania

MIX
Paper | Supporting responsible forestry
FSC® C021394

Kimberly Van Meter wrote her first book at sixteen and finally achieved publication in December 2006. She has written for the Harlequin Superromance, Blaze and Romantic Suspense lines. She and her husband of thirty years have three children, two cats, and always a houseful of friends, family and fun.

Books by Kimberly Van Meter

Harlequin Romantic Suspense

The Coltons of Owl Creek

Colton's Secret Stalker

Big Sky Justice

Danger in Big Sky Country
Her K-9 Protector
Cold Case Secrets

The Coltons of Kansas

Colton's Amnesia Target

Military Precision Heroes

Soldier for Hire
Soldier Protector

Visit the Author Profile page
at Harlequin.com for more titles.

Chapter 1

Sixteen years ago, the bruised body of Echo Flying Owl Jones, a young Macawi girl, was found partially submerged on a frigid creek bed near the Macawi Reservation in Montana.

There were no suspects, no leads, and her case was closed but, according to her aunt, never solved.

Sayeh Proudfoot Griffin aimed to change all that.

Funny thing about change, though.

Sometimes change is ushered in on a whisper, other times, a roar—and for Sayeh Proudfoot Griffin, the youngest of the Griffin sisters, a cacophony.

In the space of a year, an intruder killed her adoptive father in her childhood home, her sister Kenna narrowly escaped a psychopathic ex and her other sister, Luna, lost a best friend but found the love of her life.

And while all that was going on, Sayeh faced an Internal Affairs investigation within her department in the FBI Narcotics division and left the Bureau to take the new position on the Cold Case Task Force within the Justice Department of the BIA.

An ordinary person would probably need a long vacation, but Sayeh had never been ordinary and wasn't about to start now.

"Change is good. Change is good. Change is good," Sayeh repeated as she walked the hallway to the briefing room in the office for the Bureau of Indian Affairs located in Billings, Montana.

She'd never been known as a "people person," and starting fresh with her particular personality was a daunting prospect.

She paused, took a deep breath, lifted her chin and walked into the briefing room to meet her new team.

The task force was created due to public pressure to address the growing outrage of Indigenous people, mostly women, being victimized without consequence. The Powers That Be decided cold cases were the best use of available funds and made for good headlines if resolved. Sayeh's cynical nature saw right through the thin machinations of the PR machine at work, but if playing the game made progress happen, she'd suit up. Rusted wheels often turned with stops and starts and it took a while to get the grease.

Each member had a vested interest in seeing the task force succeed, but they were already briefed privately on what was expected of them going forward. Funding was tight, and resources were always at a premium, so failure to achieve discernible results was not an option. But Sayeh was coming to the table with a cold case worth cracking open.

At first glance, Sayeh saw their task force superior Isaac Berrigan, two Indigenous women and a broad-shouldered white man with a shock of dark hair and a set of brilliant blue eyes, which immediately took her aback.

Given the sensitive cultural nature of the cases involved, she'd assumed the task force would comprise all Indigenous people.

Don't judge a book by its cover. She didn't look as Native as her sisters with her dirty blond hair and blue eyes, while the other girls were olive complected with dark eyes. Sayeh's nickname had been "Yellow Hair" for the longest time because her hair turned golden in the summer, but her blood still ran with the Macawi heritage.

Isaac got straight to business. "Introduce yourselves, you're about to spend a lot of time together. I don't have to remind you that there's a lot of eyes on this task force right now given the current political climate. I can't say I'm not glad that the issue is finally getting the attention it deserves, but it's going to make our jobs that much harder. I don't want to sugarcoat it for you. It's going to be a hard road but hopefully, worth it."

There was no time like the present to set expectations, so let's get it going. Sayeh boldly took the lead, impatient to get started. "I'm Sayeh Proudfoot Griffin, Macawi Reservation but I was raised in Cottonwood, pleased to meet you," she said, taking a seat.

A woman with long dark hair and dark eyes nodded, introducing herself, "Dakota Foster, Flathead Reservation," and the other woman, a caramel brunette with amber eyes, followed with, "Shilah Parker, Turtle Mountain."

And then all eyes swiveled in question to the other man seated. He compressed his lips—no getting around that elephant—introducing himself, "Levi Wyatt. No Native blood but I grew up on a ranch close to the Blackfeet Reservation and my respect for the people runs deep. Happy to be part of the team."

Sayeh drew a deep breath, trying to shift against the immediate discomfort that having a white man on a BIA task force created for her. It was all well and good to have "respect" for the people, but he couldn't possibly understand the issues the Indigenous people faced.

She questioned whether or not he would be a help or a hindrance, but seeing as she wasn't in charge of the hiring, she'd have to defer to someone else's judgment—which she hated.

Breathe in, breathe out, don't say anything that'll land your ass in HR's office on the first day.

Her oldest sister's voice rang in her head, warning her to play nice. Not that she knew how to do that, but she'd give it a shot.

Isaac, a gruff older man with a dark complexion and graying curly hair, was all business. He didn't waste time with more pleasantries—something Sayeh appreciated—and got straight to the meat of the meeting.

"Great, now that we're all acquainted, we can talk about my expectations. You were hired for a reason. Each of you has something you bring to the table. You're all hard workers with top-notch investigative skills, but a few of you, you know who you are, have chafed in group settings." Was he talking about her? Sayeh kept her expression inscrutable, and he continued, "But that's in the past. We're fighting for something important. Remember that."

Sayeh's gaze darted around the table, wondering if maybe there was someone else he might've been referring to.

"Right. So, moving forward, we're looking for cold cases involving Indigenous people that have a chance of being solved. Like I said, I don't have the time or the energy to sugarcoat the truth—we need wins. There's a lot of pressure to see this task force get some newsworthy results, and lucky me, the responsibility to make sure the BIA looks good landed on my desk. We've got all eyes on us. Let's not end up with egg on our face."

Sayeh frowned. What was he saying? Isaac had all the weariness of a public servant who was too far from retirement and too in debt to quit, but the job had leached all interest from his soul. *Off to a great start*. "Be that as it may, it's about damn time someone started caring about the fact that Indigenous women are being murdered at unprecedented numbers—"

He waved away the rest of Sayeh's statement, cutting in, "Yeah, yeah, of course. You're missing the point. I'm saying there are *political* strings being pulled, which means it's not so much about the cause but what someone can use for a sound bite."

Sayeh couldn't help the tensing of her jaw as she held back a hot retort, but Isaac didn't miss a thing.

He shrugged. "Look, it is what it is, but we'll use it to do some good while we can. However, I'll put it to you straight—the minute this cause loses political or public favor, funding will dry up quicker than a mudhole in the African desert. Understand?"

So much for putting aside her natural cynicism for a fresh start. She bit down on her tongue before saying something she regretted, but she had a mouthful of opinions on the usefulness of bureaucracy.

Isaac heaved a short sigh, continuing, "I don't expect to do much hand-holding. You know what we're looking for." He gestured to the massive stack of files on the table. "There are plenty of case files in the state of Montana to go through to find your diamond in the rough. Bring me something good."

This was her chance. "Actually, I've already done some digging and found a case worth chasing down."

Isaac's gaze warmed with subtle appreciation at her initiative. "All right then, take the floor. Let's hear it."

Sayeh pulled the file from her briefcase. "Echo Flying Owl Jones, sixteen, Macawi tribe. Sixteen years ago, she was last seen at an Urgent Care, hysterical and looking as if she'd been beaten, but when the nurse returned to the room, she was gone. Two weeks later her body was found in a half-frozen creek. No suspects, no leads."

"And what makes you think it's a good fit for our first case?" Isaac asked.

"Because that sixteen-year-old girl deserves justice," Sayeh answered without hesitation. "This is exactly what we're trying to draw attention to—young Indigenous women being murdered without consequence. Someone killed Echo and for sixteen years has gotten away with it. Her young life was cut short, and she deserves justice. Her family deserves closure."

"As compelling as that is, how sure are you that it's a case we can solve?" Levi asked.

Isaac awaited her answer. Sayeh hated being questioned on her investigative instinct. She stiffened, cutting a short look at her team member. "I'm an investigator. I don't look at cases and weigh my interest based on their solvability factor."

"You better start," Isaac said. "We need to strike the balance between resources, solvability and the optics, or else this task force will become a defunct line item in the budget."

Sayeh started to defend her case when Levi asked if he could see the file. She slid the file across the table, and he scooped it up, taking a minute to skim the notes, directing a murmur at her as he read. "Former FBI, right?"

Sayeh nodded. "Narcotics."

Finished, he looked up, admitting, "Tough division," but followed with, "Here's the deal, your case tugs at the heartstrings. You'd have to have an empathy chip missing to not feel something for a case like this, but Echo's case isn't a cold case—it was solved. The original investigators concluded Echo had likely been partying and died of exposure. She had a history of running around, ditching school, et cetera. It's tragic, sure, but more of a cautionary tale than an unsolved murder."

Don't call your team member a jackass on the first day. Sayeh reined in her quick temper. "If you read between the lines, you'll see the investigators barely did any field work. They didn't even collect any forensics to support their *bad girl* theory and every year her aunt Charlene has asked for Echo's case to be reopened but no one is willing to touch it. There's something rotten about this case and all you need to do is take a whiff to smell it."

Isaac watched their exchange with a sharp eye. "Do you have something better to pitch?" he asked Levi.

"I do." Levi pulled a case file and read, "Forty-eight-year-old Crow man, Tom Sam, lived here in Billings, found dead in his bar, skull crushed. He was known to have a roving eye and a drinking problem. No suspects were named in his murder, and it remains unsolved."

"What makes this case better than Sayeh's?" Shilah piped in, curious.

"Enough forensics were taken at the scene that we could retest using more sophisticated DNA testing that wasn't available at the time of death. Seems a crime of passion, so it's likely it wasn't premeditated. Impulse kills are often sloppy and leave behind a trail. All we need is the right tools to lead us straight to the killer."

"So, just being honest, if it's between a cheating bar owner and a sixteen-year-old kid—my vote is for the kid," Shilah said. "I agree with Sayeh. Sounds like the original investigators didn't put much time or effort into the case."

"I'm not saying it's not a tragedy what happened to the

girl. I'm saying it might not be the best start for a new task force needing a win," Levi pointed out.

Isaac frowned. "You've got a point, but so does Sayeh. To be blunt, your case lacks emotional weight. It's difficult to drum up much sympathy for a man with a reputation for messing around getting whacked in the head. Hell, some might even believe he had it coming—and before you say it, yes, every victim deserves justice, but we need public support and this case just doesn't press those emotional buttons. You feel me?"

Levi disagreed, holding his ground. "The bigger picture is about solving crimes against the Indigenous people, including the men."

Pulling the sexist card is typical. Sayeh pressed. "Look, what would it hurt to do some field work? Talk to the aunt. Get a feel for the case and then decide?"

"I think the file has sufficient information. Of course the aunt is going to push to reopen the case. It's emotional for her but it shouldn't be for us. That's all I'm saying. With Tom Sam's case, we could send off the forensics and have results within a few weeks if we put a rush on it. With any luck, we could have a case solved and a person in custody before spring. That's good optics."

Sayeh narrowed her gaze—that first feeling she got from this guy? Yeah, it just intensified. "There are more than five thousand cases of missing Indigenous women and murder is the third leading cause of death. It's not *all* about the optics. It's about justice. My vote is for Echo."

Shilah and Dakota nodded in agreement.

Levi realized he was outnumbered and looked to Isaac to weigh in.

"You both make good points," Isaac said gruffly, already displeased with having to play the referee. "Sayeh, you're right, your case is meatier but could end up with a big fat zero for the team if all you catch is ghosts. Levi, your case has a better chance of getting an arrest but it's not likely to make even a ripple of public interest. Let's split the difference. Levi and Sayeh, I want you on the girl's case while Dakota and Shilah can take the dead bar owner."

"Oh, I can handle—"

Isaac cut her off, knowing where she was going. "I said what I said. Bring me results, not excuses."

Sayeh snapped her mouth shut as Isaac left the debriefing room. *Making friends already.* She appreciated Isaac's blunt style but didn't much care for being pushed into a partnership she hadn't asked for.

Rising, she grabbed the file and stuffed it in her briefcase, saying to Levi, "Listen, I'm good with chasing this down on my own if you want to help Dakota and Shilah with your case."

"Not a fan of authority, I see."

She cut him a short look, ignoring his statement. "I work better alone."

"Well, that's not an option. Isaac wants us both on this case."

Sayeh ground her teeth against the urge to say something inappropriate. Luna's voice popped into her head—*Don't go making enemies on your first day*—and she smothered the sharp quip on her tongue. "Right, I was just giving you the chance to work on the case you preferred."

"I don't have an emotional attachment to either case. I'm ready when you are."

"Are you two always going to be sniping at each other?" Dakota asked, shouldering her bag. "Because that kind of energy is disruptive. We're all on the same team, with the same goal."

This was how it always started and what she wanted to change about herself. Sayeh had a reputation in the Bureau as a lone wolf because no one wanted to work with her for long.

Was she supposed to apologize for being passionate about stuff that mattered? She didn't know the play here, but before Sayeh could respond, Dakota added, "But for what it's worth, I think you're right about this case. Too many people think Indigenous women are disposable, and they don't care what happens to them. The only way to make it stop is to go after the people responsible."

Exactly. Sayeh shot Dakota an appreciative smile for the support, even though the woman had called her out first.

Levi frowned, realizing he was putting himself on the wrong side of the argument. "Let me clarify—the case has merit," he said. "I'm just trying to keep the bigger picture in mind."

"So am I," Sayeh said. "I think we're just looking at different pictures."

"Have fun with that," Shilah quipped as she and Dakota left the debriefing room.

Okay, so change is hard. Maybe she's not cut out to play nice. *Focus on what matters.* "Echo's aunt Charlene still lives on the Macawi Reservation. I'm heading out there now."

"We can ride together."

Oh, goody, an awkward car ride. My favorite. "Suit yourself but I pick the music."

"As long as it's not country."

"Country it is," Sayeh affirmed, even though she hated country music. Some habits were hard to break. *Eh, work in progress.*

First impressions? The woman was a firecracker with a quick temper lurking behind those blue eyes. The turbulent energy roiling off her in waves was enough to knock a man over. "Quick question—are you always this adversarial or is this your reaction to something about me?" Levi asked, climbing into Sayeh's car. "If I've offended you in some way, I'm sorry."

Sayeh chuckled with dark humor, pulling her dirty blond hair into a low pony before starting the car. "Don't flatter yourself. I'm always like this."

"How's that working out for you?"

"Depends on the metrics you're using to determine success. If you're asking if I have friends, not many. If you're asking how many cases I've closed, quite a few. Look, I know I'm not easy to get along with but I have a good nose for cases. There's something about Echo's case that has my nose tingling. I guess I'm asking you to trust me but even if you don't, I'm still going to go after what I know needs chasing."

"How are you still alive?" Levi asked. "You worked in the most dangerous division in the Bureau and somehow you weren't killed by your reckless attitude? Your guardian angels must've been working overtime."

"You're not the first person to say that. My sister might've said it a time or two, actually."

"You have a sister?"

"Two."

"Are they like you?"

"Not really. I'm a limited edition." She cast a curious glance his way. "You got any family?"

"An older brother, works the ranch where I grew up."

"You said you grew up near the Blackfeet Reservation?"

"Yeah."

"Ranching life wasn't for you?"

Levi hesitated. Thinking about growing up on the ranch

brought some of his best memories, but they were tangled with moments that stung to remember. "My path went in a different direction," he finally answered.

"Each to their own. I've always walked to the beat of my own drum. I like it that way."

"I'm starting to see that about you. You don't find that can get a little lonely?" he asked.

"Too busy to be focused on anyone else," she answered.

"So, not married?"

She cast a short look his way. "Are you hitting on me?"

"No, I just like to know what I'm getting into with a partner. Like Isaac said, we're going to be working closely together. I need to factor in other considerations."

"Not married, not looking to date. I'm focused on the job. How does that sum things up for you?"

Worked for him. He preferred a focused partner—and Sayeh needn't worry about him fishing around her for a date. For one, she wasn't his type; and two, like Sayeh, he liked to stay focused. Bigger picture.

Besides, whoever said time heals all wounds was full of shit.

It'd been over a handful of years since losing Nadie to a drunk driver, and he still couldn't talk about it.

So much for healing that wound.

He studied Sayeh for a minute, testing a theory. "What would you have done if Isaac hadn't approved checking into Echo's case?"

Sayeh's slow smile answered before her mouth did.

"I'd do exactly what I'm doing now—what I feel is right."

"That's what I thought." There was something to be said for conviction, but her headstrong attitude could create problems.

Sayeh was like a wild hare, willing to chew off its foot when caught in a trap.

And that's what worried him.

Chapter 2

Sayeh firmly believed that small talk should be listed in the Geneva Convention as a verboten torture tactic.

An hour and a half drive with a stranger was pushing her limits of being able to pretend she knew how to socialize like most people.

"Not a people person, I take it?" Levi surmised after twenty minutes of silence. "Seeing as we're going to be working together, maybe we ought to get to know each other a little bit."

"Why?"

Her bald question seemed to take him by surprise. Objectively, he was a good-looking guy and probably wasn't accustomed to people being disinterested in his company. She was happy to expose him to new experiences.

"Okay, let's try again, we need to work together and that usually requires a certain level of trust—"

"I don't trust anyone I don't know and seeing as I just met you—I definitely have no reason to trust you."

"You also have no reason *not* to trust me," he countered.

Fair point. She shrugged. "I'm just not interested in making friends on the job, and creating a false sense of trust gets in the way of the investigation."

"Narcotics must've done a number on you," he said, shaking his head as if she were damaged, which she took offense to because only her sisters got to call her out on that score. "No, I get it. Working Vice, Narcotics, anything with kids, changes a person—but you got out of Narcotics for a reason, yeah? Maybe it's not smart to bring your old baggage to a new gig. Just sayin'."

"Did my sister hire you to say that to me?" Sayeh asked with dark humor. "Because that was an uncanny impression of her."

"Your sister must be a smart woman."

"She is, but she's also a pain in my ass so don't go crowing too loudly on that score. Look, I'm not the touchy-feely type. I won't ask you about your day, because I don't care. All I care about is the job. Our task force has a chance to make a difference and that's what matters—not if we're holding hands by the end of our shift. You want to know the real reason I left Narcotics? Because it never made a difference what we did out there. No matter how many perps we dragged off the streets, how many kingpins we took down—there was always ten more waiting to swoop in and take their place. It got exhausting knowing that it didn't mean a damn thing. If I'm going to put my life on the line—I want it to mean something."

Sayeh shifted against the internal discomfort of revealing too much, returning her attention to the road, hoping Levi got the hint that she was done sharing. She should've declined his offer to hitch a ride together. That's what she got for trying to be accommodating on the first day with new people.

"You've got passion," Levi said, his gaze trained out the window as they drove, watching as the wild grass bowed beneath the wind's caress beneath an unusually blue sky for this time of year. "Reminds me of myself when I was a young agent, fresh on the job."

"Yeah?" She was grudgingly curious. "What's the catch?"

"No catch. I might not have been in Narcotics but I saw enough to get jaded quick enough. I think everyone goes into this job with an idealized vision in their head about how it's going to be but then reality punches you in the gut and you're forced to adjust your expectations. I want to make a difference, too, but I'm also not blinded to the reality. Not every case has a happy ending."

"None of these cold cases have happy endings if they're already dead," Sayeh said. "What I'm looking for is *justice*—there's a difference."

"Fair enough. I'm just saying, if we want to do the most amount of good, we have to be prepared to accept that some cases aren't going to do anything but drain resources."

"And that's what you think Echo's case will do?"

He shrugged. "Not sure yet. I guess we'll see. I'm willing to keep an open mind but I'm also prepared to cut our losses."

It didn't sit right to shelve the death of a sixteen-year-old girl because the edges didn't line up nicely, but she knew he was speaking from an analytical point of view—something she had zero talent in doing.

During her time in Narcotics, her hot head was her biggest Achilles' heel, one her supervisors were constantly harping on her about, but her ability to drive that emotion into action worked in her favor. One thing that couldn't be disputed—her stats.

Probably why she lasted as long as she had in the Bureau, but that's not to say that the BIA would have the same opinion.

Better to throttle down her natural inclination to tell everyone to piss off when they didn't want to do things her way than lose a chance to make a real difference.

"Did you know the victim?" he asked.

"No."

"How'd you come across this case?"

"Dumb luck." She pulled off the main highway onto the lonely dirt road into Macawi territory. The reservation was large, sprawling across two million acres through Montana. Echo's aunt Charlene lived outside of the reservation proper, like many tribal members, in an old trailer that was held together with rust and duct tape. "I've recently been spending more time at the reservation for personal reasons, and when talking to the tribal chief, Echo's aunt Charlene came in to try to get the chief to reopen Echo's case."

"So, you've already talked to the aunt?"

"Briefly. Nothing official. Just enough to pique my interest and start poking around on my own time. When I got the job with the BIA, I pulled the files so I'd have something to present at the meeting."

"Smart to come to the meeting with a case already primed."

"Thanks. I guess you were smart to do the same."

"I knew Isaac was looking for closable cases so I used that as my compass. Even though it's not as compelling as yours, I'm willing to bet it'll close before yours."

She couldn't deny he might be right, but she didn't care. She wanted justice for Echo and would get it—one way or another.

Sayeh fascinated him. She would be a challenge as a partner, but he respected her sharp intellect, even if that intellect came with claws. She might not want to let anyone in, but she must learn to trust her team if they hoped to make the task force successful.

And he was going to have to find a way to reach her.

There was a desolate beauty to the reservation, nestled in the south-central portion of Montana with miles of rolling plains backing up to ancient sloping ridges.

Early spring in Montana still retained a bite to the air. Even though the hills were just starting to sprout with tender green shoots, the threat of snow was never far from the forecast.

They followed a lonely dirt road through nature's untouched beauty. The whisper of cottonwood trees called out to them as they passed through the Macawi proper and drove the distance to where Echo's aunt Charlene lived.

Life on the reservation was hard—resources were always in short supply. It was much the same at every reservation in the States. His family's ranch bordered the Blackfeet nation, and he'd seen the ravages of poverty and generational trauma firsthand. His fiancée, Nadie, had been proudly Siksika, and he'd learned much through her. He missed her gentle guidance and the way she'd had of giving him a look that told him he was being an ass. Nothing about life was fair, that was for damn sure.

People clung to the only lifestyle they knew, but a thread of cultural pride ran through the land that Levi couldn't help but respect.

The car rolled slowly over gravel as Sayeh pulled into the driveway. A small beat-up rusted tin can of a trailer perched on an uneven foundation. It was a miracle it wasn't condemned. Yet, in defiance of that abject poverty, a row of potted petunias faced the sun, drinking in the rays and spreading joy with their brilliant petals.

An older woman with skin burnished by years in the sun

opened the door, eager to meet them. Her grateful smile created crinkles around her eyes as she ushered them into her home.

In spite of its outward appearance, the trailer was tended with love and attention to create a homey vibe. Fresh plants crowded the living room and spilled off into the tiny kitchen, but it smelled like green growing things and vibrated with life. A framed picture of a beautiful young girl took center stage in the room, almost like a shrine, and he knew it must be Echo.

Sayeh claimed not to be a people person, but her demeanor instantly softened around the elderly woman.

"Hello, Auntie, thank you for meeting with us today. This is my partner, Levi Wyatt. We're here to get some more information about Echo's case. Do you mind sharing details?"

"I'd be happy to have someone finally listen," Charlene said, her eyes welling. "For sixteen years, my sweet Echo has gone without justice, and I don't know how much longer I'll be around to bang the drums. I hope you can find who did this terrible thing and make them pay for their sin."

"That's what we want, too," Sayeh assured the woman, pulling out her phone and explaining, "If you don't mind, I'm going to record our conversation so I don't miss anything. Are you okay with that?"

"Anything that helps is fine with me," Charlene said with a resolute nod. "I might be old but I don't mind the convenience of technology."

"We appreciate the opportunity to learn more about what happened. The tribal police reports don't leave much to go off from," Levi said.

Charlene's expression wrinkled with distaste. "Corrupt and crooked, all with their hand out to look the other way.

There are good people and there are terrible people out there running things for the tribe and I can't say nothing good about the old tribal police chief."

"How do you feel about the new chief? Joe Dawes?" Sayeh asked.

Charlene shrugged as if Dawes was fine but hadn't been much help. "He doesn't believe my Echo was murdered. He thinks she was a wild spirit that got carried away."

"Was she?" Levi asked, earning a subtle scowl from Sayeh.

But Charlene didn't flinch, meeting Levi's stare. "My girl was spirited and she made some wrong decisions but she wasn't reckless. She knew better than to stay out all night when it's storming like it was. She always came home."

"You raised Echo? Where were her parents?" Levi asked.

"My sister died when Echo was three. There was no one else to take her in so I did without question. I never had kids of my own so Echo slid into that spot like she was meant to be there. I couldn't love her more than if I'd grown her myself."

Something flickered across Sayeh's expression, but she pushed on. "The report said that Echo went to the Urgent Care for cuts and bruises… Did you see Echo before she went to the medical center?"

Charlene shook her head woefully. "If I'd known, I would've made her tell me who hurt her. I didn't even know she'd been to the Urgent Care until a few days later when I kept pestering that old chief to go look for her. He's the one who said she'd shown up at the clinic smelling like booze and making a racket before taking off in the night. I don't believe that for a second and I told him that straight to his face."

"According to Echo's file, she'd been cited a few times

for underage alcohol possession," Levi reminded Charlene. "Is it possible the chief was telling the truth?"

"No," Charlene returned flatly, daring Levi to question her belief.

Sayeh shot Levi a look and took over. "Was Echo seeing anyone at the time?"

Charlene sighed, admitting with a slight frown of regret pinching her forehead, "There was a boy, but she never brought him around. I didn't even know his name. She was real private about that stuff, and I didn't want to push my nose into her business. I just told her to be smart about it. I had plans to get her to the clinic for birth control, but I never got the chance to follow through." A tear slipped free, and Charlene wiped it away with a weathered hand, sniffing back the rest. "When you get to be my age, you realize there are a whole lot of things you could've and should've done, but there isn't much that can be done about nothing that's in the past."

Sayeh was sympathetic as she asked, "Is there any way we could find out who Echo was dating? Any friends of Echo's who might know?"

Charlene sniffed again, pausing to grab a tissue. "It's been so long since I knew any of them kids that she used to run with. Many have left the reservation, looking for better opportunities, not that I blame them. Not much to keep the young ones around anymore. No jobs, no way to make money unless it's illegal. You hardly can't fault no one for doing things wrong if it's the only way to put food on the table."

It was an ugly catch-22 that caught a lot of people in the endless loop of crime and poverty. Levi knew there weren't easy answers to the problem, but being on the other end of that equation was also challenging.

"Any name might help," Sayeh pressed. "We'll do the chasing. Someone might remember something."

Charlene nodded, taking a moment to search her memory. "Well, she was real close to a girl named Yazzie—Yazmine King, I think that was her name—but I'm pretty sure she moved away after she graduated."

Levi jotted down the name. "We'll look into it. Anyone else?"

"Well, I know she was real close to another kid, a boy named Chaska Johnson, called him Chaz, but he went down a bad path. Last I heard, he was in prison. Can't remember where, though."

Charlene's heavy sigh told a story Levi was familiar with. He saw a lot of young men spiraling into bad choices when stunted potential turned sour. Addiction issues continued to plague the Indigenous people, now more than ever.

"Echo left that Urgent Care and then her body wasn't found until two weeks later in a half-frozen creek bed nowhere near anywhere Echo would have reason to be. Now, tell me how that makes any sense? Someone hurt my girl—and got away with it. Why doesn't anyone care?"

"We care," Sayeh assured her, reaching out to gently clasp the older woman's hand. "I promise we're going to do everything in our power to find out what happened to Echo."

Levi didn't like making promises to victims' families, but it was hard to be unaffected by the palpable grief and frustration. Even if the answer was exactly as the report stated, closure would be worth the effort. Echo deserved a true investigation, not the shoddy half-ass job she was given—in that he agreed with Sayeh.

"Is there anything else you can remember that might help point us in the right direction?" he asked.

"Echo was a strong-willed girl. Too smart for school. When she got bored, she got into trouble but nothing mean-spirited. She always stuck up for the underdog, and helped anyone who needed it. She was a good girl with a big heart," Charlene shared, her voice cracking at the end. "And I miss her bad."

Levi felt a lump in his throat. Losing a child was never easy. Losing a child the way Charlene had lost Echo? He couldn't imagine.

Sayeh rose, signaling the end of the interview, promising to be in touch. "One way or another, we'll let you know what we find out."

"Thank you for listening," Charlene said, walking them out. "I know Great Spirit will guide you to the answers. I can feel it."

Sayeh's short smile made Levi wonder where her personal beliefs landed, but he knew better than to ask. She barely tolerated sharing a vehicle; she wasn't about to share her belief structure.

The fact that he was curious made him shut that door real quick.

The last thing he needed was anything more than a professional interest in a prickly partner.

He had his hands full with that alone.

Chapter 3

Thoughts raced through Sayeh's mind as they left Charlene's house. Before her behind hit the seat, she was talking about the next step.

"We need to find her friend Yazzie and follow up on the boy, too. Kids may keep their parents in the dark but their friends always know what's happening. I'll bet Yazzie knows exactly who Echo was dating and there must be a reason why Charlene didn't know the kid's name. A reason to hide the fact that they were dating."

"You thinking someone older?"

"Definitely thinking that. You saw Echo's picture on the table—beautiful Native girl with a wild streak? Men of all ages would've been swarming all around her—probably even before she was old enough to understand what was happening."

"Speaking from experience?"

Sayeh cut him a short look. "You could say that." She pulled out of the driveway and returned to the road. "Me and my sisters all got chased by shitty men at one point or another. They learned real quick that I don't play like that and I don't have a problem defending myself. My sister Kenna, on the other hand, is sweeter than me and her ex nearly killed her."

"I'm sorry," Levi murmured. "Is she okay?"

"Yeah, she's doing great now. Hooked up with the local K-9 cop and he treats her like a queen, but it could've ended real bad and she would've ended up another statistic like Echo's case."

"I need you to level with me," Levi said. "Is this case personal to you? Because I'm getting a vibe that it is—and if that's the case…that worries me."

Anyone else might've danced around admitting emotional ties, but she didn't flinch or try to deny it. "Of course it's personal and it should be. Maybe the problem is maybe it hasn't been personal enough. People need to care. I'm a Native woman. Why wouldn't it be personal when another Native female is victimized, not only by another human but then again by the system. You're goddamn right it's personal, and I won't be made to feel like I'm doing something wrong by caring."

"I'm not saying you shouldn't care," he returned gravely.

"Sure sounds like it."

"You and I both know that emotion gets in the way of objective thinking," he said, shaking his head.

"Says you. Maybe being emotional about a case gives a person that extra fire needed to keep pushing when it feels hopeless. Dedication—passion—obsession—they're all powered by *emotion*. Tell me I'm wrong."

He couldn't, but his gaze narrowed as if he still didn't agree with her viewpoint, which was fine. He had the right to be wrong as long as he didn't get in her way.

Still, it would be better if they could find common ground. She'd spent her career fighting her own team at the Bureau. She wasn't keen on making the same mistakes with her new team.

"Tell me right now that you didn't get the feeling that

more could've been done for Echo's case." When Levi didn't deny it, she continued, "Exactly. And why is that? Immediately something felt shady, and if something's shady, that means someone is trying to hide the facts. If Echo was truly just a case of a wayward kid who was reckless and ended up dead by natural causes, the facts would've held up the story, but we don't know that because the investigation—if you can call it that—was done quick and sloppy. And why is that? Because it was a Native woman. Plain and simple. Facts are facts—even when they're ugly."

Levi blew out a long breath, digesting her statement. She could tell he was chewing on a rebuttal but held back because she'd made her point, and he was smart enough to know when to cede the argument. She'd give him that. Some people, like the jackass at the Bureau who'd earned an up close and personal meeting with her fist, didn't know when to quit and doubled down on their crappy position.

"It was definitely lazy investigating," he agreed. "The poor kid deserved more."

Mollified, Sayeh throttled down a notch. "Look, I understand where you're coming from. We all want the task force to succeed. If I think Echo's case is going nowhere or it feels like my instincts were wrong, I'll cut the loss. But we're not there yet, okay?"

Levi nodded, accepting her terms, grudgingly admitting, "I suppose making it personal, as long as it doesn't impede your investigative instinct, isn't always a bad thing."

It took a minute to let the vinegar leach from her system. She was so used to fighting tooth and nail for every victory that it felt odd to reach an accord so quickly.

Her saving grace was the knowledge they didn't have time to mess around with grudges. Sayeh believed in giving people enough rope to hang themselves. Either Levi was being sincere, or he wasn't. She'd have her answer either way, but it wouldn't change what she'd come to do.

To his credit, Levi switched gears just as smoothly. "Since we're here, we should pop back into the tribal station and see what we can get with the new information. Chief Dawes will probably be able to locate Chaska Johnson in his system."

Pleased and a little impressed, Sayeh agreed. "My thoughts, too. If he was busted on drug offenses, he might not even still be incarcerated."

Levi nodded. "Either way, Chief Dawes might have some insight. The kid might still have family around here, too."

"Quite possible. It's hard to leave the reservation when there aren't many opportunities."

Sayeh felt a familiar pinch. She and her sisters were born on the Macawi Reservation, but they'd grown up in the comfort of a stable home with loving adoptive parents in the neighboring town of Cottonwood. She'd always felt disconnected from her adoptive family—she and her dad had always butted heads from the start—and discovering the details of her biological parents' deaths had only heightened her need to find a genuine connection.

Let's just say, finding out that your biological parents may've actually been murdered instead of dying in a chemical explosion had a way of messing with your head—and to add a little spice, their murder was likely covered up because no one cared to ask the right questions.

Well, she was asking the right questions now—*talk about being unpopular*. No one seemed eager to poke at that sleeping bear but she was in too deep to stop. Not that she would, anyway. Running a parallel investigation on her own time was expensive, time-consuming and exhausting, but she wasn't going to quit until she had answers.

However, she couldn't ignore the privilege she'd enjoyed of never knowing hunger, wondering where her next meal would come from or worrying about her parents' ability to pay for her extracurricular activities.

Life would've been much different if she and her sisters had stayed on the reservation.

"How'd you get into law enforcement?" Levi asked, curious.

It was on the tip of her tongue to decline sharing personal information, but another bit of advice her sister Luna had given her was to be open to trusting new people—as if that were the easiest thing to do.

Sayeh wanted to be part of a team, even if she hadn't a clue how to do that and it went against her very nature.

"I...went to college, got a degree in criminal justice and then realized that I didn't want to be a beat cop or work my way up the ranks to admin so I took a shot at the Bureau. It might've been dumb luck—or the fact that I tested crazy high—but I got in. Worked my way up to field agent pretty quick and then seemed to have a nose for sniffing out bad guys. My supervisor called my intuition *uncanny* and sometimes I wasn't sure if that was a compliment. I think it freaked him out but it got results."

"I've never known a supervisor to take issue with something that works," Levi said with a small smile.

She chuckled. "Yeah, he liked the results but definitely didn't care for my personality style—or the fact that my tolerance for bullshit was practically nonexistent."

"Nothing wrong with being a straight shooter," Levi said, shrugging. "It's refreshing if you ask me."

"We'll see how refreshing you find it when I'm calling you out on something," Sayeh quipped with dark humor.

"It's all fun and games until shit gets real. That's been my experience, anyway."

"I guess we'll just have to see how it shakes out," Levi said, but he wasn't pressed or bothered by her statement. Maybe he was the real deal. Time would tell.

They pulled up to the tribal police station and went inside.

The tiny office was barely big enough to qualify as an official agency. It had the look of a place time had forgotten. Everything was dusty, old and past its expiration date. A single uniformed officer looked up from the crossword in his hand with a questioning expression. "Can I help you?"

Sayeh didn't recognize the young man from her previous visits and introduced herself along with Levi. "Sayeh Griffin and Levi Wyatt. We're part of the newly formed BIA task force looking into a cold case from your jurisdiction."

"Nice to meet you. I'm Officer Russell Hawkins."

"Likewise. Is Chief Dawes around?"

"He stepped out to get a bite to eat. You can't beat the fresh fry bread down at The Truck. He ought to be back in a few minutes. Anything I can help you with?"

"Maybe. We need information on a man named Chaska Johnson, went by the name—"

"You mean Chaz?" the man interjected.

"Yes, that was his nickname," Levi confirmed. "You know him?"

"Yeah, I mean, we weren't friends or anything but we went to school together. Tough break what happened to him."

"What do you mean?" Sayeh asked.

"He died in prison. Took a shiv to the liver, bled out in minutes. Poor bastard never had a chance."

Sayeh shared a sharply disappointed look with Levi. "That's too bad. Where was he incarcerated?"

"Montana State Prison."

"Can you pull up his record?" Levi asked.

"Yeah, sure," he said, firing up the computer. "It'll take a second… This old thing is powered by a hamster chasing a piece of cheese. We're hoping to get a rural grant for new equipment but it's slow going getting the grants filed and all that. Joe's doing better than our last chief but none of us are what you'd call real tech-savvy."

Sayeh chuckled. "No worries. We can wait."

"So why you looking into Chaz?" the man asked, curious.

"He was friends with our victim, Echo Flying Owl Jones," Sayeh answered.

"Echo. Man, I haven't heard that name in forever." He whistled. "That was a real tragedy."

"Were you friends?"

"With Echo? No, she wasn't interested in someone like me. I remember how pretty she was, though. I think every boy in our grade had a crush on Echo at some point or another."

That was interesting information. "Do you know who Echo was dating at the time?"

"No one at our school, that's for sure. Honestly, when her body turned up in that creek, it sent a shock wave through the reservation. Echo had a wild streak, sure, but she wasn't a partier like that…but I guess all it takes is one stupid mistake to lose it all. Alcohol and below-freezing temps don't mix."

"Did you know her best friend, Yazmine King?" Levi asked.

"Yeah, if you grow up on the reservation and you're around the same age, you pretty much know everyone.

Yazzie took Echo's death real hard. She left as soon as she was able and I don't think she's been back since."

Just then, the door opened and Chief Dawes walked in carrying two plates loaded with fry bread topped with taco fixings. His expression went from focused on lunch to surprised. "Sayeh? What brings you here?"

"Hey, Joe, good to see you. This is my partner, Levi Wyatt. We're actually here on official business. Can we talk in your office?"

"Yeah, sure," he said, handing Russell his lunch plate and gesturing for them to follow him into the cramped office. He placed his plate down and settled behind the desk. "You mind if I eat while we talk? I'm starved."

"Be my guest," Sayeh said. "It's a sin to let good fry bread get cold."

Joe grinned in agreement. "Amen to that, sister."

"We're investigating the cold case of Echo Flying Owl Jones," Sayeh shared.

Joe's immediately puzzled expression wasn't a surprise, and she was prepared for any pushback. "Echo? That case was closed years ago." He shook his head as he wiped his mouth. "I had a feeling that you were going to start poking at that bear the minute you heard Charlene talk. Look, I feel for her, I really do, it was a terrible tragedy what happened to Echo—way too young to pass like that—but it was an accident. Plain and simple. It's not often we can say that when girls end up dead but it's what happened. She passed out from alcohol consumption and died from exposure. That night the temperatures were below freezing."

"I'm aware of the report. Can I be frank?" At Joe's nod, she said, "The investigation—if you can call it that—was shoddy as hell. No one asked any questions about why the poor girl had been at the Urgent Care prior to her disappearance, looking beat-up and scared. There's not a single mention of any follow-up on that angle. Not to mention, there's no report of any interviews of her friends at the time, Yazmine King and Chaska Johnson."

Joe couldn't deny it, nodding with regret as if suddenly remembering those details. "I was just a young officer at the time, too green to question the chief's handling of the case, but I remember suggesting we ought to talk to her friends. The old chief didn't think it was necessary and shut me down."

"You didn't think that was suspicious?" Levi asked.

Joe sighed, a little embarrassed. "Yeah, a little, but Echo did have a history of mischief and it didn't seem far-fetched that she could've gotten herself in trouble like that. I guess I was too unsure of myself to press the issue. I didn't want to make waves, being so new. Maybe I should've pressed harder."

"Well, there's no time like the present," Sayeh said. "We talked to Charlene a bit ago. She seemed to think Echo was dating someone at the time when she died but she didn't know who. We think Yazzie might've known."

"Maybe so," Joe said, doing a quick search in the system. "Let's see… Yazmine King. Looks like her last known address is in Great Falls." He scribbled the address and slid it over to Sayeh. "Can't say that's where she's still at but it's a start."

Sayeh appreciated the effort. Joe had always been helpful when she was asking questions about her birth parents, even when it'd brought up the sore spot of the drug network that'd operated on the reservation.

"How's Luna?"

"Great," Sayeh answered with a short grin, pocketing the slip of paper. "She spends most of her free time riding up and down the state with her boyfriend, Ben. They're like teenagers. It's a little gross but cute."

"Good for them. She deserves a good man after everything that went down."

She caught the quizzical look from Levi, knowing he was probably scratching his head at all the inside talk. "Anything else you might be able to share?"

"Can't think of anything offhand but if I do, I know where to find you."

"Thanks," Sayeh said, nodding to Levi. "We better hit the road. I don't trust those storm clouds on the horizon."

"Oh, yeah, it's supposed to rain pretty good tonight. You'd better get back to Billings before it gets here."

They climbed back into the car, and Levi asked, "You know the tribal police chief?"

"Not exactly. A little over a year and a half ago, I did some digging into the deaths of my birth parents here on the reservation. Joe helped me out. He's a decent man, just trying to do some good for his people, but I can't say his predecessors were cut from the same cloth."

"Corrupt?"

"Yeah, money is a great motivator," Sayeh said. "And for some, being king in Hell was preferable to being a servant in Heaven."

Levi nodded. "I can't help but ask, what happened to your parents? I understand if that's too personal."

"It is personal," Sayeh returned, but she relented. "My biological parents were involved with a drug operation that ran through the reservation when me and my sisters were young. I was only two when they died. I don't remember anything about my time spent on the reservation but I've since learned that it's likely that my parents were murdered to protect secrets involved with the drug operation."

"That's heavy," he murmured, appreciating the gravity of her revelation. "What made you want to dig into the past?"

"I had time on my hands," she admitted. "Actually, I'm not trying to hide anything but my time with the Bureau wasn't without its challenges. I was cleared of any wrong-doing but I was the subject of an Internal Affairs investigation."

"Why?"

"A colleague got handsy with me. I warned him—he didn't listen—and I knocked his lights out. Seemed pretty justifiable to me but there's all sorts of rules about violence in the workforce."

He surprised her with a chuckle, admitting, "Seems like he got what he deserved if you ask me."

"Yeah, that's how I felt, too." The unfamiliar tug of a smile caught her by surprise. She didn't know how to adjust to having a partner that wasn't up her ass all the time. "Anyway, the timing was perfect—or terrible, depending on how you look at it—because at the same time I was put on administrative leave, my apartment building had to be evacuated for some kind of major maintenance ordered by the city, which sent me home for a few weeks. Me and my adoptive father… Well, we were always at odds, and I needed something to occupy my mind. One thing led to another, and the next thing I knew, I stumbled on more questions than answers. I couldn't resist pulling at that thread—and here we are."

"Still pulling on that thread?"

"Yeah. It's been harder than I thought it would be, uncovering answers to a decades' long case that no one seems interested in poking into."

"Sounds like Echo's case."

She chuckled, realizing there were similarities. "I guess so. I hadn't thought of it from that angle. The difference being my biological mother was an adult when she made her choices. Good or bad, she was old enough to know what she was getting into. I don't think that's what happened with Echo. She was just a kid. Maybe even a kid who thought she was in love."

Levi fell silent, digesting everything that'd been shared. The silence felt easy between them, another shocking difference for Sayeh.

Maybe working with Levi wouldn't be the nail in the foot she thought it would be.

Maybe.

Chapter 4

The ride back to Billings was relatively quiet as they took their time to process the facts they had just learned. Levi appreciated Sayeh didn't feel the need to fill the silence with noise, including music. Sometimes he needed silence to mull things over, and extraneous sounds created an unnecessary distraction.

He was curious about her parents' past, but he didn't push further than he sensed she was willing to share. Sayeh reminded him of a mare back at his parents' ranch. If given half a chance, that mare would've taken a chunk out of your arm, and before his parents acquired the horse, she'd gained a reputation for being a problem. She'd been headed to the glue factory if his mom hadn't taken a shine to the chestnut mare.

But the funny thing about that mare…once she realized she was safe and no one was out to hurt her, she was the best horse on the ranch. Definitely his mama's favorite.

That horse taught Levi to not take everything at face value, to dig a little deeper before rendering judgment, but he would be lying if he didn't have some reservations about Sayeh's methods.

The day was nearly over, but Levi wanted to transfer some notes to his work computer before heading home.

When they got to the office, he suggested checking in with the team since they were all still there.

"Why?" Sayeh asked, confused.

"We're still getting to know each other as a team. Even though we're running different cases, it would do some good to keep connecting with each other."

Sayeh's dubious expression told him she found that consideration beneath her focus, but she followed him into the debriefing room, where Shilah and Dakota discussed notes.

They looked up as Levi and Sayeh entered the room, pausing to ask about their findings.

"So, you find anything worth chasing after?" Shilah asked.

"You first," Sayeh countered. "I'm dying to know whether or not the philandering bar owner was a victim of his wandering eye."

Shilah chuckled. "He wasn't real liked, that's for sure."

Dakota smirked in agreement. "Hard pressed to find a more disagreeable victim. It's hard to remember that every victim deserves justice when the victim is a real asshole."

It felt wrong to laugh when talking about a dead guy's unfortunate end, but you got jaded in this line of business, maybe just to save your sanity. In mock defense, Levi lifted his hands in surrender. "I never said he was in the running for Man of the Year."

"That he definitely wasn't," Dakota agreed. "We talked to his widow—she wasn't real happy to talk to us, either—and his business partner, also not happy to talk to us. All in all, no one seems to care that Tom Sam isn't on this plane anymore."

"Sounds like people with motive," Levi suggested. "They got alibis for the night the victim died?"

"Working on it," Dakota said. "Like I said, no one was

super happy to dig up the past when it comes to this guy. Roving eyes and hands, alcoholic, and suspected of skimming from the till—this guy was living fast and loose with zero cares given as to where he might end up in the afterlife."

Levi caught the subtle smirk from Sayeh even though she remained quiet. As he said, he knew the guy wasn't winning personality awards, but finding who was responsible for his death was possible. "Something will turn up. Doesn't sound like the murder was a sophisticated event. Smash and go, crime of passion, likely."

"Maybe. We'll see. Okay, how about you?" Shilah asked, lobbing the question back at them.

Levi already knew that Sayeh identified with the "lone wolf" syndrome, so sharing case details wasn't high on her list of "Things We Love," but she grudgingly participated.

"We managed to talk to the aunt and the current tribal police chief. We've got some leads to chase down—it's possible Echo was dating an older man but there's some secrecy around his identity, and that seems suspect to me—so we're heading to Great Falls tomorrow."

Dakota asked, "What makes you think she was dating an older guy?"

"If not older, definitely someone who Echo didn't want anyone to know she was dating," Sayeh said. "Either way, I want to know who she was dating. That'll give us more information as to why it was a secret."

Shilah swiveled in her office chair, chuckling ruefully. "Man, I remember being young and thinking the attention of an older guy was such a flex. Now I know it was predatory, but young girls…sometimes they unknowingly walk straight into the lion's den."

Sayeh nodded. "And in my experience, anyone that you

need to keep secret from your loved ones…isn't worth having around."

"No lies detected," Dakota quipped, shaking her head. "Well, keep us in the loop. Tomorrow we get to interview a former lover of our vic. Should be interesting. Ten bucks says this woman has nothing nice to say about our dearly departed."

Sayeh cracked a small smile. "I'd take those odds."

Levi left Dakota and Shilah in the debriefing room, detouring to his own office to finish his notes.

He was surprised when Sayeh poked her head in, lingering for a minute. "Hey, I just wanted to say…you weren't half bad today. I mean, the jury's still out for the final verdict but *today*—yeah, you were okay. I didn't feel the overwhelming need to jump out of the moving vehicle, which is saying something."

High praise. He smiled. "Thanks. You weren't bad, either. Great Falls is three hours from here. 0800 tomorrow?"

"Yeah, sounds good. Maybe I'll even let you drive."

He chuckled, shrugging. "I don't mind being driven. Makes me feel important. I'll tell you what, if you drive, I'll pick up the coffee. How do you take your poison?"

"Strong black hot tea—not that disgusting green stuff—no sugar, two lemon slices."

"Noted."

Sayeh softly rapped the door frame three times with her knuckles and pushed off. "Okay, then, g'night."

Levi ducked his head and waved, returning to his notes, but his thoughts remained on Sayeh.

The saying "still waters run deep" came to mind. Sayeh didn't reveal much, but he knew below the surface churned an undercurrent that could suck a man under.

He wished he could say he had zero interest in discovering what lay beneath, but he was intrigued—almost against his will. Sayeh wasn't the kind of woman that invited casual curiosity, and he wasn't the kind of man who indulged in that kind of thing, anyway.

After losing Nadie, he was sure his heart was numb to anything beyond professional courtesy, but there was something about Sayeh that prodded at that cold lump of muscle in his chest, trying to see if anything could make it jump alive.

Hell, an ungainly and ill-timed interest in the world's most prickly woman wasn't on his agenda.

Unless tanking his career was on his bucket list.

Still, Sayeh was intriguing.

And he'd leave it at that.

Driving had always been her way of organizing her thoughts. There was something about the road that put things in perspective in ways sitting at a desk never could.

Thank God Levi wasn't the kind of person who fidgeted beneath the weight of silence. She'd been cringing, waiting for the inevitable moment when he flipped on the radio or started chattering away during the drive back to Billings.

But he'd seemed content to watch the scenery, absorbed in his thoughts, too.

She'd give him points for that.

Sayeh walked into her Billings apartment, the smell of new paint still lingering in the air, and dropped her keys in the bowl by the door, locking the dead bolt and the chain immediately after.

She didn't know anyone who worked in any law enforcement sector who didn't believe in good locks, which was a vast difference from her childhood upbringing.

Growing up, her parents never locked up the house,

trusting their neighbors to watch out for each other and feeling secure in their community.

A lump rose in her throat at the memory of her dad.

It seemed like a sick twist of irony that an intruder killed him in his own house last year.

But Cottonwood was changing. It wasn't the town she grew up in, which was probably to be expected, but you couldn't help but wish for the days when life was much more straightforward.

She was impressed that despite everything Luna had been through, she decided to remain a Cottonwood cop. No one would've begrudged the decision to retire, but Luna still enjoyed the job. Speaking of, Sayeh's cell phone chirped to life just as she grabbed a beer and cracked it open. Dropping onto the sofa, she answered on the second ring.

"Are your ears burning?" Sayeh teased. "I was just thinking about you."

"I was going to wait for you to call me but I couldn't take it anymore. How was your first day on the new job?"

"Decent."

"And?"

"And what?"

"Did you make any friends?" Luna asked with the exasperation of a parent trying to pull information out of a teenager.

Sayeh responded in kind. "Gee, Mom, it's only the first day. Give me some time."

Luna laughed. "No, seriously, though, what do you think of your team?"

"I think they're okay, no one stands out as particularly annoying yet."

"That's a good sign," Luna said. "Promising start."

Sayeh agreed. "Actually, you'll be happy to hear that I took your advice."

Luna was interested immediately. "Oh, yeah? Which advice is that? Because I gave you a lot."

Sayeh rolled her eyes. "Yeah, you did. You act like I'm incapable of being around other human beings."

Luna was unapologetic. "Being a people person isn't one of your strengths."

Okay, valid point, but Sayeh was proud of how she handled herself today. And seeing as Luna was the only person who would understand how hard it was for her to go against her nature, she wanted to share.

"So, my team is small, but tentatively, I can say they seem like cool people. Two of the women—Shilah and Dakota— are Indigenous, which I think is appropriate given we're tasked with solving cold cases involving Native people, and the other is a man named Levi. Even though he's as white as sourdough toast, it seems like I'll be able to work with him. I mean, he didn't make me want to go back in time and snuff out his ancestors so that's a good sign."

"Sayeh…" Luna warned, and Sayeh could almost see her sister shaking her head. "I can't believe you just said that."

Sayeh chuckled, accepting her sister's judgment with good humor. "Anyway, tomorrow we're heading to Great Falls to chase down a lead."

"Anything you can talk about?"

"Nothing much to tell yet but I think there's something behind whoever Echo was dating at the time of her death. It's suspicious that she didn't want anyone to know who her boyfriend was."

Luna agreed. "Secret relationships never bode well."

"My thoughts exactly. Remember when Taryn Stillwater

was supposedly dating that college boy no one had ever heard of?"

"Yeah, and it turned out her *college* boyfriend was actually a married forty-year-old man she'd met on a teen chatting site," Luna recalled. "That was some cringy stuff."

"At least her cringy, inappropriate boyfriend didn't end up killing her," Sayeh said derisively.

Luna agreed with an "mmm-hmm" sound because they both knew how those situations could go sidewise. "I'm pretty sure that guy did some time for having an inappropriate relationship with a minor and now he has to register as a sex offender."

"Serves him right. I hope his wife took him to the cleaners, too."

"If I'm remembering correctly, she actually stood by him, choosing to believe that Taryn was some kind of Lolita who seduced her poor husband."

Sayeh shook her head in disgust. "I guess it's hard to swallow that your husband is a pervy predator. Much easier to believe that a shy teenage girl is some kind of seductress."

"Yep. Denial is a powerful thing."

That was something she was familiar with. The thing about being in law enforcement at any level, it can wear down your faith in humanity because you see people at their worst.

"How's the apartment?"

"Small but functional," Sayeh answered, her gaze wandering the tight space, snagging on the unpacked boxes stacked against the living room wall. The ink was still fresh on the lease agreement, but now that she was working in Billings, staying in Cottonwood didn't make sense, even though it'd been nice not having a rent payment. "You still thinking of selling the house?"

"Maybe. I go back and forth. Ben thinks I should wait a bit longer, see if the housing market will stabilize, but for years the place has been paid for so anything we sell it for will be all profit."

"Yeah," Sayeh murmured, unsure how she felt about someone else living in their childhood home. Even though any money made from the sale would be split three ways, she and Kenna agreed to let Luna decide because she'd spent most of the time helping their dad out when he needed it. "How's Kenna?"

Luna was happy to switch gears. Talking about selling the house was a tough subject for all of them. "Doing great! I love seeing her so happy. She deserves it. Ty absolutely killed it on his first year with the ski team. I'm so proud of how far he's come."

Their nephew had a bit of a rough patch, but he was back on track, and for that, they were all grateful. He was a great kid, but trauma had a way of messing up even the sweetest hearts.

It went without saying that they wanted their sister to be happy, but after what Kenna and Ty went through last year with that psycho ex of hers, as far as Sayeh was concerned, they deserved nothing but blue skies and butterflies from here on out.

After a bit more chitchat, Sayeh's social battery was about empty, but Luna understood, and they said their goodbyes.

Before the shit show their family experienced last year, Sayeh's relationship with her sisters had been distanced. Mostly she'd found Luna to be overbearing and bossy, and Kenna, while less so, had been wrapped up in her own life, going MIA due to that aforementioned psycho ex.

It made Sayeh sick to her stomach that she hadn't pressed

harder to find out why Kenna hadn't kept in touch with her family for so many years, but Sayeh had been self-absorbed in her own troubles.

Some of which had been of her own making.

She understood that now, so she was determined to do things differently this time.

She just had to remember to get out of her own way.

Chapter 5

Rising with the sun, they started the drive to Great Falls in easy silence. Levi sipped from a large take-out cup of coffee while Sayeh nursed a hot cup of tea with lemon. She glanced at his coffee, curious. "So, how do you drink your coffee?"

He took a sip before answering. "With lots of flavored creamer to cut back the bitterness. I don't actually like the taste of coffee but I can't function without the jolt of caffeine."

She laughed at his answer. "Why not try tea?"

Levi shook his head. "Not a fan of that, either."

"Have you ever tried chai?"

He nodded slightly, and the faintest hint of a smile touched his lips. "Uh, yeah, once or twice. It was my fiancée's drink of choice."

Was? As in past tense?

Sayeh pulled her gaze away from Levi and back to the road ahead. "Oh, I didn't realize you were engaged. I guess we really don't know anything about each other."

Levi regarded her with an inscrutable expression before reminding her, "By your choice, as I recall."

Called out, Sayeh chuckled awkwardly, admitting, "Okay, you got me there. Yesterday, I wasn't sure if I was going to like you but you passed at least one test so, go ahead and tell me about your fiancée."

A pained expression clouded his features briefly before he cleared his throat and said quietly, "She passed away two years ago. Car accident…drunk driver. The only saving grace I have is that it was quick—likely, she never even knew what hit her."

The air between them felt heavy with grief as Sayeh tried to think of something comforting to say but realized nothing would ever be enough at this moment; instead she simply murmured an apologetic, "I'm sorry, that's terrible," before looking out the window again.

Levi offered her a faint smile—one reserved for moments of courtesy when you don't want to be rude but honestly would rather eat a rusted nail sandwich than continue the conversation—before turning his focus back to the open highway.

This was why she thought it best to keep the lines drawn. Her "emotional distance" rule from her coworkers had always worked to keep the lanes uncluttered. Now she had a long uncomfortable car ride ahead of her, all because she asked one personal question.

But Levi surprised her by breaking the tension, admitting, "I don't like to talk about Nadie, but if we're going to be working together, I should probably let you know a few things about me. Sorry if I shut down just then. It's a bit of a knee-jerk reaction."

She could understand that. Everyone had their limits when it came to talking about their past. Sayeh nodded with understanding and said, "It's all right. I'll never push someone beyond what they're comfortable discussing."

"Thank you."

"And you know what, we don't need to know anything

about each other aside from what affects us on the job. That was on me. I should've minded my own business."

Luna had always said Sayeh was born without an empathy chip, but Sayeh knew better than that. She felt too much of what others were feeling, and her own well-being depended on keeping those feelings at bay.

Even now, trying to remain detached, Sayeh felt his unspoken pain. He buried it deep inside himself as if speaking its name would make it real. Grief was a vicious animal that burrowed down deep, latching on with sharp claws, making it difficult to shake loose.

Catching a glimpse into his business felt like trespassing.

If she were even halfway more well-adjusted, she might know how to offer some level of comfort or condolence, but that stuff left her dangling in no-man's-land.

Best to change the subject—that always worked.

"I couldn't sleep last night so I tried to find some information on Yazzie online. I'm sure pretty soon we won't even need our background programs, we'll be able to find everything we need on social media."

"Hence, the reason I don't have social media," Levi said.

Sayeh agreed. "Same. Plus, I don't like anyone knowing my business and I don't care about anyone else's business, either. Like I really want to know if your aunt Clara's potato salad won some award at the county fair."

Levi's smirk of agreement felt like a good shift in their energy, prompting her to continue. "So, Yazzie is in Great Falls, works as a nurse at the pediatric oncology clinic. Seems she did all right for herself after leaving the reservation."

Felt good to see someone succeed. One less shitty statistic—and that felt like a hard-won cultural win for their people.

Levi nodded, pulling up his cell phone. "I got her phone number. Hopefully, with some luck, she's home and not at the clinic today."

"I called the clinic already and confirmed she's not on shift," Sayeh said, earning a subtle frown from Levi, anticipating his concern. "And yes, I followed protocol and identified myself. Although, if she's not keen to talk to us, knowing we're coming could give her a heads-up to not be around when we show up."

"We'll just have to take our chances. I'd prefer if you kept the rule-bending to a minimum," he warned. "We need to be able to present our findings in court and if you do something that inadvertently renders evidence inadmissible, we could lose our case."

"This isn't my first rodeo. I know which rules can bend," she told him.

"Sure, practice makes perfect and all that, but I'd prefer if you didn't do that on our cases."

His simple request landed in a different place in her head. If anyone else had said that to her at the Bureau, she would've reacted with a snarl and a silent vow to show how far she could take things without breaking the case.

Rule-bending was her thing—also the thing that'd enraged her superiors at the Bureau. Admittedly, there were times she may have pushed the boundary too far and narrowly missed tanking months' worth of work, but luck had been on her side.

Which, in hindsight, may have only enabled her to keep pushing.

But after the IA investigation, she was embarrassed to realize that no one would miss her at the Bureau. She might act like she didn't care what people thought of her, but she did.

And, damn, if that wasn't excruciating to admit.

She wanted to be different this time around. She didn't want to mess up her fresh start at a new agency by acting the same way as before. The task force was doing important work—work that mattered not only to her but to so many people.

The quote "the definition of insanity is doing the same thing over and over again and expecting different results" was running through her head like a ticker tape.

Gotta be different if I want different results.

Swallowing her ego, Sayeh nodded with a short, "Noted," and returned her attention to the road.

He wished he could forget the pain of Nadie's death, but every time her name was spoken, a fresh wave of grief swept through him. He had been told that his sorrow would begin to heal at some stage, but he felt as if it were just as raw as the day she had passed away. The world around him kept telling him to move on and not linger on his loss, but all their words seemed futile against the empty void in his heart.

But something about Sayeh made him want to loosen his grip on that pain—which scared him.

What was it about his new partner that tried to pry the tight grip of his fingers away from that hot coal burning his palm?

"C'mon, man, Nadie wouldn't have wanted you to spend the rest of your life mourning her loss," his older brother, Landon, said one night as they shared a beer after a hard day of calf branding at the family ranch. "I see you going through life, a part of you shut off, and you're too young to clock out like that."

Levi appreciated his brother's candor but wanted to tell him to mind his own business. He had no idea what losing a part of yourself was like. Landon was too wrapped up in the ranch's day-to-day to make time for friends, much less dating.

Nadie had been Levi's best friend, lover, confidant and go-to person whenever he needed advice or a swift kick in the ass.

Now she was gone, and he was supposed to just get over it?

No, not possible.

But, like so many people, his brother was just trying to help.

"I appreciate the advice," he'd said, finishing his beer, "but it's just not in the cards. Nadie was my person. No amount of time or circumstance will ever change that. I'd rather just focus on my career. That makes sense. Nadie's death never will."

The memory of that conversation echoed in his empty heart, and it remained true to this day.

The job was everything that mattered.

He'd warned Sayeh about letting personal feelings get in the way of the investigation, but he was a hypocrite. It was personal for him, too.

Nadie had been an incredible woman—intelligent, funny, sexy and ambitious. Raised on the Blackfeet Reservation, Nadie had been fiercely determined to help her people by raising awareness of the lack of critical services they needed to thrive instead of withering away on the vine.

God, he'd loved her drive. Watching her in action had been intoxicating.

As sweet as she was, no one intimidated Nadie. She'd go toe-to-toe with anyone who dared to try to push her down.

That included crooked politicians—and there were a

few—to well-meaning but timid elders who'd been beaten down by the system and feared retribution.

She'd always known the only way to effect change was from the inside.

Right before she died, Nadie had shared she was eyeing a seat in the political arena.

"Baby, activism is great but is it doing what needs to be done?" she asked him one night, cuddled against him as the rain pelted the rooftop of their tiny rental home. "I want to do so much more."

"And you think politics is the way to do it?" he'd asked, unsure. "You hate politics."

"I do," she affirmed, "but sometimes you have to think like the enemy to beat him at his own game. There has to be someone advocating for the First Nations. I'm willing to be that person."

"It's a big commitment…expensive, too," he said, apprehensive at the dollar amount attached to a political campaign. "We'd have to put off buying a house to fund your first campaign… Are you okay with that? It's a huge risk to bank on a career that might not even happen."

"Always the voice of reason," she teased, kissing him on the nose. "But you have to swing for the fences if you want to go for that home run."

"Oh, darlin', keep talking sports analogies, it's doing something for me," he said with a playful chuckle as he pushed her down into the plush sofa, leaning over her. "Give me some more."

Nadie laughed as she wound her arms around his neck, murmuring, "You're ridiculous," even as she pressed her lips to his.

But Nadie had never had to worry about his support because she'd had it, no matter how expensive or against the odds her dreams happened to land.

He'd believed in her ability to change the world.

And some jackass with zero sense of responsibility had taken Nadie before she'd even had the chance to make her mark.

It didn't seem fair.

He cut a short glance at Sayeh. She didn't look anything like Nadie—from her dirty blond hair to her blue eyes—aside from the strong jawline and high cheekbones, they were opposites.

But Sayeh's spirit reminded him of Nadie.

Sayeh was bold and fearless, determined to do the right thing, even at significant personal cost.

His Nadie had been the same.

Maybe that's why he was drawn to Sayeh despite pushing against the feeling. He felt comfortable in her presence, more at ease than he had with anyone since Nadie, but that made little sense.

And he didn't want to untangle the knot that figuring it out would take.

When Sayeh didn't press for any more conversation—benign or not—he was glad.

Better to focus on the job.

It was safer that way.

Chapter 6

As force of habit, Sayeh immediately scanned the area when they exited the car, looking for anything or anyone suspicious, noting every detail.

Cars and trees dotted the aging suburban tract. A red pickup truck sat empty in the driveway of the small house. A worn rubber ball bounced across the sidewalk and onto the grass when no one caught it. The ball rolled down the lawn toward a jungle gym play set where two children chased each other around its metal bars.

The older neighborhood showed signs of a sluggish economy but still retained some charm. The small house was probably built sometime in the 1960s when one income could comfortably support a family of four.

But considering Yazzie's roots, her modest home might as well be a castle.

"Nice quiet place," Levi said as if trying to tell her it was okay to let down her guard. They weren't approaching a drug dealer's house, and there weren't likely armed assailants waiting behind the door.

"Yeah, I don't trust quiet," she admitted, but she didn't trust loud, either. He was probably right, though. Drawing a deep breath, she consciously tried to relax the tension from her shoulders. They weren't interrogating a suspect, just conversing with someone who might've known their vic.

Sayeh knocked on the front door.

Several minutes later Yazzie opened the door, expecting someone else, but was immediately taken aback by the strangers at her threshold. "Something tells me you're not delivering my new microwave."

"No, ma'am," Levi confirmed with a disarming smile as he and Sayeh flashed their credentials. "We're with the BIA, here to ask you a few questions about a girl you used to know back in high school, Echo Flying Owl Jones. May we come in?"

She blinked in surprise. "Echo? She's been dead for years. What questions could you have?"

Sayeh understood her confusion. "We're looking into her case. We're hoping you might be able to clear up a few things. Her aunt Charlene said you two were close."

At the mention of Charlene, she softened and nodded, ushering them into the living room. A shy cat skittered from the room to hide from view.

"Don't mind him, he's terrified of strangers," Yazzie said, gesturing to the sofa and sitting across from them as she pulled her long black hair around to the side so it trailed nearly to her waist. "How can I help?"

Sayeh was a firm believer in getting straight to the point. No sense in wasting anyone's time. "Agent Wyatt and I are members of a new task force with the Bureau of Indian Affairs. We're looking into cold cases involving Indigenous people that might've been overlooked and deserve a second chance. I met Echo's aunt Charlene by chance and when I looked into her case, there were too many unanswered questions to agree with the official report of death by natural causes. The only issue is we need to go over the case with a fine-tooth comb to find what was missed sixteen years ago."

"You really think Echo was murdered?"

"Do you?" Levi countered.

Put on the spot, Yazzie shook her head, uncertain. "I don't know. Echo was…like a force of nature back then, but sometimes she could get into trouble." Yet the memory of Echo seemed to poke at a sensitive spot as her eyes immediately welled up. "A day hasn't gone by that I haven't missed her. I've always wondered how things might've turned out if she would've left the reservation with me like we planned or if she would've stayed with Charlene. I know Echo didn't feel right about leaving her aunt all alone—but in the end, that's exactly what happened."

The sad irony was not lost on them.

"Did anyone interview you after Echo died?" Levi asked.

"No," Yazzie answered, shaking her head. "Not a single question."

"I know it's probably difficult, but we'd like to ask you a few questions that might seem personal, but I promise you, they're important to the investigation," Sayeh said.

"It was so long ago," Yazzie murmured faintly. "I don't know how useful my information will be—and honestly, Echo's death hit me pretty hard. I blocked a lot of that time out of my memory. It was the only way to get through the pain of losing her. I feel bad, I didn't even keep in contact with Charlene and wish I would've. Echo was all she had."

"No one grieves the same. I didn't get the impression Charlene held any bad feelings about you," Sayeh assured Yazzie, hoping to ease that small worry. "She said you and Echo were thick as thieves back in the day, practically joined at the hip."

Yazzie chuckled, nodding. "Yes, very much so. Echo was

the cool sister I never had. She was always so full of spirit and charisma. I swear, Echo had whatever quality movie stars have—that certain something that makes people stand up and notice wherever they go. I used to tease her that she was going to be walking down the street and some Hollywood producer was going to notice her right away and snatch her up to be a star."

"Was Echo interested in becoming an actress?" Levi asked.

"No, not really. She had terrible stage fright. Hated speaking in front of a group. I can't imagine she'd enjoy performing in front of a bunch of strangers. No, she was just special, even if she didn't plan on doing anything with it."

"So, she didn't have plans for college or anything like that?"

"Oh, she did—with me—but sometimes I felt that I was just dragging her along and she was happy to go with the flow because I was the one dragging her. Maybe even just humoring me. I don't know what Echo wanted to be in life. Maybe she didn't know, either."

"Sixteen is pretty young to have it all figured out," Sayeh said. "I think at sixteen I still wanted to join the military and become a helicopter pilot—but then I realized I wasn't cut out for the military lifestyle and I switched gears."

Yazzie agreed, admitting, "I wasn't exactly sure what I wanted to do yet, either. I just knew I was going to get off the reservation and make something of my life because there was no way in hell I was going to live my life in poverty if I had a chance to get out. That was one thing Echo and I agreed on—we had to leave the reservation, one way or another."

"Charlene mentioned that Echo had a boyfriend. Do you know who she was seeing?"

"She wouldn't tell me but I had my suspicions."

"Why wouldn't she tell you?"

Yazzie fell silent, swallowing a lump as she tried to work around the pain of the past. "Sorry, it's just… I haven't talked about Echo in so long. It's like ripping off a bandage and finding out the wound is still bleeding."

"I'm sorry," Sayeh said with understanding, but had to press. "I wish there was another way but you're our best lead right now."

Yazzie took a deep breath, nodding as she recalibrated. "It almost feels like a lifetime ago that she was alive, but if talking about her helps find who killed her, I'm willing to do it."

Sayeh appreciated Yazzie's bravery. "We're going to do our best to find her killer."

"So, you don't have any idea who Echo was dating at the time of her death?" Levi asked.

"No, Echo was real tight-lipped about who she was seeing. Chaz and me were putting bets on who we thought it was because we figured eventually she'd have to spill, but she took that secret to the grave."

"Do you think it was somebody that her aunt wouldn't approve? Maybe like an older man?"

Yazzie wasn't sure. "That's the thing, it could have been, but she and her aunt were so close. It feels weird to think that she wouldn't share that information with her. But then we were close, too, and she didn't share it with us, so I honestly don't know why she kept that information private."

"Was Echo generally a private person about her personal stuff?" Sayeh asked.

"Yeah, I guess you could say so. She had a really big heart but she kept her private stuff pretty close to the chest. I think she had trust issues."

"Charlene told us that her mother died when she was three. Although it sounds like Charlene did the best that she could to give her as good of a life as possible," Sayeh said.

Yazzie nodded in agreement. "Charlene was wonderful. She was kind but firm, and she had a great sense of humor. She was more like an older sister, but not one that just let Echo do whatever she wanted. She definitely had rules and structure but not so strict that Echo felt boxed in. Honestly, they had a great relationship. Much better than me and my parents, that's for sure."

"You said that you had suspicions. Who did you think was a contender?" Levi asked.

Yazzie tried to recall names. "Gosh, it was so long ago. I can barely remember. When I walked away from the reservation, I didn't look back. I do remember this one kid…from the neighboring town of Cottonwood that we thought *maybe* because he came around a few times. Cottonwood kids always showed up at the Rez to party because they knew no one was going to bust them for underage drinking."

A chill rushed Sayeh's spine. "I'm from Cottonwood. Maybe I know the person that you're thinking of. I'm not much older than what Echo would be if she hadn't died."

"He and a buddy used to come to the reservation on occasion, and I saw Echo talking to them. I never saw her with either of them in a romantic way, but there was something there."

"Did you see them flirting or something?" Levi asked.

"Yeah, a little bit. Nothing serious but…just a vibe, you know?"

Sayeh knew exactly what Yazzie was trying to say.

"I remember thinking, *this is bad news*, because rich Cottonwood kids were nothing but trouble on the Rez and I didn't want nothing to do with it, but Echo didn't pay attention to all that. She thought it was all a bunch of bullshit and part of what kept people drawing lines. She used to tell me, *Yazzie, we're all Great Spirit's people, we need to stop acting like it's us against them. That's how things change for the better.*" Yazzie shook her head sadly. "God, you'd never guess it but beneath it all, she was an idealist with a romantic heart."

"The best always are," Sayeh murmured in commiseration.

Levi had his notepad ready. "Do you remember the names by any chance?"

Yazzie took a minute, thinking hard. "Sorry, it's been so long. I don't want to give you the wrong name and inadvertently put the spotlight on someone innocent."

"Don't worry, we're not putting anyone under a hot bulb yet. We're just talking, gaining intel right now. Anything that you can remember would be very helpful," Levi said.

Yazzie nodded, blowing out a short breath. "Okay, so one of the guy's name was Chris—tall, shaggy blond, an athletic kind of guy—and the other was a redhead. I remember teasing her about hooking up with a ginger and I know that's terrible but we were kids and it just seemed so different from the guys that we were used to having around."

Sayeh chuckled. "I think we've all said and done things as kids that would make us cringe as adults. Do you remember the redhead's name by any chance?"

Yazzie thought long and hard and then snapped her fingers as recall came to her. "Yes, his name was Logan—something. Sorry, I don't remember his last name."

Sayeh was already thinking. She remembered Chris and Logan from school, older by a year and popular. All the girls—except Sayeh—tried to get one or both of their attention.

"Is it possible their names were Logan Caldwell and Christopher Roth?"

Yazzie wasn't sure but admitted, "That sounds familiar but I wouldn't bet my life on it. How did you know?"

"I remember those boys. They were really popular at school. Both were a year older than me, but we knew a lot of the same people."

Levi looked to Sayeh. "Did you keep in contact with either of them?"

Sayeh barked a short laugh. "I said I *knew* them, I didn't say I was *friends* with them. Theirs was not a crowd I ran with. I was a sports jock, but they weren't interested in girls who could whoop their ass. As I recall they were more into girls who were soft and kind of shallow."

"Well, maybe these aren't the same people because that was the opposite of Echo. Echo was tough as nails and could decimate someone with a look. She was the ultimate champion. Which is why it was so bizarre to me to even consider the fact that someone got the jump on her. I just have a hard time wrapping my head around that and I always have."

"According to the report, the night she died, she went to the Urgent Care with cuts and bruises, like she'd been in a fight. Do you know anything about that?" Levi asked.

"The night Echo died I wasn't even in town. I always wondered if things might've been different if I'd been here."

Levi beat Sayeh to the punch, gravely advising, "Don't bother going down that road, it's a dead end."

Sayeh agreed. "Thoughts like that will likely drive you crazy because you can think until your head pops off about how you should've, could've, would've, and none of it will matter. So, don't do that to yourself, okay?"

Yazzie nodded. "I know that's good advice, but it's hard to put into practice. She was my best friend and suddenly she was gone. For a long time I felt like I was living in an alternate reality. Everything felt surreal and nothing made sense."

Sayeh gave Yazzie a minute to collect herself, then brought up another sad topic. "You mentioned your friend Chaz... We've since learned that he went down a different path and ended up in prison on a drug offense and later died. Were you two close?"

Yazzie drew a shuddering breath, wincing as regret crossed her expression. "Ohh, man, today seems to be the day of emotional reckoning," she said, her hands fluttering to her long hair and stroking it in a self-soothing gesture. "Chaz struggled on the Rez. He never fit in with his family. I know it's easy to assume what kind of person he was because he went to prison, but he was a really good person. I think he got into drugs to self-medicate the pain of not fitting in and ended up falling in with the wrong people."

"So you didn't keep in contact?" Sayeh asked.

Yazzie shook her head. "When I bailed on the reservation, I was so eager to get out of there that I didn't check to see if Chaz was going to be okay. I just assumed he'd figure it out. When I heard that he got busted and then went to prison, I couldn't deal with the guilt and I just kind of shut all of that off. When I heard that he'd been killed, I went into a deep depression. It felt like everything was crashing in on me. I was overwhelmed with the realization that both my best friends were dead and I hadn't been there for either of them when they needed me. It took a lot of therapy to pull myself out of that hole."

And Sayeh knew, without Yazzie saying it, that their questions had just dredged all that pain back to the surface. She didn't doubt Yazzie would have her therapist on the line as soon as they left.

She shared a look with Levi. What a horrible burden to carry all these years.

"Why did Chaz struggle to fit in?" Levi asked.

Yazzie hesitated but revealed, "Even though he's gone, it doesn't feel right to share a secret that isn't mine. All I can say is that his family never would've accepted him as he truly was and he knew it. He was terrified of being alone so he hid his true self. The only people he felt secure with to be his true self was me and Echo. And, let me tell you, Echo would've beat anyone into the ground if they dared to pick on Chaz. Echo's death affected us all differently. I lost my best friend, my soul sister, but for Chaz it was like he lost the light in his life, and he never recovered. I know for a fact that if Echo was still around, there's no way Chaz would've ended up the way he did. She would've found a way to get him off the reservation and into a safe place."

The more Sayeh learned about Echo, the more she wished she could've known her.

"Thank you for sharing with us. If we have any additional questions, would you mind if we called?"

"I don't mind. I think it's good that you're looking into her case and I hope you find what you're looking for."

Sayeh took a chance and offered, "I have Charlene's number. She'd probably love to hear from you."

Yazzie nodded, her eyes welling up. "Yeah, maybe I'll give her a call."

Sayeh wasn't sure if Yazzie would follow through, but at least she'd have the opportunity. Sayeh jotted the number down, and then she and Levi took their leave.

As they climbed into the car, Levi said, "Looks like we're headed back to Cottonwood."

Sayeh nodded. "Looks like. I guess you'll get to meet my

sister Luna. She's a Cottonwood detective—and before you ask, yeah, she's nicer than me."

Levi chuckled and wisely remained silent.

Chapter 7

Seeing as Great Falls was three hours from Billings, they agreed to tackle Cottonwood tomorrow, which worked for Levi because he was ready to put his feet up and watch the sunset with a beer in his hand while going over case files.

Listening to Yazzie talk about Echo made him realize that Sayeh might be right about this case. A whole picture was starting to emerge of a girl who wasn't the party type, as the report made her out to be, which meant she likely never would've simply gotten wasted and fallen asleep in the cold.

Someone likely murdered the kid and walked away scot-free as if her life never mattered.

And that created a slow burn of anger that he wasn't expecting.

Maybe it was because that's how it'd felt when Nadie died, like her life hadn't mattered, and he felt the black hole of her absence every day.

So, yeah, she goddamn mattered.

The man who'd killed Nadie had gotten off with manslaughter charges and only spent a handful of years behind bars before he got out on good behavior. Now the man was living his life as if he hadn't stomped out the light of another, free to start fresh.

But there was nothing that he could do about it, so he tried to put those feelings in a box and stash them away.

In his most savage moments, usually after one too many beers, Levi thought the only acceptable sentence was to put that man behind the wheel of a car to experience the terror of another person careening into him on the road.

But then he sobered up and boxed up those thoughts nice and tight once again.

Would there ever come a day when the thought of Nadie wasn't like taking a hot poker straight to the chest?

It hadn't happened yet.

He felt for Yazzie having to relive the pain of losing her best friend at such a young age, only to lose her other best friend not long after.

He was an adult when he lost Nadie; he couldn't imagine what it was like to experience such loss as a kid.

His cell phone chirped with a text from his brother, Landon.

Are you free to come to the ranch this weekend and help go through Dad's things?

Levi sighed, knowing he couldn't keep putting off that chore—it wasn't fair to Landon to expect him to shoulder the entire job, but the idea of sifting through their dad's things was enough to turn his stomach.

Jack Wyatt died suddenly of a heart attack a year ago. It was a staggering blow to the family but even more so to Levi. It was devastating to him, having to deal with another tragedy.

But no one got a pass to check out from life when you're an adult.

Life goes on—that much became abundantly clear after losing Nadie.

People expected a limit on acceptable grieving timelines, and when you didn't adhere to that expectation, they lost compassion.

So, the grief for his dad got shoved in the box labeled "heartbreak and other shit I can't deal with right now," and he moved on.

And he was afraid that going through his dad's things, deciding what to donate, what to keep and so on, would rip that box to pieces, and he didn't know what that would mean to his sanity.

Sorry, I'm booked this weekend. Working on a new case. I'll text you when my schedule clears up.

Levi felt like an asshole for dodging his brother, but the lie was honesty in disguise. He couldn't afford to lose himself in grief with this new case just starting. Maybe after the case closed he'd have the extra mental fortitude to tackle that job.

In the meantime he wanted to immerse himself in the job of background research. He'd start with the Macawi Reservation. He didn't know enough about the reservation and wanted to learn more.

He grabbed a beer, a slice of cold pizza and his laptop, settling on the sofa. First, he searched for news articles about the reservation. Immediately, one recent article in particular jumped out—involving Luna Griffin, a Cottonwood detective.

Interesting. He read on, instantly engrossed.

Griffin managed to bust up a complicated drug network that was using the protection of the reservation's sover-

eign nation status to shield its illegal drug trafficking—
interesting that it was so similar to the investigation that
busted open the Mexican mafia ring doing the same thirty
years prior.

What started with the investigation of a gruesome murder involving a local Cottonwood family turned into a
gnarly and twisted investigation netting a sophisticated
drug operation.

He shook his head, impressed. He wanted to pick up the
phone and ask Sayeh for more details about the investigation, but they weren't on that level of familiarity. His questions would have to wait until tomorrow.

Finishing the articles—which had reached national news
coverage—he closed up his laptop and then the house.

It was times like these that he wished he'd followed
through on Nadie's request to get a dog. She'd joked that
since they weren't having kids anytime soon, they ought to
get a dog as a test run.

"A dog? Nadie, neither of us is prepared to take on a
dog," he said, trying to appeal to her sense of logic. "Both
of our schedules are jammed. How are we going to squeeze
in something that needs to be regularly fed, watered and
taken outside to do its business? Maybe in a few years when
things settle down."

"There's always an argument against getting a dog or
having a baby. You just have to go for it."

He chuckled. "Yeah? Just go for it and hope for the best?"

"Yes, exactly," she said, grinning.

Somehow he'd distracted her from that particular argument, and they hadn't ended up at the shelter to find a dog,
but now he wished they had.

Sometimes the house seemed so empty he did everything
he could to avoid going home.

At his old position as a tribal operations specialist within law enforcement, working late nights was a welcome distraction from the reality that no one waited for him at home.

Not even a wilted houseplant.

Stop being so damn morose, he thought with irritation, shutting off the lights and climbing into bed. *All that ever matters is the job.*

Sayeh rooted around in the refrigerator and found a container of leftover take-out Chinese. She stuffed the cold metal fork into her mouth and rummaged through some mail until she spied an envelope addressed to her by name, tucked behind a bill for the water company. She sat back on the couch and sifted through a couple of days' worth of mail: junk from grocery delivery services, credit card offers, bills from the gas company and an invitation to attend a birthday party pub crawl with a friend of hers. At this rate it would be a few weeks before her stack was reduced by half. Luna was always getting after her about checking her mail every day, but to be honest—although she'd never tell her—it was one of those chores that definitely slipped through the cracks.

Staring at the official envelope, her dinner was forgotten in anticipation. It was a response from TerraLab Soil Solutions, the company she'd hired to examine the sample from her biological parents' old home. She had been thinking someone was blatantly ignoring her attempts to uncover the truth, but it was probably just an overwhelming backlog that had caused the delay in getting back to her.

Her fingers trembled as she ripped open the envelope to read the response:

We are pleased to present the findings of the comprehensive soil analysis conducted on the soil sample provided by you. Our expert soil scientists have diligently examined the sample to determine its composition and characteristics. The soil sample in question was collected from an area on the Macawi Reservation in Montana.

Soil Composition:
The soil sample consists of various components commonly found in the region. The predominant soil composition includes:
• Sand: 45%
• Silt: 30%
• Clay: 25%

pH Levels:
The pH level of the soil sample was determined to be 6.2, indicating a slightly acidic soil condition. This pH range is typically suitable for a wide range of regional agricultural activities.

Nutrient Analysis:
The soil analysis revealed the following nutrient levels in the sample:
• Nitrogen (N): 0.08%
• Phosphorus (P): 0.05%
• Potassium (K): 0.12%

These nutrient levels indicate that the soil has moderate fertility, which can support various crops and vegetation with appropriate management practices and fertilization.

Organic Matter:
The soil sample contains approximately 2.5% organic matter, which is within the expected range for the region. Organic matter is crucial in enhancing soil structure, water-holding capacity and nutrient retention.

Texture and Drainage:
The soil texture was classified as loam based on the particle size analysis. Loam soils are generally well drained and balance water retention and aeration well.

Recommendations:
Considering the characteristics of the soil sample, we recommend the following:
- Conduct regular soil testing to monitor nutrient levels and pH, ensuring appropriate fertilization and soil amendments.
- Implement crop rotation and cover cropping practices to enhance soil health and minimize nutrient depletion.
- Properly manage irrigation to prevent waterlogging or excessive drying out of the soil.
- Consider soil conservation practices, such as contour plowing or strip cropping, to minimize erosion risks.

Please note that these recommendations serve as general guidelines. For more specific advice tailored to your intended use of the soil, we recommend consulting with an agricultural specialist or agronomist.

We hope this report provides valuable insights into the quality and characteristics of the soil samples submitted. If you have any further questions or re-

quire additional information, please do not hesitate
to contact our team.

Sayeh stared at the words on the page until they blurred.
Her heart thundered in her chest as the implication of
that letter hit her like a donkey kick.

The letter in her hand confirmed her parents hadn't been
killed by any hazardous chemical accident. Someone had
gone to great lengths to fabricate a story and conceal what'd
really happened. As relieved as she was to discover the truth,
she felt overwhelming despair—what would justice be for
them now?

According to the autopsy report, their bodies were burnt
beyond recognition, and without exhuming their remains,
there was no way to know if they had suffered any defen-
sive wounds before death.

Not to mention the technology needed to do more ex-
tensive forensic testing simply wasn't available back then.
Sayeh didn't have enough money in her bank account to
fund a private audit into her biological parents' deaths.

Luna had asked her if she thought finding out their parents had been murdered would make her feel better or worse.

She was confident the truth was preferable at the time,
but she felt worse.

How was she supposed to find answers to a case nobody
wanted to solve? Her biological father had had a drug rap
sheet. There'd been no question that he'd been involved
with drugs, but what about her mother?

From the sounds of it, Mika had been very sweet and
loving. Her main offense had been falling in love with the
wrong man.

Inexplicably her thoughts turned to Echo. Was that

Echo's story, too? Had she simply fallen in love with the wrong man?

It was such a clichéd story, but love had a way of twisting feelings into a liability. How many battered women stayed with their abusers because of what had started as love turned into fear? Some women were trapped by circumstance and the very real threat of being murdered if they tried to escape.

Before what'd happened to her sister Kenna, she couldn't imagine staying with someone who dared to raise a hand against her. She would've taken great joy in breaking their fingers if they tried.

Now she had a newfound sense of empathy. Sometimes the most loving people gave villains chances they didn't deserve, which ended up costing them. Maybe, like Mika, that's what happened with Echo, too.

Her thoughts drifted to Levi. Tomorrow he would meet her sister Luna. Was she nervous about that meeting? Maybe a little, though she couldn't quite pinpoint why. It's not as if she needed Levi to make a good impression. He was just her teammate, not a significant other or even a romantic consideration.

He was good-looking, though. Objectively, she could admit that. There was something about him that spoke of stoic vulnerability, a contradiction she found intriguing.

She told him she didn't want to pry—and that was true on the surface—but there remained a nagging interest to hear about his life before he lost his fiancée that she couldn't quite quit.

She sensed that he'd been a different person then than how he was now. It was as if Levi felt he couldn't laugh anymore; the pressures of grief had squashed his joy like the stomp of an elephant. She could see it in the tightness around his mouth and how his gaze seemed intensely distant out of a reluctance to get close to anyone.

After losing her dad, she'd been numb for quite a while. There was a lot of guilt wrapped up in her feelings. All the times she'd been unfairly harsh, said things she didn't mean or flat-out picked fights with the man who'd done his best to give her a good life made her wish she'd been a better daughter.

She missed him more than she let on. He'd had a great yet quirky sense of humor that always made her laugh, even when she wanted to kick him in his stubborn ass.

Still, death was a weird thing—and how one dealt with grief was incredibly personal.

Why was she interested in Levi's personal life, anyway? It was a foreign feeling.

Also, the fact that she was looking forward to spending time with him tomorrow made her give her own feelings the side-eye.

Let's get down to brass tacks—was she attracted to him? Was that what this was? Surely, it couldn't be that simple. It'd been so long since she'd dated anyone that she'd forgotten how this worked.

Not to mention she'd never dated a coworker. She was treading in unfamiliar territory. Thank God they had a complicated case to focus on. Best to keep their minds on the job to limit distractions.

A long sigh rattled out of her as she folded the letter and tucked it into her bag so she didn't forget to show it to Luna tomorrow.

Maybe Luna would have an idea of what to do next.

For once, she was looking forward to her big sister's advice.

Ha! Best to keep that revelation to herself. Sayeh didn't need Luna knowing that she actually appreciated her advice.

Chapter 8

This time around, Levi offered to drive, and to his surprise, Sayeh agreed. Even more surprising was she showed up with his correct coffee order and breakfast sandwiches for both, saying, "It felt rude to eat alone," as she put a serious dent in hers.

It was a simple gesture, but the fact that she thought of bringing him a sandwich touched him in a place he didn't want to think about too deeply because it felt wrong on several personal levels.

Even if everyone else in his life thought the opposite.

You're going to give yourself an aneurysm. Just focus on the case.

Going back and forth between Billings and Cottonwood gave a serious déjà vu vibe, but at least it wasn't as far as Great Falls.

"I did some research last night and came across your sister's case from last year. She was responsible for blowing up an international drug ring?" he asked, impressed.

"Yeah, my sister is reluctantly badass. She doesn't like to toot her own horn, preferring a quiet career without a lot of fanfare. She was happy when the FBI took over the bulk of the investigation but I was pissed on her behalf. She did all the work and then they came in and took the glory."

"Sounds like the Bureau," he said with a knowing chuckle, though he found it interesting that Sayeh saw it that way, being former Bureau herself. "Were you still an FBI agent at the time?"

"Technically, yes, but I was on administrative leave pending the IA investigation," she answered with zero embarrassment. Most people skirted around admitting they'd been the subject of an IA inquiry but not Sayeh. The woman had sass; he'd give her that.

He liked that about her.

"Was it luck that she cracked the case?" he asked.

"No, my sister is an incredible investigator. She chased the leads until she found who was responsible for her friend's death."

"Oh? She knew the vic?"

Sayeh quieted with somber respect for the dead. "Yeah, they'd been best friends in school. They'd grown apart but not because of any kind of squabble. Life just took them in different directions. Charlotte got married and had kids, became queen of the PTA social network, and Luna went the law enforcement route. They lost things in common."

"That happens," he commiserated, though it seemed to hit women harder. He had buddies from school who got married, and it didn't stop them from talking shit to each other whenever they met up again. But then, as Nadie used to remind him, men were notorious for only caring about the surface-deep stuff—and it was true. Levi didn't know his buddies' hopes and dreams, but he knew who would almost always lie about their fishing haul and who couldn't handle their liquor on a Saturday night.

"I read about the details of the murders—terrible tragedy. Especially with the kids."

The murder of the Leicki family had rocked the small

Montana town, throwing the tight-knit community into an uneasy frenzy to find the killer.

"Yeah, it was a crap-sandwich situation. I think that's what also pushed Luna to solve the case because it was so personal."

He nodded, accepting the not-so-subtle jab at their earliest conversation about personalizing things and how it could negatively affect the case.

"And she still works at the local police station?" he asked.

"Oh, yeah, the FBI actually courted her, wanted to offer her a position, but she wasn't interested at all. It's just not my sister's vibe. Besides, she's happy as a clam right where she's at. Her current position gives her the freedom to spend her free time with her boyfriend, Ben. He's a retired marine…and Charlotte's brother."

"Oh?" *Talk about making it personal.* She went all the way. "And it's working out okay?"

"Yep. Deliriously happy—not quite as nauseatingly happy as my sister Kenna with her guy—but they're gooey in love."

"You don't sound like you're a big fan of a solid relationship status."

Sayeh barked a short laugh. "You caught that, huh? Yeah, it's just never been my thing. Look, do I enjoy having someone to cuddle at the end of a crappy day? Of course. But that comfort comes with the expectation that you're going to be at their beck and call, which is just not my scene."

He chuckled ruefully. "It doesn't have to be like that. A good fit with another person should complement your relationship style, not smother it."

"Hasn't been my experience."

Now he was immediately curious about what her past relationships were like to give her that crooked viewpoint, but it wasn't his business. Still, he couldn't help but add, "I never felt stifled or smothered by my commitment to Nadie and vice versa. We were a team, not opponents."

"I guess you were lucky," Sayeh said, shrugging. "What I've found is most men in the dating field are intimidated by my career and those who aren't are usually in law enforcement, too, which is definitely a hard pass for me."

"Why?"

"Because stereotypes exist for a reason and I don't need that kind of drama."

"Painting with a wide brush doesn't leave much room to discover new colors."

Sayeh's belly laughter at his attempt at being philosophical coaxed a smile from him, too. "Okay, that was a bit much," he admitted. "But you get my point."

"Yeah—you shouldn't quit your day job," she wisecracked.

Levi accepted her ribbing with a grin. The constant tight band around his chest loosened momentarily, and it felt good to just laugh at something stupid.

After a short pause, Sayeh shared, "I might've mentioned, my sisters and I were adopted by a Cottonwood family but we were born on the Macawi Reservation. I recently discovered that our biological parents may have been murdered to cover up evidence against the Mexican mafia running drugs through the reservation thirty years ago."

Levi cast a sharp look Sayeh's way. "I came across that case info when I was doing some research on the Macawi Reservation. Your biological parents were involved with that?"

"Well, I'm not sure. That's the thing—the official report said they were killed by a chemical explosion under the assumption that they were mixing toxic chemicals for illicit drug manufacturing but I just received a letter from the independent lab I hired to examine the soil samples taken from the site and there were no chemicals found."

"Are you sure the soil samples were taken from a large enough perimeter?"

"Yes, I sent four separate samples taken from different quadrants, as well as one taken directly from the blast site."

"So, based on the results, you're concluding that the crime scene report was…"

Sayeh smirked, knowing full well what she was implying. "I think the word you're looking for is *falsified*."

"That's a serious accusation," he warned.

"I know it is but hear me out. My parents' bodies were burnt to a crisp and it was just assumed that the story held water. No further forensic testing was performed to corroborate the theory. There's also the theory that the former Cottonwood police chief was crooked and involved somehow but I'll have a snowball's chance in hell of proving it."

"And why's that?"

"Well, he just died but before that, his brain was mush. He was in a Memory Care facility and didn't even remember his own name. Alzheimer's is a nasty disease."

He murmured in agreement. "Surely someone might remember details from that time who isn't gone yet."

"Maybe. I was waiting until I got the confirmation from the soil sample before going forward. I didn't really get a solid vote of support from the tribal council to push an inquiry. They think the past needs to remain in the past. But I'm not okay with letting the world think that my parents blew themselves up playing bathtub chemists."

"They didn't have a history with drugs?" he asked.

"No, they did—which only made them easy victims. It's like, you can't be a victim if you make bad choices in your life? That's not true."

Levi answered, "No," adding, "But it makes it harder to help them."

"Morality should never be the sticking point between helping someone and letting them twist in the wind. Justice is supposed to be blind, right?"

"True enough but you and I both know that's not how it always works."

She didn't have time to argue the point further because they'd arrived at the Cottonwood police station.

But before they entered the station, Sayeh asked, "Is that how you work?"

He didn't pretend to misunderstand. He answered clearly and without hesitation, "No," and she nodded, seeming relieved.

And for some reason, that mattered to him.

Sayeh entered the Cottonwood police station and immediately visited Luna's small office. She'd texted ahead of time to give her a heads-up they were on their way, but she'd left out the reason for the visit.

Ordinarily, Sayeh would never dream of letting a coworker know her business, but it felt oddly comforting knowing Levi was privy to what she'd discovered about the soil samples.

"This looks official," Luna said, looking up with a smile as her gaze darted to Levi and back to Sayeh. "This must be your new partner."

Sayeh made a quick introduction. "Levi Wyatt, Luna Griffin, yada yada yada, and so on. We are here on official business but I have personal business to discuss, too."

To Levi, she said, "Pleasure to meet you," and to Sayeh, she said, "Immediately intrigued. What's going on?"

They settled in the chairs opposite Luna's desk, and

Sayeh got right to the point. "Business first—do you remember two kids by the names of Logan Caldwell and Christopher Roth? We went to school with them. They were a year older than me so a year younger than you."

Luna frowned, searching her memory, recalling, "Well, I think Logan Caldwell still lives here in Cottonwood. He does seasonal work for the logging industry if I'm remembering correctly. I don't know what happened with the other one but I can check and see if he's in the system."

Luna did a quick search, shaking her head. "No criminal record for Roth. Why are you looking for them?"

"You remember that case I was telling you about? Well, we got a lead that the two boys used to party at the Rez back in the day and might've known our vic. We just want to question them and see if they remember anything about Echo."

Luna shook her head. "Parties at the Rez. Remember Dad getting so hot under the collar about kids doing that? He swore if he ever found out we were doing that stuff, he'd ground us until the state started questioning if we were truant." She chuckled at the memory. "He said it was disrespectful and he wouldn't have any daughters of his acting like that."

Sayeh had forgotten how fired up their dad got about that stuff, which had always struck her as odd, seeing as he wasn't even Native. Now she realized he'd been teaching them to respect their heritage even if they were raised away from the land. Her sinuses tingled in warning, and she blinked back the sudden show of tears. Sometimes she never knew when a pocket of hidden grief would show up.

She sniffed and rubbed her nose, acting as if her allergies were acting up, quick to get back on track. "Got an address for Caldwell?"

"Yeah, sure." Luna scribbled an address and slid it over to Sayeh. "Do you want some backup? Caldwell's file indicates a history of violence. Mostly misdemeanor stuff but you never know."

"Thanks for the heads-up. I think we'll be okay," Sayeh assured her sister. "Anything else you can tell us about him?"

Luna rocked back in the creaky old chair. "Well, according to his arrest record, he seems to get out of control when he drinks. As long as he's sober when you talk to him, you should be fine."

Sayeh chuckled. "Good to know."

Luna looked to Levi, gesturing to Sayeh. "How do you like working with your new partner?"

"She's a sharp investigator with quick instincts," he answered. "Can't ask for a better person to have your back in the field."

Sayeh tried not to be overly flattered, but his praise made her want to grin from ear to ear, so she deliberately frowned, saying, "Okay, tone it down. She's not in charge of your promotion so no need to kiss ass."

Luna rolled her eyes as if to say, *Geez, Sayeh, can't you just be nice?* but Levi chuckled, shaking his head as the comment rolled off his back like water off a duck.

"So what's the personal business?"

"I got the soil sample results."

Luna sobered immediately, leaning forward. "And?"

"And no evidence of chemical contamination."

Luna looked conflicted. "I guess this means someone lied back in the day."

"Yeah, that's my feeling, too. Makes you wonder why someone would go to such lengths to make an explosion look like one thing when it was clearly another. Burnt up bodies are hard to examine, especially with limited forensics available."

Levi asked Luna, "Do you agree with Sayeh that your biological parents were likely murdered?"

"I don't know yet, but the sheer number of lies we've been told about what actually went down that night makes things real suspicious."

Levi nodded, looking to Sayeh. "What's your next move?"

"Um, well, if I were treating this like an investigation, I would start talking to people who would've known Mika and Darryl, my biological parents, see if I could find a reason why they'd end up on someone's hit list."

Luna looked unhappy with that answer but agreed it was the best place to start. "You're going to stir a hornet's nest and you still might end up with nothing to go on," she said with a resigned sigh, "but I'll do what I can to help."

Sayeh appreciated her sister's support. "Thanks, sis, I might need it."

Levi stood. "In the meantime, we've got our own case to chase down. You ready to talk to Caldwell?" he asked Sayeh.

Sayeh nodded, rising. "Let's see how good Logan's memory is."

And hope the man was sober. Sayeh hated the idea of throwing hands before lunch.

Chapter 9

Logan Caldwell lived in a small cabin on the outskirts of town that looked like it was built in the 1800s by a home-steading trapper and every occupant since had been fearful of upgrading to modern conveniences.

"Quaint," Sayeh said, her sharp gaze taking in every detail. "How much you want to bet there's a functioning outhouse out back?"

"I'd take that bet," he said as they approached the front door. Levi stepped forward and rapped three times on the solid oak. Several minutes later a crash and a litany of swearing followed before the door swung open and a bleary-eyed, disheveled man appeared, squinting into the morning sun as he pulled on a ratty T-shirt.

"What the hell do you want?" Logan growled before realizing they weren't the run-of-the-mill callers. They flashed their credentials and Logan rubbed at his eyes as he straightened and tried again. "I already checked in with my probation officer. I'm square, I swear it. Check my file."

"Logan Caldwell?" Levi confirmed. At Logan's uncertain nod, his gaze darting between Levi and Sayeh, Levi smiled and gestured, saying, "Mind if we step inside and talk a bit? We have some questions about a girl you might've known back in high school."

At that, Logan's face screwed into a confused frown. "High school? Yeah, I guess?" He stepped aside and motioned for them to follow him. He scooped up a clump of dirty clothes, trying to tidy up, but it was a lost cause. Realizing this, Logan tossed the clothes in his arms into his bedroom and shut the door. His gaze returned to Sayeh, and a glimmer of recognition tried to flare. "Hey…aren't you… uh, Selma, Sarah, damn, I'm bad with names…"

Sayeh helped him out. "Sayeh Griffin."

Logan snapped his fingers with a grin as if he'd been responsible for the recall. "Yeah, Sayeh, damn, girl, you look like you've done all right for yourself. You a cop now?"

"Bureau of Indian Affairs, Investigations. How are you, Logan?"

Logan dropped down on the lumpy sofa, scrubbing his face with his hands before answering. "Can't complain. Living the dream, you know?" he quipped, gesturing to his cabin as he cracked a yawn. "Sorry, went out with the boys last night. Might've gotten a little rowdy. You know how it is." He sniffed and sat up a little straighter. "So, who'd you want to ask me about? High school was a long time ago, you know? Like, I can barely remember last week sometimes."

Of that, Levi didn't doubt. From the bloodshot eyes, puffy face and blotchy complexion, Levi could tell the guy was heading for full-blown alcoholism if he wasn't there already.

"We're investigating the case of Echo Flying Owl Jones. Do you remember her?" Sayeh asked.

Logan's blank stare didn't bode well. "Echo? Did she go to school with us?"

"No, she lived on the reservation but someone said that you and your friend Christopher Roth came to the reservation to party sometimes and saw you guys talking."

"Shit, I'm going to be honest, nights at the reservation are mostly a blur, but the best parties usually are, am I right?" Logan joked, but when neither Sayeh nor Levi found the humor, he sobered and tried again. "Uh, no, I don't really remember her. Why? She in trouble or something?"

"Echo died sixteen years ago. You don't remember hearing about it?" Sayeh asked.

Logan didn't have the emotional intelligence to be ashamed. He shrugged. "Naw, I didn't really pay much attention to what happened on the Rez beyond the next party. Let's face it, when the Natives get restless, shit happens. Sorry to hear that she died, though."

If Levi felt steam building beneath his collar, he could only image what Sayeh was feeling. "Have you kept in contact with your friend Christopher Roth?"

"Shit, I haven't talked to that cat since high school. His family left our senior year and I haven't seen or talked to him since."

This was starting to feel like a dead end.

"You didn't keep in touch?" Sayeh asked, surprised.

Logan shrugged. "I mean, I would've liked to but Chris's family was a snobby bunch. I guess they never much approved of our friendship to begin with, so yeah, not surprised when Chris didn't call."

"Snobby? Why do you say that?" Sayeh asked, interested. "Did they have money?"

"They were rich as hell. They had one of them fancy ranchettes that's easy on the eyes but doesn't actually make any money. Like, not a real working ranch but it looked real good. You know what I mean?"

Sayeh nodded. "I'm familiar."

"Yeah, well, that's money for you. It's all about how it looks and I don't know if you can tell by looking around, but I ain't living in the lap of luxury. I inherited this piece of shit cabin when my old man died, and basically the only thing going for it is that it's paid for. Other than that, it could burn to the ground and I'd happily take the insurance money without losing a lick of sleep."

Levi couldn't say he blamed him, though if the place suddenly went up in flames, Levi would find that suspicious, given Logan's statement. "So, you don't remember Echo at all," he confirmed, disappointed.

Logan scratched his head as if that might dislodge a memory but ultimately shook his head. "Sorry, I don't." However, Logan sat up, confused. "So, why you looking into such an old case? Nothing better to do?"

Levi ignored the question, posing his own. "Do you know where the Roth family relocated?"

"Nope, can't say that I do. Like I said, when they cut bait, they didn't look back. Good riddance, you know?"

"Do you remember his parents' names?" Sayeh asked.

"Uh, sorry, just Mr. and Mrs. Roth is all I ever called them, when I saw them, which wasn't often. Chris didn't like to spend too much time with his folks. They were all up in his business all the time so we usually stayed away from the house so he could catch a break."

Sayeh pulled up a picture of Echo on her phone, showing Logan. "I know you said you don't remember but maybe take a look and see if it jogs your memory."

Logan stared at the picture; something flickered across his gaze, but he shook his head. "Sorry, nothing pops up. I wish I could help you more but I really don't remember the chick. Sorry she died, though. That's pretty young to kick the bucket."

"Yes, way too young," Sayeh agreed, shooting Levi

a glance that conveyed her annoyance. Rising, she said, "Thank you for your time, Logan."

Logan rose on unsteady feet, shoving his hands in his jeans pockets. "Yeah, sure."

Levi handed Logan a business card. "If you think of anything that might help, give us a call."

"Sure thing."

They left the cabin and climbed into the car. He wasn't surprised Sayeh had something to say once they were in the privacy of the vehicle. "He's just as much of a dickhead as I remember," she said with a scowl. "Talk about peaking in high school. He definitely didn't age like a fine wine—more like milk left out to curdle."

Levi chuckled, turning onto the road. "And he was popular with the ladies?"

Sayeh barked a short laugh. "Not this lady."

He laughed and started heading back to Billings.

Something about their interview with Logan kept coming back to Sayeh. Even though Logan swore he didn't remember Echo when she showed him the picture, she saw something in his eyes—quick enough to miss if you weren't paying attention—and Sayeh was willing to bet Logan was lying.

"I think he remembered Echo," she said.

And if he was lying about knowing Echo…what else could he be lying about?

"We need to do a deeper search in the database for Christopher Roth. Even if he doesn't have a criminal record, he's bound to have a driver's license, and as long as he hasn't had facial reconstruction surgery, I'll be able to recognize his picture."

"That could take a while, combing through the scores of Christopher Roth identities out there," he said with a frown, and Sayeh could practically hear his reservations about the time spent on what he felt was probably a dead end. But he surprised her when he offered, "I could order a pizza. Cut the work in half."

"I mean, I'm never one to turn down pizza but you don't have to. I can handle it. There's no reason for both of us to sacrifice our night."

"I don't mind. Also, I agree with you. I think he remembered Echo, too. His micro-expression gave him away. He was trying real hard to seem like there was nothing there but I saw the flicker that he couldn't disguise."

Sayeh was pleased Levi had seen the same as her. "Exactly. So do we go back and call him out? Or sit on it until after we find his buddy?"

"I'm curious as to why the Roth family split town. Seems odd. Let's chase down this lead first and see where it goes."

Sayeh agreed, good with that plan, adding, "I think we need to head back to the creek where Echo was found. I want to see the location, get a feel for the scene."

"It's unlikely any forensic evidence is still around. I say we go to the hospital and talk to the staff, see if anyone remembers the night Echo was brought in."

Of course, that was a good plan, but it was hard to explain without seeming like a crackpot that Sayeh often listened to an inner voice that guided her. She called it instinct, but if she tried to verbalize the exact mechanics, it just sounded woo-woo, and people gave her the side-eye. Not that she blamed them. She wasn't trying to claim any psychic ability—she wasn't even sure if she believed in that stuff—but her inner voice hadn't steered her wrong yet.

"It won't take long," she said, refusing to be deterred. "Besides, you never know, evidence has a way of showing up when you least expect it. In my rookie days, we came across a pen that'd been used to stab a person in the neck. It was stuck in an alley beneath the window the perp had thrown it out of and by chance I found it. Something about it grabbed my eye and I bagged and tagged it. Turned out the vic's blood was encrusted on the inside of the pen and voilà, we had the murder weapon."

"Death by ballpoint?" Levi deadpanned before cracking a grin. "Sorry, that was right there for the taking. It was almost served up on a platter."

"A real punny comedian," Sayeh drawled, fighting the urge to laugh with him. It was a really stupid joke, but there was something about Levi that she couldn't quite shake… She liked it.

"So, we're heading back to the reservation tomorrow, then."

"Wear your hiking boots," Sayeh returned with a short grin.

"If I'd known I was going to be putting so many miles on the car, I would've booked a hotel room in Cottonwood."

"What? And miss out on that sweet federal mileage rate?" she teased. "Just think, if we keep up this pace, by the end of the investigation you'll be able to splurge on a diner hamburger with fries."

He chuckled. "Well, when you put it that way…"

"It's all in the perspective."

They rode in easy silence the rest of the way to the office, and true to his word, Levi followed Sayeh to the debriefing room with his laptop tucked against his side, ready to cut the workload in half.

Ordinarily, Sayeh would've run the other way if a coworker had suggested working together after hours, but Levi wasn't half bad.

And he wasn't hard on the eyes, either.

His fiancée had probably been a lucky lady to have a guy like Levi adore her as he had.

She'd never given anyone half the chance to love her that deeply—the idea made her squirm.

Any situation that implied vulnerability made her want to run in the opposite direction.

Her last boyfriend, Trevor, what a mess that'd been. A weird combination of needy and distant—and an excellent reason why she didn't want to date cops.

Great sex hadn't made up for the fact that being with him was emotionally exhausting.

Then, she'd broken up with Trevor, swearing off relationships until she was retired or needed a companion to feed her medication when her arthritis kicked up.

Ahh, hell, who was she kidding? She always thought she'd end up with one of her sisters because she didn't think there was another person alive who could put up with her.

But Levi... Well, he made her wonder what it might've been like to have someone like him as a romantic partner.

Dangerous—and useless—thoughts that needed to die a horrible death.

Immediately.

Alarm spiked through her, and she faked a sudden yawn as she checked the time. "You know what, I'm going to head home and crash. The day really wiped me out. See you tomorrow?"

"You sure?"

"Yeah, I'm beat."

Levi nodded, watching her pack her laptop and grab her things before she waved and practically ran from the office.

No—*correction*—ran from Levi.

It was best to remove yourself from a situation if you felt yourself slipping into dangerous territory.

Why was she thinking about Levi in any way that wasn't strictly professional? She wasn't that person, and it made her intensely uncomfortable that those thoughts had even contaminated her brain.

They'd head to the creek tomorrow and see what Sayeh could pick up. Maybe, with any luck, the Evidence Gods felt magnanimous, and they'd find something worth the trip.

And something that might get her mind off Levi, and the way he filled out those jeans.

Good lord...help.

Chapter 10

Levi watched as Sayeh hustled from the building as if her backside was on fire, and he wondered if it was something he had said during the day. She was hard to figure out, but he was fascinated by her unusual personality.

He could see how others might find her prickly or hard to work with, but he only saw a damn good investigator who didn't care what stood in her way, even if that meant someone's feelings.

He couldn't fault her for that.

He also couldn't help but wonder what kind of relationships in her life had twisted her opinion on commitment because what she described was nothing like what he'd had with Nadie.

Not that Nadie had been perfect—no one was—but they'd been well matched.

Except when it came to opposing opinions on better organizing a closet. Nadie had been adamant about doing it her way; he'd been positive his way was more efficient.

Of all the stupid things to argue about…that was probably at the top.

He didn't want to go home, and he wasn't tired. Powering up his laptop, he started to search for Christopher Roth. He didn't have much to go on, but he managed to find three or four possible choices that he earmarked for Sayeh tomorrow.

Then he returned to Echo's case file, reading over what the Urgent Care report said. It was unfathomable to him that a child could show up battered and bruised to an emergency room and not receive better care.

What happened to you, kid?

Isaac paused at his doorway on his way out. "How's the case looking?"

"Slow. We've hit a few dead ends so far but we're inching in the right direction."

"Inching. Yeah, I was afraid of that. Maybe I should've shut down Sayeh's request to reopen this case. Dakota and Shilah are already making headway on the dead bartender."

"Yeah?"

"It might've been one of the girlfriends that smashed the old bird over the head. They're running forensics on a possible murder weapon. We'll see."

"That's good," he murmured, adding, "Echo's case is full of inconsistencies. Sayeh was right that it wasn't investigated worth a damn. Basic protocol was essentially thrown to the curb, which begs the question, why?"

"Yeah, sure, it's a real head-scratcher but if we can't solve it, our failure won't help anyone, much less the dead girl."

"We're working on some new leads," Levi said, trying to ease Isaac's fears. He knew all eyes were on their task force, and Isaac was reacting to the pressure. "It's going to take time."

"Yeah, sure, of course. I don't expect a miracle," Isaac returned gruffly. He checked his watch and then waved off. "Keep me in the loop."

"Yeah, will do."

Levi sighed, wondering if he was letting his personal feelings cloud his judgment about this case. The leads were wispy at best.

Emotion was leaching into his ability to stay impartial. Listening to the girl's aunt and talking with the people attached to this case, he was finding it hard not to chase any lead that might seem promising.

He wanted justice for the kid.

And not just because it seemed to matter to Sayeh.

He was going to need coffee if he was going to stick around the office for a bit longer. Rising, he entered the break room to find Shilah warming up a half-eaten burrito. He reached for the coffeepot, and she grimaced. "I would brew a fresh pot. I think that stuff has turned into tar."

"Thanks for the tip," he said, dumping the old pot and making a fresh one. "You working late tonight?"

"Yeah, me and Dakota are going with the local sheriff to serve a search warrant tomorrow on the bar and I want to make sure I'm ready."

"Evidence lead you in a different direction than the ex-girlfriend?"

"Possibly. We need to rule out the wife. But honestly, either woman could've had motive—the man was a toad."

He chuckled. "Yeah, I got that impression from the initial report."

"Not that I feel this way but…it's not far-fetched to feel that he got what he deserved." After a moment of shared humor, Shilah switched gears. "How's your case coming along? You getting anywhere yet?"

"If we were in a race to solve cases, you would definitely be in the lead but Sayeh was right—there's something to this case. That poor kid… A lot of missed steps up the chain. She deserved better."

"How's working with Sayeh?"

Levi knew the pitfalls of office politics. Working together as a team was paramount to the task force's success. He wasn't going to hobble the team with gossip. "She's great—real professional and a sharp investigator."

Maybe it was a test he hadn't realized he was taking, but Shilah seemed pleased that he'd passed. "Good to hear it. Have a good night." She grabbed her burrito and returned to her office.

Human beings were complicated.

What was Sayeh doing tonight? Something told him she hadn't been truthful about being too tired to put some OT on the case.

Or she was doing her "lone wolf" routine and didn't want him involved with whatever she was running down. He didn't like that idea. For one, safety was an issue on that score, and two, he was her partner and trust was a two-way street.

As the coffee maker finished percolating, he poured a fresh cup and returned to his office, settling into his chair, only to discover a text message on his personal cell.

He stilled as he read the anonymous text.

One rotten case can spoil a promising career.

What the hell? He narrowed his gaze at the ominous sentence. Was that a threat? His heart rate kicked up a notch. Someone had gained access to his personal cell number to intimidate him.

Well, that just pissed him off.

Then his work cell rang. It was Sayeh. He picked up immediately. Sayeh didn't waste time. "Someone just tried to scare me off—"

"With a coyly intimidating text to your personal cell? Yeah, I got one, too," he finished for her. "Make a report to IT. They might be able to trace the text and find the coward."

"On it."

"And then power your cell down for the night. You got a good security system at your place?"

"I live in an apartment complex, so no, but I can take care of myself. How about you?"

"I'm good," he assured her. "Someone doesn't want us poking into Echo's case and we've barely started turning over leads, which means someone's real nervous. Joke's on them—threatening me is a surefire way to keep me interested. How about you?"

"Oh, yeah, doubly so. I actually got excited. Means we're on the right track."

He barked a laugh. Only Sayeh would get fired up by an intimidation tactic. "See you tomorrow."

"Don't forget to wear your hiking boots," she advised with residual laughter.

He clicked off and immediately reported to IT to follow up on the sender, then powered his cell down.

Whoever sent that text must think they've got connections strong enough to affect their careers. Was this an inside job? Someone within the BIA with secret ties to a murdered girl? It was possible. The crime happened sixteen years ago. A lot could happen in that time frame.

So far they'd only talked to a handful of people about Echo's case—Yazzie King, Logan Caldwell and the aunt. Of the three, it seemed doubtful the aunt or Yazzie had ulterior motives to keep the investigation quiet, and Logan didn't seem the type to have connections to anyone in a powerful position.

There was also Joe Dawes and his rookie officer, Russell

Hawkins. He didn't know enough about either to understand where their characters landed.

Maybe it was time to take a deeper look.

After the mystery text Sayeh slept fitfully, only managing to snatch a few solid hours before she gave up and decided to shower and get ready ahead of schedule. She arrived thirty minutes early and waited for Levi to show up at the office. She knew without having to ask he hadn't slept well, either.

She recognized a grittiness to his energy, and it excited her to find the commonality between them.

Some people got loopy with lack of sleep; for Sayeh, it honed her senses.

"I'll drive," he said, handing her a hot tea as they climbed into his vehicle.

She didn't argue, too pleased to be on the same page. "I got to thinking, whoever sent that threat, they seemed more refined than your average street punk. So, that knocks Logan Caldwell out of the lineup. Can you really see Logan choosing metaphor to get his point across? The man's brain is probably way too pickled to remember how to string together a complex sentence."

Levi nodded. "Not to mention, whoever sent it thinks they have enough connections to affect our career. I don't see Logan rubbing elbows with anyone influential down at the local bar."

Pleased he was already running down possible suspects, Sayeh asked, "Okay, so who are you thinking? The number of people who know we're investigating Echo's case is very small."

"I'd like to take a closer look at Joe Dawes and his rookie officer. Do you know much about either of them?"

"I'd hate to learn Joe is a bad apple like the chief before him. He's been real helpful to me and my sister. As first impressions go, I like him. I don't know his rookie officer. Let's start there."

"Fair enough, but that saying, 'keep your friends close and your enemies closer,' could apply. Joe might want to play nice to gain your trust so that you don't look closer later."

Sayeh knew that could also be true, but her gut didn't want to believe Joe could be a crooked cop. Still, this business always had a surprise waiting in the wings.

Sayeh brought along the original crime scene photos, paltry as they were, for visual guidance. She'd already studied the images so many times she had them memorized.

"According to the GPS, Echo's body was found in a place called Yego Creek, which is pretty far from the reservation proper," Sayeh said, reading the directions from her work phone. "That's another reason I always found the narrative of the report to be suspect. What kid is going to wander around in the freezing cold and end up in an out-of-the-way creek? Feels more like a body dump to me."

Levi agreed. "Is it a seasonal creek or does it run year-round?"

"Looks to me like it's seasonal. It should have some water running through it right now but it'll dry up by late summer, or depending on the rainy season, slow to a sluggish, murky trickle."

"The likelihood we're going to find anything is small," he warned, "but I'm open to luck being on our side."

Sayeh wasn't expecting a miracle, but she also believed in things being overlooked, especially if Echo was dumped quickly, as she suspected. People doing things in a panic often left behind clues. The time passage was the element working against them. Anything biological would be long gone, but physical clues could still hide in the area, just waiting to be discovered.

They pulled off the main highway onto an unmaintained road, the rough ruts washed out from previous storms making it slow going until they reached the point where they'd have to walk the rest of the way.

The smell of grassland tickled her nose as they trudged through the tall grass until they reached the banks of Yego Creek. Using the GPS coordinates, and the photos, they started looking for anything to catch their eye.

Yego was a tributary to the Little Big Horn River, feeding the winding river with winter runoff and providing plenty of fresh drinking water for grazing cattle and local wildlife. Green ash trees dotted the banks, the leaves rippling as the wind raced through the branches.

It was a peaceful enough place in the spring but probably not in the winter. Something caught Sayeh's eye across the bank. "Check it out," Sayeh murmured, gesturing with a head bob. Levi followed her gaze and nodded.

"Looks like some good old-fashioned homesteading," Levi said.

Someone was camped out by the creek's edge, and by the looks of it, they'd been there some time.

"Let's cross over there and see if anyone's home," Sayeh said, heading for the section of the creek with enough rocks rising above the water to cross without having to swim.

As they got closer, they saw a man stretched out on an old cot, snoring loud enough to wake the dead. He could've been in his thirties, or he could've been in his sixties— hard to tell when someone spent 90 percent of their time in the elements.

Levi cleared his throat. "Excuse me, sir," he said, trying to wake the man up. "Can we talk to you for a minute?"

The man snorted and woke with a start, his gaze disoriented as he struggled to his feet. The smell of alcohol seemed to leak from his pores, and Sayeh immediately felt for the older man who'd obviously lost control of his demons if he'd ended up in a tent by the creek.

"Who are you?" the man croaked, shoving a shaking hand through his hair, causing it to stand on end. His bloodshot gaze darted with mistrust between Sayeh and Levi. "What do you want?"

Levi immediately put the man at ease. "We're not here to make trouble," he said calmly. "We're looking for something that might've been left behind. What's your name?"

The man took a minute, unsure if he trusted either of them, but answered, "Daniel Irontail. What are you looking for?"

Sayeh spoke up. "Sixteen years ago, a girl was killed and dumped here. Her name was Echo Flying Owl Jones. We're trying to find anything that might help find who killed her."

"Echo…" he repeated, his mouth moving as if chewing on an imaginary piece of gum or trying to hold back a wave of emotion. "I know her."

Both Levi and Sayeh weren't expecting that. Levi asked first, "How did you know Echo?"

"She's nice to me," Daniel answered as if Echo were still alive. "Brings me food sometimes. Fry bread and beans."

Sayeh's hopes sank. The man wasn't well. Either he suffered from mental illness, or his alcoholism had taken its toll on his brain. "Do you have family that visits you here and brings you food?" she asked, thinking Daniel was mixing up Echo with someone else in his life.

But he scowled and shook his head. "No family. Just Echo."

That didn't make any sense. Echo had been dead for sixteen years.

"Eyes like coal. I keep her secret safe."

Secret? "What do you mean?" Sayeh asked.

Daniel's gaze lost clarity, and he ignored them as he disappeared into his tent, leaving them baffled and unsure how to proceed.

"We could call tribal services and let them know an elder with mental instability is camped out at Yego Creek," Sayeh said, biting her lip, unsure if that was the right choice.

"Let's give him a few minutes. Take a look around like we planned, and then circle back. His faculties might reset and we may get a few answers out of him."

Mental illness was a terrible thing.

Sayeh knew that statistically there were more mentally ill tossed out on the street than those who'd made poor choices in life.

Daniel Irontail had a story to tell, but it was locked inside the chaos of his mind.

And there was no telling how much they'd be able to pull out before his faculties shut down again.

Chapter 11

They were back on the other side of the creek when Sayeh said, "You were really good with him. How did you know to talk to him like that?"

Levi smiled, sharing, "Back at my family's ranch, there was an old-timer named Ridgewater Tom. He had dementia brought on by a head injury from the Vietnam War. Before his brain injury got too bad, he was one of the most loyal and hardworking men I've ever known. Even though all the ranch hands had a place in the bunkhouse, in the summer Ridgewater Tom preferred to sleep out in the field with the cattle, and during the winter, he slept in the barn with the horses. Said he liked animals more than people and my dad said that was something he could understand."

Sayeh chuckled, engrossed in the story.

"Anyway, he was never late to work and never stole anything from the ranch so my dad said that he could have a place to live until such time that he chose something different."

Levi had fond memories of Ridgewater Tom. He was like the uncle he never had. "He started to have bouts of mental instability, so my dad paid for him to see a doctor. They did an MRI and discovered that his brain injury had created chronic encephalopathy, which then led to his mental deterioration."

"But your dad kept him on the ranch even after discovering he was falling apart?"

"When my dad took someone under his wing, he didn't let go. My dad said that it was important to invest in people and people come with all sorts of trials and tribulations. He made sure that Ridgewater Tom had a home until the day he died."

Further impressed, Sayeh murmured, "That was very kind of your dad."

Levi's throat threatened to close up, but sharing something of his dad's legacy with Sayeh felt good. "My dad always knew how to get through to Tom when he was having a moment. He would say, *Give him a minute, and he'll come back around*, and he was right. When it got to the point that Tom couldn't work, he just let him be and would take food out to him every couple of days. They'd sit, chat, and then my dad would leave him to watch the livestock, count bugs or whatever Tom wanted to do that day."

Then came the day they'd all known was coming. "One day my dad went out to bring him food, and Ridgewater Tom had passed in the night. Honestly, I think that was exactly how he would've wanted to go. He was happiest out there with the livestock, watching the sunrise or the sunset, with nothing but the wind to keep him company."

"That almost sounds very peaceful," Sayeh mused. "Except the 'living outside with the cows' part."

Levi chuckled. "Yeah, not everyone is cut out for that life. Anyway, I figured Daniel might respond similarly."

"You're handy to have around," Sayeh said, winking as she pulled the crime scene photo from her back pocket, returning to the case. "This is where Echo's body was found.

Except…" She frowned, studying the picture and comparing the creek today. "The water is much higher now. I'd say by maybe two feet?"

He nodded in agreement. "An above-average snowfall followed by an unseasonably warm spring has caused a lot of the snowpack to melt early."

Sayeh frowned with disappointment. "It was a long shot but the odds of finding anything to help our case seem to be in the same realm as winning the lottery on a scratcher. Damn it."

Levi agreed, but Sayeh continued to study the creek banks with a critical eye, tuning into whatever sixth sense or instinct she claimed helped her solve cases. He wasn't one to believe in the woo-woo stuff, but he also wasn't one to discount methods that worked, either. He preferred not to label everything, accepting that he wasn't meant to understand some things.

"Do you think it's possible that Daniel knew Echo?" Sayeh asked, pausing in her search.

It seemed highly unlikely, but he wouldn't rule it out. "It's possible he fixated on Echo at some point, and now that someone is bringing him food, he's transferring the memory of Echo onto the new person."

"So that would mean we need to find the person bringing Daniel his food," Sayeh said. "Got any tricks to do that?"

He shook his head. "It's not likely we'll get a name out of him that makes sense."

"That's why I'm wondering if we should take him to a facility so he can get the help that he needs, which in turn, might also help us."

He thought of Ridgewater Tom and how being confined would have crushed his spirit. Levi shook his head. "I know you think it's for his own good, but if he's not hurting anyone and he's not a danger to himself, I think we should just leave him alone."

Sayeh seemed conflicted between agreeing with his logic and fighting against the impatience that pushed an investigator to seek answers. To Sayeh, Daniel might seem like an obstacle in her way, but if Levi had learned any- thing from his experience with Ridgewater Tom, you had to give people space to be who they were, not who you wanted them to be. "Let's head back to his camp and see if he's lucid again," he suggested.

Sayeh blew out a short sigh and nodded, realizing they weren't going to find anything with the water this high.

They crossed in the same place they had before and found Daniel eating out of a can of beans as if he'd forgot- ten they'd spoken not more than thirty minutes ago. He wasn't startled awake this time and smiled, gesturing for them to join him. "Hungry? I got another can."

Sayeh smiled. "I think that's my favorite kind. Where did you get those?"

"Oh, a real nice girl always brings me the best ones. She knows all my favorites. I don't know where she gets them, though. I'm just happy that she brings me presents. Not like the others who are mean and throw rocks at me."

Sayeh exchanged a look with Levi, approaching Daniel from a different angle. "You said you were friends with a girl named Echo, and you were keeping her secrets. What kind of secrets?"

Daniel shook his head as if he couldn't be tricked. "Can't be telling secrets. That's a no-no, but I can share my beans. That's all I can share today."

Daniel started talking to himself as if the conversation had continued without them, stopping to intermittently hum a nonsensical tune. The man was a far cry from the one they'd stumbled upon, sleeping like the dead, but he also wasn't giving up anything of value.

Levi let a few moments pass, then asked, "Hey, Daniel, can you tell us about yourself? How and when did you come to live at the creek? You sure have the best view."

Daniel scooped a spoonful of beans into his mouth, nodding in agreement. "Nothing beats what Great Spirit has created, no sir. I am blessed."

That's what Ridgewater Tom used to say, too. It was amazing how life became so simple when you stripped away everything that made it complicated. "Are you from the Macawi Reservation?"

"I am Macawi," Daniel said, proudly thumping his chest. "The blood of the ancestors runs through my veins."

"Does your family know that you live here?" Sayeh asked.

"No family. Just me."

Levi was willing to bet that Daniel had family somewhere on the reservation, but he'd either had a falling out with them many years ago and his brain had erased them from his memory, or his family had left the reservation and he didn't remember where they went.

"Tell me, how'd you get so lucky that Echo trusted you with her secrets?" Levi asked conversationally, as if they were just two buddies shooting the breeze and sharing a beer.

It was a method his dad had used with Ridgewater Tom.

"Not everyone around here respects the old ways. Being an elder don't mean much when the young'uns don't care to listen to any wisdom that we have. I knew from the start she was different. She was always real nice, always willing to listen. And when she saw I didn't have nothing to eat, she brought me something for my belly. She didn't make fun or yell at me when I got confused and that's something."

Levi shared a look with Sayeh. From everything they'd learned about Echo, it sounded as if Daniel had known her. Was it possible that Echo had brought Daniel food sixteen years ago, and the old man's brain had no concept of time passing? That would make sense as to why he thought Echo was still alive. Was he here the night someone dropped her body off on the creek bed?

Levi thought of something. "Daniel…have you always been in this particular spot?"

"Oh, no, but I came close when she needed me. Had to. It was cold. Real cold. Her fingers were blue and hard as a creek's rocks. I told her, it was too cold for her. She wasn't strong like me. I'm used to the cold. I got a special blanket."

Levi stilled, afraid to ruin the momentum. Daniel had seen Echo's body. He could feel the vibration of Sayeh's excitement, but she wisely remained silent, letting him steer the conversation.

"That was real nice of you," Levi said. "Did Echo say why she was out in the cold that night?"

Daniel opened his mouth, and then the confusion overtook his limited cognitive abilities. He started to mumble. "It was too cold. She was frozen all over. I… I tried. I'll keep her secrets. I will."

"Of course you will," Levi assured him in a moderated tone. "You're a good friend to Echo."

"Yes. Good friend."

"Daniel…did Echo ever bring anyone else with her when she brought the food to you?"

Daniel looked conflicted, finally saying, "People are bad."

"People are bad," Sayeh agreed with a murmur. "I'm so glad Echo has you as her friend."

That seemed to calm Daniel down for a minute, but something was troubling him; the memory of seeing Echo's body sixteen years ago…was probably confusing him even more.

Daniel said Echo had been frozen all over. What did that mean? Was he being literal? Or was he just saying her body was cold, which he would've attributed to the freezing temperatures?

One thing was for sure…they needed his help.

And if Daniel couldn't get help, they'd help him.

Sayeh could barely contain her excitement. She was willing to bet her eyeteeth that Daniel had the key to their case locked in his jumbled brainpan.

Another thought jumped to mind.

What if Daniel was their killer, but his mind had blocked out the memory of what he'd done to Echo?

She needed to talk to Levi to determine what they would do next.

Gesturing to Levi, she dusted off the seat of her pants and said, "Well, we're going to take off, but is it okay if we visit again another time?"

Levi followed her lead, though he could tell she was up to something.

Daniel nodded, and within a blink, he was lost in his own world again.

Once they were far enough away, Sayeh looked at Levi, her mind racing. "I know you have a soft spot for this guy because of your experience with Ridgewater Tom, but we can't ignore the fact that we could be talking to Echo's killer right now."

"What makes you think Daniel is our suspect?"

"Hear me out. Obviously, Daniel had feelings for Echo because she was kind to him, but he might have hurt Echo without even realizing what he'd done. His fractured mind might've manufactured some fiction because he couldn't face the reality of his actions. Cognitive dissonance. Maybe it wasn't his fault, but we have to find out if Daniel is the one who killed Echo. You have to admit, that theory makes a hell of a lot more sense than Echo landing in some random creek in the middle of a storm and freezing to death."

"I'm not saying you're off base," Levi conceded, "but let's come at this from a different angle first. I think we can get a psychologist out here to talk to Daniel on his own turf. He'll be more likely to open up if he's in familiar territory. We'll bring some food, like we're all friends, and we might get some more answers out of him. If that doesn't work, we will take him into custody, do a DNA swab and see what happens. I'd really rather not do that because it'll be very traumatic for him but you're right, there's a possibility Daniel is our guy."

Sayeh softened. "I can tell you hate the idea that Daniel might be our guy but we can't ignore all possibilities. Echo deserves justice."

Levi chuckled with wry amusement, putting her fears to rest, saying, "If Daniel is guilty, I'll handcuff the man myself and take him into custody. I won't let sentiment get in the way of justice."

A shiver of awareness tickled her backside. There was something intensely alluring about the way Levi could be kind, yet his spine was made of steel. What an inconvenient time to realize her partner was relentlessly sexy.

Calm down, girl. Get your hormones under control— before you hog-tie the man to your bed.

Shaking off the inappropriate thoughts, she allowed one small concession. For Levi's sake, she hoped Daniel was innocent. She didn't want to arrest a man whose marbles had gone on a permanent walkabout.

Chapter 12

"I could use a beer," Sayeh admitted as they drove back to Billings. An unfamiliar thrill at spending more time with Sayeh jumped to his gut at the casual mention, and his discomfiting visceral reaction stalled his response. She took his silence as rejection and quickly amended, "Hey, cool your jets, I'm not asking you to go with me. I was just making conversation."

But he suspected that's exactly what she was doing, and he felt like a jerk for leaving her hanging. He was tempted to take her up on the offer—and that's when a wave of guilt threatened to capsize him.

What the hell was wrong with him that he was thinking of his partner in any way that wasn't professional?

He wasn't that guy.

He was the opposite of *that* guy.

And yet the idea of returning to his apartment, facing that constant emptiness, made him almost desperate to agree, and he didn't like that, either.

Sayeh deserved better than what he had to offer—which was not much.

Not to mention messing around with a colleague; hell, there were so many reasons why that wasn't a great idea that even an idiot without much critical thinking skills could puzzle it out.

But he was drawn to Sayeh in ways he hadn't felt since Nadie.

Red flag, right?

No, *he* was the walking red flag, and maybe he ought to be honest about that fact. *Act like an adult and communicate like you're capable of stringing together a complete sentence without retreating to awkward silence.*

Great advice, except his mouth remained stubbornly sealed shut. Why was this so hard to do? He was inexplicably tongue-tied.

"I like you," he blurted out. *So much for finesse.* His cheeks burned. Swallowing his pride, he shook his head and put it all out there. "But I don't have anything to offer you, Sayeh. My heart is a broken mess after losing Nadie, and despite everyone telling me it's time for me to let her go, I can't. She's always there in my head and my heart. Every time I even think of trying to move on, it feels like I'm cheating on her memory, and then I feel sick to my gut. Am I attracted to you? Hell yes. Damn, who wouldn't be? You're stunning. But what can I offer besides sex? You deserve better than that. I would never disrespect you like that, and I sure as hell would never do anything to jeopardize our working relationship. We're both professionals, and we're both committed to seeing this through. I think sex would just muck things up."

He should've felt relieved, but he felt worse—and catching her incredulous expression made him feel like he'd misread everything.

"Dude, like I said, it was just a beer. Sex was never on the table. You're not even my type. I'm oddly flattered...

kinda…but yeah, brokenhearted dudes who are stuck in the past are not my jam."

Well, this is embarrassing. "Uh, right. Okay, glad we got that out of the way," he said, trying to speak normally around the size elevens in his throat. "I mean, this is good. Communication is important. Being able to talk to each other about uncomfortable things is good. Healthy."

"Yeah, sure," Sayeh agreed, though her expression was dubious. "Anything else you want to get off your chest?"

"Nope. I'm good."

"Great."

Silence stretched between them as the tires ate up the distance between the reservation and Billings, but Levi's brain was anything but quiet.

Had he imagined the growing tension between them? Had he misread that look she'd given him earlier? Sure, it was there and then gone in an instant, but he wasn't so far out of the game that he'd forgotten everything he'd ever learned about women.

Or had he?

A moment of panic seized him as he wondered if he'd completely lost any sense of game he'd ever had.

Or maybe he'd never had a game.

Nadie used to joke that if it hadn't been for her making the first move, he'd still be watching her from across the crowded bar, too petrified to even talk to her.

He'd always countered that's not exactly how he remembered it, but now he had to question if Nadie had been right all along.

Was he clueless?

"Just for the sake of asking…what is your type?" he asked, feigning nonchalance as if he could take it or leave it with her answer.

"Take a guess," she countered, turning it into a game.

A game he didn't enjoy, but he'd play along. "The 'bad boy' type," he supposed.

She barked a short laugh. "Sure, during a phase *in college*. Bad boys are exhausting and almost always broke. My dad taught me that if a man can't afford to take you to dinner, he can't afford to build a life. Of course, I was rebelling against my dad at the time, so I deliberately found the bad boys alluring. Until one nearly ruined my credit and I narrowly escaped catching an STD. I like excitement but not that kind of excitement."

He chuckled despite himself. "Okay, so not a bad boy. You've already told me you don't like men in law enforcement...so perhaps a white-collar type? A lawyer or something?"

She made a face. "I would eat a lawyer for lunch. Besides, in my experience, lawyers are in the same category as doctors—functional and necessary but ultimately suffer from a God complex. No thanks."

At that, he laughed. He had a buddy from school who became a lawyer, and that was pretty spot-on as to his personality trait. "Okay, so that leaves what? Blue-collar? A plumber, carpenter, or..."

"I like a guy who can make me laugh," she said, surprising him. "I guess I'd be willing to overlook a problematic profession for a guy with a good sense of humor."

"And why is that?"

Her smile softened, sharing, "Because if there's one thing I learned from my parents, it's that when everything else fades, if the laughter remains, so does the love."

That was ridiculously profound—and oddly sweet. It was a philosophy he appreciated. "Your parents were wise."

She chuckled softly. "Yeah, they really were. I wish I'd

realized it way earlier. My mom died of cancer six years ago but I lost my dad suddenly last year. Home invasion gone bad. I've since realized that I wasn't always the best daughter to two people who'd been nothing but good to me all my life."

That rare show of vulnerability from a woman as tough as Sayeh choked him up, and he didn't know why, but it meant something to him.

"I'm sure they knew what a good daughter they'd raised," he assured her.

Sayeh blinked away the telltale sheen in her eyes, returning her gaze to the road as she said, "Well, if I ever make it to Heaven, I'll be sure to ask them. Until then… I'll just have to hope."

Levi felt the heaviness of her quip and recognized the weight of banked grief. He wanted to ask her more about her dad but backed off. That was enough sharing for today.

Sayeh hadn't meant to get all mushy, but there was something about Levi that made her want to bare her soul, like it felt safe in his hands, which in itself made her intensely unnerved.

Arrrgh. She hated that feeling.

And she *had* been fishing for a hint that he might feel the same way about her—that the attraction wasn't a one-way street—but the embarrassment of being shut down had taken control of her mouth.

She should've been honest—like Levi had been with her.

Hell, what was wrong with her?

She knew better than to mess around with a colleague. *Recipe for disaster.*

Not to mention an HR nightmare.

It was easier to act like he'd completely misread her

body language and that her gaze had lingered one too many times, sending a silent message straight to his primal brain that she was interested and willing to see where it went.

Like a cat in heat.

Mortification threatened to swallow her whole.

Finally they arrived at the office parking lot, and Sayeh popped from the car and waved goodbye, pretending to feel nothing but airy indifference to that excruciating conversation, but inside she was cringing.

And she needed advice.

Before she'd even cleared the parking lot, she was on her cell to Luna.

Thankfully, her sister answered.

"I need advice," she said before even saying hello.

"Are you okay?" Luna asked, alarmed. "Who is this? My baby sister never asks for my advice so that leads me to the next logical conclusion that you've either been kidnapped and you're being coerced, or an alien has taken over your body."

"I'd take the alien option if I had a choice because what I just experienced was enough to make me want to fall through the earth's crust and disappear."

"That sounds dramatic. What happened?"

She cut to the chase. "Something awful. I'm attracted to my partner."

Luna didn't seem surprised. "Well, he's hot so I can't fault you. Why is that awful?"

"Luna, I'm not dating a colleague. Not really my style."

"Me, either," she agreed, clarifying, perhaps for her own benefit, "Benjamin wasn't my colleague but we were working together so I think that might qualify. I don't know, it's a gray area."

"It's not the same. My paycheck and Levi's paycheck

are signed by the same person," Sayeh said. "Benjamin could've walked away from your case at any point, and it wouldn't have affected the outcome of your investigation."

"Agree to disagree but go on."

"I don't even know when it happened," Sayeh admitted. "It was a sneak attack. One minute I felt my normal, stand-offish self and the next I was picturing how it would feel to kiss him. I've never wanted to kiss a coworker before. What is wrong with me?"

"There's nothing wrong with you," Luna assured her softly. "You like him—and from what I've seen, he seems like a great guy. Sure, dating a coworker can get tricky, but you're both adults. Just don't let it affect your working relationship."

"Because that always works out," Sayeh said dryly, reminding Luna, "When emotions get involved, all rules and common sense go out the window. C'mon, I need you to haul out the big guns and really let me have it like only a big sister can. Tell me what a stupid idea it would be to mess around with Levi. Oh, did I mention, he's still hung up on his ex?"

"Oh, that's not good," Luna said, concerned. "How long have they been broken up?"

"Well, technically, she died, so…it's not like they broke up on their own accord."

"Yikes, that's even worse."

"Tell me about it."

"And, how long ago did she pass?" Luna asked cautiously.

"Two years ago."

"Oh. Okay. So, it's been a little while, not that there's an expectation for an acceptable grieving timetable but… how does he feel about you?"

"Uh… I mean, he said he likes me but then he also said that he can't give me what I deserve so he pulled that card, which always feels like a cop-out, and usually when a guy says that to me, I power walk in the opposite direction. But there's something about him that makes me want to wrap my arms and legs around him like a baby koala and squeeze all of his pain away."

At that, Luna laughed. "I've never heard of that method before but I'm intrigued."

"You know what I mean. There's just something about him that makes me feel safe enough to be soft, which I hate, by the way, but at the same time, I crave. Good gravy, if Kenna could hear me right now she'd start chirping on about getting into therapy. Like *everybody* needs therapy just because *she's* started going."

"Which isn't a terrible idea for other reasons, but for this reason, probably not necessary. You like him, Sayeh. I mean, you *really* like him—that's not a bad thing. He seems like a good man. Maybe be willing to see where it goes."

"It goes straight into the HR office for a mountain of paperwork," Sayeh said.

"Our jobs are filled with paperwork—one more stack isn't going to kill you."

"I was hoping you'd tell me to snap out of it and to stop being a reckless idiot, like old Luna would. Instead, you're being all supportive and while it's nice, I'm not sure if it's the best advice in this situation."

"This feels like a lose-lose situation for me," Luna said with a laugh. Sayeh blamed Benjamin for this change in her sister, even if it was good. "Look, it can be scary to take a chance on something new when your last relationship wasn't so great but don't shut yourself off to experiencing something potentially better than what you had before."

Sayeh sighed unhappily. Of course Luna was right. Her mature brain agreed wholeheartedly with the advice but the immature, damaged part of herself that was afraid of being vulnerable wanted to ignore every syllable.

"I don't even know why I'm stressing about this… Levi isn't open to anything more than professional, which should be a blessing but it leaves me feeling rejected and I hate that feeling, too."

"Maybe he's scared, too."

Sayeh sensed the truth behind that simple statement. Levi was attracted to her but still grieving his fiancée's loss.

So where did that leave them?

Unsure.

"I hope that helped," Luna said, "but I have to get going. I'm meeting Kenna and Ty for dinner. Lucas is out of town for a K-9 training seminar, and we're going to try out that new restaurant in the plaza, Blossom Bistro. It's supposed to be really good."

Sayeh suffered a short pang of envy that her sisters were hanging out and having a good time without her, but she let it go.

"I hope it's great," she said. "Thank you for the advice. Tell Kenna I said hi, and give my favorite nephew a squeeze for me."

"Will do. Love you, sis."

"Same," she returned before clicking off with another heavy sigh.

The thing about good advice—sometimes what you don't want to hear is what you most *need* to hear.

Sliding into her parking space, she grabbed her stuff and headed into her apartment. Looked like another solo night of pizza and research for her.

Good thing those were two of her favorite things.

Chapter 13

The following day, both observing an unspoken courtesy to avoid all mention of the awkward conversation from yesterday, Levi and Sayeh waited their turn to talk with Dr. Carla Lopez.

Despite a jammed schedule, the clinical psychologist had agreed to meet with them on such short notice, and Levi was just as hopeful as Sayeh that Dr. Lopez would be willing to help.

"Have you ever noticed that every shrink has the same interior decorator?" Sayeh mused, pacing with her hands shoved in her pants pockets while they waited in the lobby.

The lobby was aesthetically pleasing but bland. Neutral paint, soothing, nondescript art and a water fountain burbling unobtrusively in a corner created a perfectly nonthreatening environment. "It's meant to put people at ease."

"Yeah, well, it makes me uncomfortable," Sayeh said.

Levi chuckled. *Ever the obstinate one.* "Well, I think you're in the minority. The study of aesthetics and how it affects mood might disagree with you."

Sayeh shrugged. "Probably." She switched tracks. "Has IT gotten back to you about that cryptic text message?"

"Yeah, last night actually. I was going to tell you today and forgot. Burner phone. Untraceable."

She snorted. "Of course it was. Remember when burner phones were only available to James Bond-esque spies? Now you can pick one up at a gas station."

Levi grinned, shaking his head in agreement. "Yeah, well, technology gives with the same hand that it takes."

"Ohh, so wisdom-y this morning," Sayeh teased.

"It was something my dad used to say," Levi shared.

Immediately sobering, Sayeh said, "Oh, sorry. I didn't mean to be an ass."

"You're fine," he assured her, "but now we have to change our personal cell numbers, and that's a pain in the ass."

"Tell me about it. Whoever sent that stupid text tried to be intimidating but all they did was add one more item to my to-do list."

The door opened and a patient of Dr. Lopez's exited, wiping at her face and avoiding eye contact as she hustled past them. An attractive woman in her midfifties, Dr. Lopez smiled congenially and waved them into her office. "You must be the agent I spoke with…" she said, looking at Levi.

Levi confirmed, flashing his credentials as Sayeh did the same. "Levi Wyatt and my partner, Sayeh Griffin. Thank you for seeing us on such short notice."

"I'm always happy to help law enforcement," she said, closing the door behind them and settling into her fat-cushioned, high-back chair, gesturing for them to sit opposite her on the matching sofa.

While the lobby was bland and neutral, her office had a subtle upscale quality. It was still soothing, but the furnishings were made of finer material and had a lush feeling.

Mental health pays well, Levi mused.

"How can I help? You mentioned a man with deteriorating faculties?"

Sayeh jumped at the chance to get things moving. "We're

investigating a case involving the murder of a sixteen-year-old Macawi girl who was found dead in a creek sixteen years ago. We think this man might've witnessed her murder or at the very least seen who dumped her body. The problem is... he seems to have advanced mental deterioration and he has issues with time. He thinks she's still alive. But when we try to get answers out of him, he gets confused and shuts down."

Dr. Lopez mulled over the information. "Yes, it's very frightening for patients when they lose their grasp on reality. Is he violent?"

"Not that we can tell but we don't know him very well," Levi answered. "We only just discovered him yesterday. He's set up an encampment beside a creek on the reservation, the same creek where the victim's body was found."

"And he's not a suspect?" the doctor asked.

"We're not ruling it out but until we can get more coherent answers out of him, we're not treating him as one."

"I see. How can I help?"

"I doubt he'd be willing to come to you and I don't want to traumatize him by forcing him into a facility. Would you be willing to speak to him on his own turf? Help us determine whether or not he's a danger to himself or others and whether or not he has information of value stuck in his memory?"

Dr. Lopez frowned, conflicted. "That's not usually how I operate. I prefer a more controlled environment for my sessions. If he's been living on his own for quite some time, his grasp of reality is likely clinging to a familiar setting. Me showing up and asking questions could wrench his fingers free from that hold. It could make things worse—and he could become violent."

It's true Levi didn't know Daniel, but he didn't get a sense that the man was dangerous. Still, he understood the doctor's reluctance. "We could provide security for your safety," he assured her. "Plus, we would be with you. If the man seemed dangerously unstable at any point, we would make sure your safety was a priority."

"And I'm assuming billable hours apply?" Dr. Lopez said, hinting that she wanted assurances she'd get paid for this adventure.

"Of course," Levi answered, putting her mind at ease. "The BIA appreciates your time."

Dr. Lopez admitted, "I'm not going to lie, I'm intrigued by the prospect of going into the field. It's been a while since I've had the opportunity to work with a patient under these circumstances."

Sayeh perked up. "You've done this before?"

Dr. Lopez chuckled ruefully. "To be truthful, I was an intern at the time, working under a doctor in California, but I remember it was a thrilling experience."

"How so?" Levi asked, curious.

"The doctor was asked to consult on a case with the LAPD. An elderly man in advanced stages of dementia was in the care of his stepdaughter when a home invasion went bad. The stepdaughter was killed but the elderly gentleman was found wandering the neighborhood in a heightened state of disorientation. We were called in to assess whether or not it was possible the elderly man had witnessed the murder and if so, what information could be pulled from his memory."

"Did it work?" Sayeh asked.

"After many months, we did discover evidence that the ex-husband had broken into the house and killed his estranged spouse. Sadly, the elderly man passed shortly after the evidence revealed the ex-husband's guilt. It felt good knowing we'd been integral in putting a bad person be-hind bars."

"Why'd you go into private practice?" Sayeh asked.

"To be frank, it pays better than civil service," Dr. Lopez answered with a chagrined smile. "However, I'm glad to have the chance to pay it forward again."

Not exactly paying it forward when you're getting paid, but Levi let that slide. They needed help, and she was the only psychologist available for months.

The doctor grabbed her iPad, opening up her schedule. "When shall we do this?"

Sayeh didn't know what to think of the good doctor.

Maybe Sayeh was generally distrustful of head docs, but something about Dr. Lopez rubbed her the wrong way. Per-haps it was the pseudo-helpful veneer that put her off. She knew damn well if Levi hadn't been able to produce the federal checkbook to pay for her time, she would've *ever so politely* and *regretfully* declined. Yeah, a real humanitarian.

But it wasn't productive to look a gift horse in the mouth, and seeing as Dr. Lopez had agreed to come out to the creek with them, Sayeh would shelve her misgivings.

"We'd like to head out there as soon as possible," Sayeh said. "Sometime this week, if you can manage it."

Dr. Lopez frowned as she peered at her schedule, which Sayeh imagined was a forest of clients, and after moving things around, said, "I can manage a trip to the reservation next week. Does that work for you?"

No, it definitely did not, but what choice did they have? Sayeh shared a look with Levi but nodded, accepting the doctor's timetable.

"Excellent," Dr. Lopez said, powering her iPad down.

"And perfect timing as my next client is waiting. My secretary can finalize the details with you on your way out."

"Thank you for your time," Levi said, following Sayeh out.

"I don't like her," Sayeh said in a singsong voice under her breath before reaching the secretary's desk.

"Yeah, well, she's what we have to work with, so smile and be nice," he responded quietly, then turned on the charm for the receptionist. Sayeh left Levi to work out the details, and then they headed to the car.

Finished, Sayeh slid behind the wheel only to hear her cell buzzing. "Agent Griffin," she answered as she snapped her seat belt in place. It was Charlene, Echo's aunt.

"Agent Griffin, I… I'm sorry to bother you…but…um, I think maybe it was a bad idea to open up Echo's case," she said in a shaky voice choked with fear. Sayeh immediately put Charlene on speaker so Levi could listen.

"Are you okay? What's going on, Charlene? Talk to me," Sayeh encouraged.

"It's… I've just been thinking…maybe it was selfish of me to keep bringing up a bad memory for our people. I should've just let Echo rest in peace."

Sayeh shared an alarmed look with Levi. *"What happened?"* she mouthed to Levi, instantly concerned. "Charlene, did someone threaten you? What are you talking about? Are you safe?"

"I'm f-fine," Charlene answered, but the reedy thin pitch of her voice gave her away.

"Charlene, stay where you are. Lock the doors. We're on our way."

Levi was already calling Joe Dawes with tribal police while Sayeh threw the car into Drive and spun out of the parking lot, heading out of town and back to the reservation.

Sayeh kept Charlene on the line while Levi spoke with Joe Dawes. He confirmed with Sayeh, murmuring, "They're on their way out there to make sure she's okay," and Sayeh relayed that information to Charlene.

"Stay put. Joe Dawes should be there within minutes and we'll be there within half an hour."

It was a forty-five-minute drive, but Sayeh would break several laws to make it in thirty.

"I'm going to keep you on the line until Joe gets there, okay?" she said, navigating the road like a pro racer. She'd been top of her class in the obstacle driving course, and growing up driving country roads had given her plenty of practice.

Levi clutched the "Oh, Jesus!" handle as Sayeh took a hard turn, shooting her a warning look but otherwise remaining silent.

As soon as Joe Dawes arrived, Sayeh felt secure enough to click off and focus her full attention on the road.

"Someone wants this case shut down," Sayeh said ominously. "First that cryptic text and now someone is threatening Charlene? I got a bad feeling."

"We don't know any of that is related to the case," Levi warned. "Don't jump to conclusions."

"I'm telling you, someone is trying to get us to stop asking questions and whenever that happens, that tells me we're sure as hell on the right track," Sayeh muttered.

"If that's the case, I agree with you, but until we get some kind of confirmation these incidents are related to our case, I'm staying neutral."

"You do that," Sayeh said, shaking her head.

They pulled up to Charlene's house in a spray of dirt and gravel, and Sayeh was out of the car and in the house within minutes. They found Joe Dawes and his young tribal officer, Russell, talking with Charlene in the living room. Charlene's eyes were red-rimmed as if she'd been crying, and her nose was pink, tissues clutched in her hand.

Sayeh immediately crouched beside Charlene to meet her gaze. "What happened?" she asked softly.

"At first, I thought it was nothing but…then the messages kept coming and they got worse each time."

Sayeh rose and looked to Joe for more information. Joe gestured for them to follow him while Russell stayed behind with Charlene.

"Charlene said when she came home from grocery shopping today, this message was on her machine waiting for her," Joe said, pushing the play button on the antique answering machine on the counter below the equally old wall phone. Joe turned the volume up so they could hear the message.

The scratch of old tape sounded as a distorted voice followed. "You dumb bitch, I told you what was going to happen if you didn't shut up about that little whore. If you don't want to end up in the same place, you better make sure people stop asking questions."

Sayeh's blood chilled and heated at the same time. The voice was disguised, so there was zero chance Charlene would recognize who was on the other end, but maybe forensics could pull something from the tape.

"Forensics might be able to get something to ID the caller," Sayeh said, frowning. "But why threaten Charlene? She doesn't have any control over our investigation. Whoever did this is a damn bully. They took the opportunity to frighten an older woman, knowing it wouldn't change a thing."

Levi agreed, but Joe said, "I hate that this happened to someone as nice as Charlene but it's probably a prank.

Some kids probably heard their parents talking about you guys stirring things up, asking questions, and they took it as an opportunity to be little devils."

Sayeh narrowed her gaze at Joe. "If it was a bunch of misguided kids, a few weeks in juvie ought to remind them that karma is a bitch. I'm going to find who did this and I'm going to make sure they are served the justice they deserve."

Joe lifted his hands in a conciliatory manner, saying, "Hold up, I'm on your side. I'm just saying, I doubt there's anyone in town truly looking to hurt Charlene. She keeps to herself, volunteers and, generally speaking, is well-liked in town."

"Charlene said this wasn't her first message," Levi said.

Joe nodded. "But she erased the others. This is the only one she's still got and only because it scared her so bad she was afraid to erase it."

Sayeh looked to Levi, tempted to ignore Joe and bag and tag the tape, anyway. But she grudgingly agreed to let Joe look into this incident, only because they had their hands full with other aspects of the case.

Sayeh returned to Charlene, her heart hurting at the sight of the older woman's lip quivering. "Joe seems to think it was probably a bunch of mean-spirited kids playing a prank," she said, trying to soothe Charlene's nerves. "What did the other messages say?"

Charlene sniffed and wiped at her eyes with a shaking hand. "Well, I can't remember specifics. At first it was just a quick message, saying something along the lines of *stop asking questions* and then it changed to stuff that was more mean, like *stupid hag*, and then that awful message today." She looked to Sayeh, confused. "What kind of person would say that as a joke?"

"A terrible person with zero sense of empathy," Sayeh

returned dryly, wanting to ring the necks of whoever put fear in the old woman's eyes. "We'll find who did this and make sure they stop."

"But what if…what if it's not just kids who sent the messages? What if it's the same person who killed my Echo? What if they're not bluffing?"

The instant rage burning in her gut made Sayeh make a somber promise, "It's going to be okay," then offering quickly, "If you don't feel comfortable staying here tonight, we can get you a motel room."

Charlene shook her head. "I'm not going to be run out of my own home," she said with a sliver of her spirit. "I'll be okay."

"Are you sure?" Sayeh asked.

Charlene wiped at her eyes, nodding. "I was scared but I'll manage."

Sayeh nodded, returning to Joe and Levi. "She's going to stay here, though I wish she'd let us spring for a hotel room, at least for the night."

"I'll have Russell do a drive-by during his patrol," Joe assured Sayeh. "She'll be okay. I truly think this was just the work of mean-spirited kids but we'll keep our eyes peeled for anything suspicious."

Sayeh didn't like how quick Joe was to brush off the situation, but she had to remember not everyone had the same suspicious mind as she did.

Levi seemed to know what she was thinking. He pulled her aside while Joe and Russell put Charlene's fears at ease, saying, "I haven't known you long but I can tell by that look in your eye that you're not happy."

"No, I'm definitely not happy," she confirmed, but was resigned to the situation. "But if she doesn't want to come with us, we can't force her. Even if it's for her own safety."

"There's a chance Joe is right about it being a prank," he said.

"And there's a bigger chance that it's something worse. I don't believe in coincidences, Levi. Someone is trying to send a message—and I don't like what they're saying."

Chapter 14

Levi sensed the turmoil beneath the surface as Sayeh reluctantly agreed to abide by the older woman's wishes. He didn't necessarily agree with Joe Dawes that it was nothing, but he wasn't entirely ready to sign off on the belief that it was someone trying to stop their investigation, even though the unease in his gut said otherwise.

However, like Sayeh, he didn't believe in coincidences, and there was enough to keep digging.

They managed to convince Charlene to let them take the recording—though how the thing still worked, he hadn't a clue. He hadn't seen anything that archaic in a decade, but then technology moved more slowly in rural areas.

"We'll get the tape to forensics and see if any of their new tech can isolate the voice and remove the disguise from the recording," Levi said. "Then, there might be a chance of identifying the voice."

"Maybe so, if it's someone local, but not if they're not from the reservation," Sayeh said. "Let's just say for argument's sake, everything so far has been connected. That means someone is close enough to the case to know what we've been up to."

"If everything is connected," he reminded her, "but yeah, that theory would hold water."

"Okay, so let's play that game. Who jumps to mind?"

"For me? Obviously, Joe Dawes and his tribal officer."

"I thought that, too, but I've dealt with Joe before this and I never got a bad vibe from him."

Levi cast a dubious look Sayeh's way. "Forgive me if I don't consider your gut the standard by which we judge someone's potential for criminal behavior."

Sayeh surprised him with a laugh. "Fair enough but when I'm right, you owe me a beer—or whatever beverage of your choice that doesn't trigger your internal alarms that I might be after more."

Levi shook his head, biting back a grin, even though she'd technically roasted him for overreacting the other day. No time like the present to make amends. "Hey, Sayeh, want to go grab a beer?"

"Are we adding burgers and fries to that order?"

"We can."

"I had pizza last night," she said, almost apologizing. "Not that I wouldn't mind pizza again but I'm trying to watch my girlish figure."

It was an innocent statement made tongue-in-cheek, but Levi immediately went to a place he hadn't been in a long time.

"There's nothing wrong with your figure," he murmured before he could stop himself. "I mean, you're in obvious good shape. Do you go to the gym?"

"Only when I'm angry and punching a human being is frowned upon."

"Are you angry often?"

Sayeh only grinned, and he grinned back. "Great. Burgers and fries, then."

It felt good to shake off the day, at least for a short while, and he'd been wanting to try the burger joint down the street from his apartment but hadn't gotten around to it.

They pulled into the diner and chose the patio with fewer people.

The service was excellent—already off to a great start—and they had beers in their hands within minutes.

Sayeh took a drink and released an audible sigh of relief. "That's hitting the spot," she murmured, the tension releasing from her shoulders. She was an intriguing woman. Each time he thought he had a handle on who she was as a person, she flipped the script. As someone who prided himself on accurately figuring people out, Sayeh presented an enigma he yearned to solve. Also he liked looking at her. "So, is this a working dinner...?"

The smart answer would be to say yes, that way things would remain professional, but he had less interest in that prospect than he should. "We need a break from the case," he decided. "A watched pot never boils. Sometimes we have to switch focus to get our brain to see a solution that might be right in front of our faces."

"I'm willing to give it a shot," Sayeh said with an unsure smile, admitting, "I'm in unfamiliar territory. I'm not really good at socializing on a superficial level. Usually, I end up asking a blunt question that's considered rude or impolite, so how about you start and I'll follow your lead."

He chuckled, appreciating her honesty. "All right, so far I've met one of your sisters and she's got dark hair and dark eyes... How'd you end up with dirty blond hair and blue eyes?"

"Great question, one I've wondered myself, but until I learn more about my birth parents, I don't know how I'll find out," she answered. "My nickname growing up was Yellow Hair because when I was young, it was much lighter. I definitely looked more like the child that could've been my adoptive parents' biological kid."

"Were you close to your adoptive parents?"

Her soft laughter couldn't hide the flicker of remorse. "Well, I was close to my adoptive mom but I think that's because she was always sticking up for me when me and my dad were butting heads. My mom was sweeter than apple pie. I don't think she had a mean bone in her body. Cancer took her way too young."

"I'm sorry. Cancer is a bitch," he commiserated, sharing, "I had a cousin close in age to me and my brother who died when he was fifteen from a rare bone cancer. It's hell on everyone."

Sayeh nodded. "It really is. Sometimes the fallout from the grief afterward is just as bad as the sickness. When my mom died, my dad just became less of himself. I mean, sure, he was still stubborn as all get-out but he spent more time in his workshop and less time with us. I think he just couldn't function for a long time after Mom died. My sister Luna was the biggest help to my dad in pulling him out of that funk."

Levi understood that all too well. If it hadn't been for his dad and brother, Landon, he might've fallen down that well of grief and never surfaced.

Thinking of Landon made him remember dodging his brother's text about helping clear out their dad's things. Damn it, he needed to buckle down and get it done.

Sayeh caught the subtle shift in his mood and questioned him on it. "Everything okay?"

He was tempted to brush it off, but Sayeh had shared something personal, and he wanted to reciprocate. "My dad died of a heart attack a year ago. It was sudden and came out of nowhere. The man seemed healthy as a horse one minute and the next he was gone. My brother's been after me to help clear out his things from the ranch but I've been avoiding his calls and texts. I feel like an ass about it but I can't bring myself to shove my dad's things in a box. I guess I'm not ready yet to admit that he's truly gone."

Sayeh knew that pain. She blinked as tears tingled behind her sinuses. Even though she and her dad had their issues, accepting that he was gone was a pain she was still trying to reconcile. "When my dad died, my sisters, Luna and Kenna, took on the lion's share of that duty," she admitted. "So, I understand how when something hurts so bad, you don't want anything to do with it."

Levi nodded, the guilt in his eyes making her want to reach out and caress his cheek, but she kept her hands to herself. "The thing is, I know it's not fair of me to put this all on Landon's shoulders—he's already handling all of the ranch business—but each time I try to bring myself to return that text and give him a solid date to get it done... I don't. I put it off, I make excuses, everything else becomes a bigger priority. And then I feel like a shitty brother."

God, she knew that feeling. She'd spent half her life feeling like the sister that was more trouble than she was worth. "Something tells me you're not a bad brother," she assured him, and this time she reached for his hand and squeezed it gently. "From what I know of you, you're a good man, which probably translates to being a good brother, too."

"I appreciate that," he chuckled, accepting her comfort. Levi covered her hand with his, the warmth of his palm sending a thrill racing across her nerve endings. Her breath caught, but she forced a cheerful smile as they pulled away simultaneously. The waitress arrived with impeccable timing with their food order, and Levi looked relieved and frustrated at the same time, but he smiled at the waitress, switching gears seamlessly. "Damn, that looks good," he said, surveying the monster burger surrounded by a mountain of seasoned fries on his plate.

Sayeh followed his lead, agreeing as she plucked a fry from her plate. "I'm starving. This looks amazing. Good call."

They enjoyed their burgers, finished their beers and paid the tab. The food was good, but the company was better. Sayeh realized, as they said their goodbyes and went their separate ways, that not only was she starting to see Levi in ways that weren't professional, but the realization was beginning to bother her less than before.

What she'd said to her sister had been true—she didn't mess around with colleagues—and it was a rule that'd always served her well.

But as clichéd as it sounded, there was something about Levi that flipped all her rules on their heads.

The knowledge made her uncomfortable, but she couldn't stop what was happening.

Luna didn't see a problem with Sayeh's growing attraction to Levi—clearly her gooey-eyed relationship with Benjamin had turned her brain to soup—but Sayeh saw many problems.

For one, new relationships flooded the brain with endorphins, and she didn't need to be distracted by thoughts of Levi's fantastic ass while chasing down leads. She needed all her faculties to close this case. Actually, no other reason mattered because reason number one was strong enough to carry the entire argument.

Yet, as solid as the argument was, it left her with a bone-deep dissatisfaction that was hard to brush past.

It was oddly unifying that they'd both lost their fathers a year ago—even though that was a macabre bonding point.

She wanted to know more about his life, what it was like

growing up on a ranch with his brother, how he got into the Bureau of Indian Affairs and even how he and his fiancée met. A funny thing happened when you're into someone— suddenly everything about them was fascinating.

Oh! You can juggle? Neat! Tell me more!

Most days Sayeh wanted to know as little as possible about the people she worked with.

Sighing, she pushed Levi from her mind, tired of the endless loop of her thoughts. She wouldn't waste time thinking about it if it wasn't productive.

She grabbed the official soil sample report and added it to her file for her parents' investigation.

Not a lot of answers on that front, either. Everyone involved with her parents' case that she knew of was dead.

The police chief at the time, Allen Paul, had taken all the answers to the grave.

However, she thought the man's family might remember something from that time. It was a long shot but one she could try.

She remembered the Paul family from her childhood, but she hadn't kept in contact after leaving Cottonwood.

She quickly searched the internet and found what remained of the former chief's family on social media. Maybe Luna would be willing to come with her to ask some questions. Allen's wife, Vera, still lived in Cottonwood. However, she was probably in her late seventies or early eighties. No telling how lucid or healthy she was or if she would be willing to talk to Sayeh.

And even if she was willing, would she know anything?

Not all men shared details of their lives with their spouses. Especially if they were harboring secrets.

Chapter 15

Levi knew that sometimes the wheels of justice moved slowly—much too slowly—but the tension in his neck was enough to keep a solid grip on the constant throbbing in the back of his skull. A week felt too long to wait to get back to Daniel, but they were stuck with Dr. Lopez's schedule.

Sayeh saw him rolling his head on his shoulders, trying to relieve the pressure, and wordlessly pulled two ibuprofen from her bag.

"Thanks," he murmured, washing them down with a swig of water as they exited the vehicle. Coordinating the team to provide support took some maneuvering, but Dakota and Shilah stationed themselves on the other side of the bank with a clear view of the encampment, along with support from the tribal police office.

Dr. Lopez, dressed casually in slacks and a button-down linen shirt, wasn't prepared to cross the creek, but after some help hopping from rock to rock, they managed to get her across without getting wet.

Levi brought a few cans of the beans Daniel seemed to enjoy and a fresh loaf of sourdough bread that was easy to pull off in chunks to eat with the beans. He wanted to do what he could to make Daniel feel at ease because he knew showing up with the doctor was bound to create a ripple in Daniel's comfort zone.

The air was crisp, smelling of fresh rain from the day before, and the birds chirped in the distance.

"What a beautiful view to wake up to every day," Dr. Lopez murmured as they navigated the tall grasses toward the encampment. "I can understand why he wouldn't want to leave. Developed properly, this could be a prime real estate location."

Sayeh regarded Dr. Lopez with a questioning look. "Moonlighting as a real estate developer?"

Dr. Lopez chuckled. "No, just a little dabbling here and there. I've always thought the reservation leaders could manage their resources a little more profitably, though. I mean, this spot is just perfect. With a little development, this could be—"

"It's exactly as nature intended," Sayeh interrupted with a short smile. "Just because a place is beautiful doesn't mean everyone is entitled to have a piece of it. Especially when it's someone else's home."

Levi wasn't sure if she was referring to Daniel or the Macawi people, but it was alluring how quickly Sayeh shut the doctor down with that kind of talk. He agreed with Sayeh. The spot was beautiful, just as it was; no improvements were needed. He smothered his grin and gestured, saying, "It's just up here," and they were walking into Daniel's camp within a few minutes.

Levi chuckled, seeing Daniel's still form beneath a blanket, just like the last time they visited. "Daniel?" he called out.

But unlike last time, the old-timer didn't jerk awake.

Levi's smile faded. Sayeh picked up his vibe, and immediately her hand strayed to her sidearm, ready. Seeing the change in demeanor, Dr. Lopez hung back as Sayeh and Levi approached the form beneath the blanket with slow measured steps.

"Daniel?" Levi tried again as he lowered slowly to the ground to grab a small corner of the blanket and pull it back. But the reason Daniel wasn't answering was immediately apparent. "Goddamn it," he growled, stepping back, confirming with Sayeh, "He's dead."

Sayeh saw the round hole in the center of Daniel's skull and pulled her cell, immediately calling their awaiting team. "Call a coroner. Daniel is dead."

"Confirmed?" Shilah asked over the speaker.

"Confirmed." Levi nodded grimly. "He's been dead at least a day or two. It's a miracle the coyotes haven't found him yet."

"Or a hungry bear," Sayeh quipped, frowning with sharp disappointment as she swore under her breath. "We were so close. I know Daniel had the answer locked in his head someplace."

"Hello?" Dr. Lopez called out from a safe distance. "Is everything okay?"

"Not exactly," Sayeh answered. "He's dead."

Dr. Lopez gasped. "Dead?"

"Yes."

"Oh, dear, that's terrible," she said, hugging herself and rubbing her arms. "Natural causes? Perhaps a heart attack or a stroke?"

"Not unless bullets to the brain are considered natural these days," Sayeh returned, looking to Levi. Sayeh ignored Dr. Lopez's gasp, saying to Levi, "You still think none of these incidents are related? The one person who might've turned this case on its head…just got a one-way ticket to the afterlife right before we were supposed to talk."

Levi was ready to tie the incidents together. "No, I think you're right—someone is trying to keep this case buried," he agreed darkly.

The team crossed the creek and walked toward them.

"Coroner is on the way," Shilah said, glancing at Daniel's body. "Straight between the eyes. Almost sniper-style. Someone is a good shot."

Russell scratched his head. "Well, almost everyone's got a gun nowadays and picking off squirrels your whole life can make you a pretty good shot. It could've been anyone. Hell, it could've been an accident. Plenty of people hunt on this land."

Levi's gut didn't mesh with that theory. Someone shot Daniel intentionally. You'd have to be a blind idiot to shoot in an area with an obvious human occupant. It wasn't like Daniel was sleeping in the grass. He had a tent, for crying out loud. It was clear someone was living there.

"Did you know the victim?" Sayeh asked Russell.

Russell frowned. "Know him? Not really. I saw him around the town a few times. He kept to himself. Never much trouble, though. You could ask Joe more about him."

Sayeh nodded. "We'll definitely do that."

"I'm guessing you don't much need me anymore," Russell said, looking uncertain about his role. "Unless you want me to wait until your forensics people show up…?"

"You don't have to stay," she told Russell. "Go ahead and let Joe know what's happened here and we'll be in touch soon."

But Russell seemed conflicted. "It happened on Macawi land. Doesn't that mean we have jurisdiction?"

"Technically, the Office of Justice Services within the BIA—which the task force is a part of—has jurisdiction, so we'll take it from here," Sayeh corrected him with a short smile.

Levi seconded Sayeh's answer. "Sayeh is right. The task force has jurisdiction but we'll keep you in the loop. We appreciate the tribal police's cooperation."

Almost forgotten, Dr. Lopez piped in. "I think I'll hitch a ride back to town with the officer. I'll just get in the way at this point."

"Actually, I know it's asking a lot but would you mind looking at his living space and see if you can see anything that stands out," Sayeh asked.

Dr. Lopez grimaced, clearly unhappy with being around a dead body. She seemed pretty squeamish for a doctor, but one might say she wasn't "that kind" of a doctor. Levi would forgive her reluctance. Not everyone was cut out for fieldwork.

"What am I looking for?" she asked, uncertain.

"We're not sure. Can you give us your professional opinion on the health of his brain based on his surroundings?" Sayeh asked.

"That's a bit of a stretch," Dr. Lopez murmured, shaking her head. "But I'll see if anything jumps out."

"That's all we can ask," Levi returned with a short smile.

Dr. Lopez drew a shuddering breath as she surveyed the encampment, her gaze darting away from the body beneath the blanket, but as she switched into a different mental mode, she noted, "The patient exhibited a need for order. Even though much of his environment was out of his control, he seemed to take great care with his own things." She glanced back at them. "Did he serve in the military?"

Sayeh answered, "We don't know much about him. It's possible. Why do you ask?"

Dr. Lopez pointed toward Daniel's food stores—a row

of canned goods, each turned with their packaging facing outward in the same way. "There's symmetry here. Damaged brains often return to the safety of long-term memory or even muscle memory. He might not have remembered why he preferred to have his things kept in an orderly fashion but it may have given him comfort."

"When we talk with Joe Dawes, we'll see if Daniel had a military background," Sayeh said, making a note in her phone. "Anything else?"

Dr. Lopez shook her head. "Sorry, without speaking with the patient myself, it's hard to make any kind of determination that isn't purely speculation, which of course makes me uncomfortable."

"Of course," Levi said, understanding. Turning to Russell, he said, "Would you mind giving the doctor a ride back to town?"

"Not at all," Russell said, relieved. "After you, ma'am."

Dr. Lopez left with Russell, and it was hard not to feel the weight of everyone's disappointment in today's outcome. He was sick to his stomach for the old man and thought he'd let Sayeh down.

And somehow, that felt worse.

Sayeh was seething with impotent rage on the inside, but she was doing her best to keep it cool. It wasn't the doctor's fault that they'd had to wait a week to get out here, but she wished she would've gone with her gut and had Daniel brought into protective custody. Maybe if they'd done that, he'd still be alive.

"I know what you're thinking," Levi said, mainly to Sayeh.

"Yeah? And what am I thinking?"

"That if I would've let you make the call to bring Daniel into custody, he'd still be alive to question."

"Okay, so you do know what I'm thinking." Sayeh let out a short breath. "I'm not mad at you, just at the situation. I get your reasons why you didn't want to do that but we just lost our best lead."

"Yeah, I know," Levi admitted grimly. "But I finally agree with you—this isn't a coincidence—and I definitely don't believe this was an accident."

Dakota joined them with an update. "Forensics team is right behind the coroner. ETA thirty minutes."

"Thanks, Dakota." Levi bracketed his hips as he surveyed the scene, looking for anything that might've been left behind, but Sayeh was more interested in studying the entry wound.

She wasn't a Forensics girl, but she'd seen plenty of dead bodies in Narcotics. Guns and drugs went hand in hand, and friendly fire happened often. "That wound is really clean," she mused. "Hardly any blood. High-powered, long-range. I'll bet the bullet is still in his skull."

"Quite possible," Levi agreed.

"So, why'd someone take out the old guy?" Dakota asked.

"Probably because they were afraid he'd talk about something he saw sixteen years ago," Sayeh answered.

"Yeah, but I thought his marbles were scrambled."

"That's why we brought the doctor. We were hoping she could help make sense of his disordered timeline and find out what he saw that night. We think he saw either Echo's murder or, at the very least, who dumped her in the creek."

"Tough break," Dakota commiserated. "I hate when that happens."

"You and me both," Sayeh said.

They couldn't touch the scene until Forensics had processed everything, but Sayeh gingerly peered into Daniel's small tent. It smelled like one might imagine a homeless man's tent might smell, but Sayeh was more interested in the little odds and ends collected like knickknacks perched on an upside-down box.

"See anything of interest?" Levi asked.

"Not sure," she murmured. Her gaze roamed the tight space, returning to the box. A tattered book, three tiny ceramic figurines and a teacup.

The teacup seemed odd.

She carefully maneuvered herself into the tent, mindful of Daniel's body and his belongings, to get a better look at the teacup.

Nestled at the bottom of the cup, an older turquoise bracelet, the silver chain darkened with time, seemed out of place. She shot a quick photo with her phone and slowly backed out of the tent just in time for a convoy of cars to pull up across the creek, signaling the arrival of the Forensics team and coroner.

Dakota announced with a gesture, "The 'Brush and Comb' team are here."

Good. She couldn't explain it, but she felt the bracelet was important.

The Forensics team quickly unloaded their gear, and Levi directed them to the easiest part of the creek to cross. Unlike Dr. Lopez, they had no problem navigating the crossing.

A man with salt-and-pepper hair and an experienced air walked up to them. "CSI Preston Howard with the Office of Justice Services. Fill me in on what we got here," he said as he looked at Levi and Sayeh expectantly.

Levi broke down what they knew so far, and Sayeh pointed him to the tent's interior, saying, "I'd like everything in there tagged, with particular attention to the brace-let at the bottom of that teacup."

"Any reason why?"

"Just a gut feeling," Sayeh said.

Howard directed his team. "You heard the lady. Bag and tag everything." Then he gestured to a woman with a camera slung around her neck. "Go ahead and photograph the body so we can get him loaded up."

Levi and Sayeh stepped back to give the team room to work, while Dakota and Shilah headed back to Billings to return to their own case.

What a complete waste of time for everyone involved, Sayeh thought with frustration.

The team worked efficiently to process the scene, then they bagged up Daniel's lifeless body and carried him care-fully across the creek to load into the coroner's awaiting van.

Once cleared, Levi and Sayeh took one final look at the encampment and crossed the creek, the last to leave.

"You think that bracelet was Echo's?" Levi asked as they climbed into the car.

"Maybe. I took a picture of the bracelet before Forensics bagged it. Let's stop by Charlene's place on the way out. She might recognize it."

Levi nodded and carefully pulled out of the tall grass and onto the dirt road.

Sayeh's gut was tingling—as if something major had just been discovered, but she had no context. Was it the bracelet or something left behind by Daniel's killer?

Hopefully Forensics would be able to give them some-thing to work with.

Chapter 16

They rolled up to Charlene's place, tires kicking up the fine dust of the weed-choked driveway, and saw her outside watering her flowers. The older woman looked as if she hadn't slept well since the last time they were here, and Levi knew it was out of fear.

They were still waiting on the IT department to break down the audio recording from her answering machine tape, but they had a slim chance of finding anything on that tape that might help their case.

Charlene shaded her eyes against the sun, instantly relieved when she realized it was Levi and Sayeh. "Oh, sorry, the sun was in my eyes. Wasn't sure who I was looking at. Do you have news on Echo's case?"

"Not exactly," Sayeh answered apologetically as they joined the woman. "We met a man who seemed to know Echo, a homeless man with an encampment on Yego Creek, near where Echo was found. Said that Echo used to bring him food."

Charlene blinked in surprise. "Oh, yes, that's Danny Irontail," she shared, surprising them both. "He's harmless. Wouldn't hurt no one. Especially not Echo."

Stunned, Levi and Sayeh could only stare. Sayeh asked first, "How did Mr. Irontail meet Echo?"

"Echo and I volunteered down at the tribal center. At the first of the month, we'd help hand out food to those less fortunate. Danny was one of our regulars. He'd never been right in the head since the day we met him. He couldn't hold down a regular job and had a hard time with people but like I said, he wouldn't hurt no one."

"Do you know if he served in the military?" Sayeh asked.

"He might've but it was hard to know what was a fact or a figment of his mind. Sometimes he was lucid enough and other times, not so much."

"And you never worried that he was dangerous?" Levi asked.

"Oh, no, he was real protective of Echo. Bless that child, she always had a soft spot for Great Spirit's lost and forlorn. She took him under her wing like he was a lost puppy. If he didn't show up on the first of the month to get his box of goods, she'd insist that we bring it to him."

"That was very kind of her," Sayeh murmured.

"That was my Echo," Charlene said with pride shining in her eyes. "She talked tough but deep down, she had the softest heart."

Levi guessed, "Have you been bringing Daniel his food lately?"

Charlene nodded. "I know it may seem crazy but it was something me and Echo did together and it made me feel close to her by continuing to see to Danny's care. He's all alone, no family to speak of, so in a way, I suppose we were his family. I've offered for Danny to set up his tent here on my property but he likes the creek." She sniffed with a small smile, revealing, "I know it might seem crazy but knowing Danny was on the creek always made me feel like he was still watching out for Echo."

Levi never questioned what brought other people solace. Even though he wouldn't say he had a green thumb, he spent an inordinate amount of energy trying to keep a plant alive that'd been Nadie's favorite. Somehow seeing that plant thrive made him feel connected to her.

And now he and Sayeh had the unenviable job of telling Charlene the bad news about Daniel. Chagrined, he drew a short breath, revealing, "We hate to be the bearer of bad news but we found Daniel in his encampment, dead from a bullet wound."

Charlene gasped and actually lost strength in her knees. Levi caught the older woman before she crumbled to the dirt. "Dead? I don't understand."

Levi helped Charlene to a small patio chair before continuing. "Unfortunately, we don't have any answers just yet. We were supposed to meet with Daniel today and found him expired. We think it happened a day or two ago. We'll know more after the autopsy."

Sayeh said, "We had no idea you knew Daniel. We actually came to ask you if you recognized a bracelet we found on the scene. Would you mind taking a look?"

Charlene wiped at her eyes, nodding. "Of course."

Sayeh pulled out her cell phone and showed her the picture she'd snapped. Charlene held the phone and peered at the image. Instantly recognition followed shock. "Y-yes, that was Echo's. Are you saying that Daniel had her bracelet all this time?"

Levi smothered the flicker of excitement at the positive confirmation. "It seems that way. It was in a teacup in his tent. Do you remember the last time she was wearing that bracelet? Did you buy the bracelet for her?"

Charlene shook her head, still reeling. "No, I didn't buy it. At the time I thought it was a gift from her boyfriend but I didn't want to press her until she was ready to share.

From the moment she got it, she never took it off. I asked about the bracelet when her body was found but the officers claimed they hadn't recovered a bracelet. I'm ashamed to admit that I thought someone in the tribal police department had stolen it. I mean, how could I prove she'd been wearing the bracelet at all? I knew I couldn't, so I had to let it go. And to think… Danny had it this whole time? I don't understand."

"The bracelet has been turned over to Forensics. Maybe we'll find some DNA that might help us in the case," Sayeh said, trying to ease Charlene's pain. "But I promise as soon as we can we'll return the bracelet to you."

"Thank you," Charlene murmured with tears sparkling in her eyes. "That would mean a lot to me."

Even though Charlene was adamant that Daniel would never hurt Echo, the fact that he had her bracelet was troubling. What if Daniel had taken the bracelet after killing Echo? And if he had killed Echo, her death would've fractured his mind even further out of guilt.

But that didn't answer why someone had gone to great lengths to silence the homeless man before they could get any answers out of him.

An entire ecosystem of questions swirled around the murder of one teenage girl.

Why?

Sayeh's heart broke at the expression of misery on Charlene's face. It must feel like her tiny slice of the world was slowly crumbling in on her. "Can we get you anything?" she asked, trying to help in some way.

Charlene shook her head, still processing the information about her friend. "I know what you're thinking," she said. "Danny having her bracelet…probably makes him look guilty as hell but Danny worked real hard to keep himself in check. He never wanted to hurt no one, that's why he stayed out by the creek. He knew he wasn't well."

"I understand you want to protect his memory but is it possible that Daniel had a mental breakdown and hurt Echo?" Sayeh asked gently. "It could've been accidental—maybe he didn't have control of his faculties when it happened."

"No." Charlene shook her head. "Not a chance. You didn't know him like I did. He wouldn't hurt a fly—much less Echo."

"And why is that?" Levi asked.

"Because Echo was kind to him in ways that went beyond just bringing him food."

"Can you elaborate?" Sayeh asked, curious.

"She used to read to him from his favorite book."

Immediately Sayeh remembered the tattered book on the box beside the teacup. "Which book was that?"

"*The Catcher in the Rye*," Charlene remembered, smiling. "There was something about that book that really calmed him, made him happy."

"Why did she read it to him?" Levi asked.

"Because Daniel couldn't do it for himself. He was severely dyslexic and never learned to read properly. He could make out certain words and string together a sentence but it took him quite a while to do it. His true reading level was probably a second-grade level at best."

Sayeh did the mental math. Judging by his appearance, Daniel was probably in his late sixties or maybe early seventies. It was quite possible to slip through the cracks of the education system back in the '50s and '60s, especially if he dropped out of school and immediately enrolled in the military.

The more she learned about Echo, the angrier she became that someone snuffed out such a precious light in the world. Echo would've done amazing things if she'd been allowed to grow up.

Tears jumped to her eyes, but she sniffed them back. "What a tragedy. He loved to read but couldn't help himself, so she bridged the gap."

"Yes." Charlene nodded, appreciating that Sayeh saw Echo's beautiful soul. "She was one of a kind."

Sayeh nodded. Returning to Charlene, she said, "Are you okay? How have you been since we talked last?"

Charlene shrugged, reluctant to admit that she was on edge, but Sayeh could see it plain on the nose on her face. "When you get to be my age, you take each day as it comes," the older woman said with a stiff upper lip. "I go about my day same as ever."

She knew they'd have zero success convincing Charlene to leave her house until things settled down, but Sayeh hated leaving her alone, especially now that Daniel had been killed. If someone was silencing people who knew Echo, that put Charlene in a dangerous position.

"I know you're not comfortable with the idea of staying in a hotel but would you consider staying at my parents' place in Cottonwood for a few days?" Sayeh offered, almost desperately. She was breaking all the rules—letting the case get personal—but she couldn't stomach the idea of leaving Charlene to fend for herself without anyone to look out for her and she didn't know if she could trust the tribal police. "There's a spare bedroom—nothing fancy—but nice enough. My sister would probably enjoy the company."

"You're a sweet girl but I'm fine right where I am."

Of course she knew that's exactly how she'd respond,

but Sayeh had to try. Levi seemed to understand her fear and remained quiet.

They weren't supposed to let a job get under their skin, but sometimes it happened because investigators were only human, not robots.

"Charlene, I'm worried about your safety out here," Sayeh admitted. "Someone is real unhappy that we're digging into Echo's case and as we get closer to the answer, they might get desperate. I don't want anything to happen to you."

Charlene smiled up at Sayeh. "You're a good girl, too. You remind me of Echo in some ways. I'll be fine." At Sayeh's protest, Charlene shook her head, saying, "Even if I'm not fine and it turns out my time is here, that just means I'll be spending eternity with Echo, and I can't be sad about that. She's waiting for me—and that makes the fear of dying fade away."

It was a beautiful sentiment, but Sayeh was more pragmatic about death. The actual dying part could be quite gruesome and painful, especially if it wasn't through natural causes. They didn't know who they were dealing with or why they wanted the secret of Echo's death to remain a mystery. Sayeh couldn't settle with the idea that Charlene might be in the murderer's sights.

She knelt beside Charlene, imploring, "Auntie…you might not be safe here right now. Please accept my offer, if not for yourself but for my peace of mind."

Charlene paused, holding Sayeh's gaze, torn between stubbornly holding her ground and relenting for Sayeh's sanity. They hadn't known each other long, but Sayeh felt a kinship with this elderly woman that poked at her banked grief, reminding her that life was short and capricious.

"Are you sure your sister wouldn't mind a stranger in her home?" Charlene asked, uncertain.

Sayeh wanted to crow with victory, so relieved. She assured Charlene, "Are you kidding? She'd welcome the company. Her boyfriend lives out of town and I moved to Billings for my job. She'd love to have you. Plus, you can meet my other sister, Kenna. She loves to bake and has wanted to learn more about how to cook more traditional Macawi dishes. Maybe you could help her with that."

Charlene brightened with wary hope. "I've always wanted to pass down my grandmother's recipe for fry bread."

"That sounds amazing—and I can promise you I'll be first in line to eat it," Sayeh said, grinning.

Decided, Charlene rose and announced she'd need a few minutes to pack a bag.

As Charlene disappeared into the house, Sayeh turned to Levi, expecting a look but seeing nothing but kind understanding, and those damn tears rose to the surface again.

"I just need her to be safe," she said, her throat threatening to close.

Levi reached for her hand and squeezed. "I know."

And without realizing it, Sayeh slipped further down the rabbit hole she swore she'd never go.

But she was too far gone to feel mad about it.

If anything, she just wanted more.

Chapter 17

Sayeh hated to admit that she had been putting off the talk with Allen Paul's widow, afraid of what she might find out.

She knew Vera Paul peripherally, as her dad and Chief Paul had been best friends. Vera had been polite friends with her mom, Nancy, but they hadn't been overly close. Nancy once shared with Sayeh that she thought Vera was terribly snooty, and they didn't have much in common besides their husbands on the force.

At the time Sayeh couldn't imagine how horrible it must be to pretend to be polite and courteous to people you didn't like. Little did she know, that was basically the premise of adulting—something Sayeh never quite mastered.

So, sitting down with Vera after all these years wasn't appealing. She feared the woman would have the power to reduce her to a teenager again with one sharp look, especially when Sayeh hit her with the questions she needed to ask.

How do you ask a woman if she knew her husband was corrupt? Usually that line of questioning went down like a turd in a punch bowl.

But if Vera had answers, Sayeh needed to know. Fear of the unknown wouldn't solve the mystery of what'd happened to her parents.

Her cell chirped and she smiled when she saw it was

Levi with an offer to check out the new bistro in town for a quick bite on their day off.

She quickly texted back, Sorry, I have plans to follow up on my parents' case. Rain check.

Levi responded nearly as quick. I'll go with you. You should have backup.

Sayeh chuckled, getting ready to text back that she hardly needed protection from an octogenarian, but she stopped short. She wouldn't mind having some moral support. She'd considered bringing Luna along, but Luna was taking Charlene for a drive to the lake to take her mind off everything.

Just as she knew she would, Luna immediately took Charlene under her care, happy to have someone in the house again.

But that left Sayeh to fend for herself in this instance.

She quickly texted back before she lost her nerve. Yeah, sounds good. Meet up at the station. I'll drive.

Sayeh knew she ought to shut down whatever was brewing between them, but she didn't want to. That stubborn part of her that didn't care about rules or protocol was eager to see where this went, even though her logical brain was making a ruckus.

No rule said they couldn't be friends and coworkers, she argued with herself.

And he was just being supportive, which wasn't a bad thing.

But to prove that she wasn't going out of her way to influence Levi in one way or another, she purposefully pulled her hair into a slick unforgiving bun and decided against even a tiny swipe of mascara.

She surveyed her look with a critical eye, satisfied. *Friends don't go out of their way to impress each other.* Collecting her keys, she locked up and climbed into her car.

Within minutes she was in the parking lot, and Levi was there waiting. A tiny thrill tickled her spine as she pulled up. Levi commanded any space he occupied, a skill Sayeh found incredibly attractive.

He climbed into the passenger seat. "Where to, boss?" he asked.

"Back to Cottonwood."

"Of course. Why would it be anywhere else?" he quipped. "At this point, it feels like a second home."

She smiled, relaxed in his company and grateful for his presence. Returning to talk to Vera after all these years lodged a pit in her stomach that felt a lot like the insecurity of youth that she'd long since evicted from her life.

With the soil sample proving the original police report was falsified, it was imperative to find out if Vera knew why.

"You think the man's widow is going to open up to you?"

"I don't know. It could be a giant bust, but I have to try."

"Of course you do—it's what any good investigator would do."

It mattered that he saw her as a skilled professional in the field. Not that she needed his validation, but it meant something that he believed in her.

Sayeh couldn't help but smile. She wouldn't admit it, but she felt protected by his presence, something she'd never needed or wanted from anyone in the past. If anything, she'd pushed away everyone who'd tried.

The house they pulled up to was pale yellow with sage green shutters around each one of its windows and a large wraparound porch that gave it an old-fashioned charm as if it had been pulled straight out from another century entirely.

It was exactly as she remembered. "Talk about a time

warp," she murmured, shielding her eyes from the sun. "Time always seems to stand still in Cottonwood."

"You've been here before?"

"When I was young. Only a handful of times, though. Vera Paul didn't much care for kids running around her collectibles."

"So, the widow and the chief never had any kids of their own?"

Sayeh shook her head. "No, like I said, I don't think that was Vera's scene. She never displayed an interest in motherhood."

"Fair enough."

They exited the car and walked up to the front door. Sayeh purposefully hadn't called ahead. She hadn't wanted Vera to give her an excuse not to meet. An ambush seemed the best way to make this happen, but it also meant she risked finding an empty house.

Luck was on Sayeh's side. After respectfully ringing the doorbell, Vera Paul answered the door.

Tall and spindly that might've looked frail on anyone else only made Vera seem imperious. Her hair looked like whipped cotton candy with gray food coloring, but her eyes were as sharp as ever. Confusion followed recognition as her gaze darted between them. "Sayeh Griffin?"

"Yes, ma'am," Sayeh said with a smile. "It's nice to see you, Mrs. Paul."

"My word, I haven't seen you in a dog's age… How are you, honey?"

"I'm good. I'm with the Bureau of Indian Affairs, Investigations. This is my partner, Levi Wyatt."

Levi dipped his head in greeting with a respectful, "Ma'am."

"Indian Affairs, well, that's quite the achievement," she

said, folding her arms across her thin chest. "But I'm a little confused as to why you're here."

"I'm not here on official business, this is a personal call. I was wondering if we could talk. With both my parents gone, you're the last person who might be able to provide some answers about my past."

Vera hesitated, torn between a glimmer of compassion and a distaste for getting involved in business that didn't concern her. "Oh, I'm not sure I have much to contribute," she said regretfully, pursing her lips and shaking her head, but her gaze strayed to Sayeh and lingered for a heartbeat as if reminded of something she'd rather forget.

"May we come in? Ask a few questions? Perhaps you might know more than you realize."

Perhaps it was the earnestness in Sayeh's tone, or she simply didn't want people in her neighborhood gossiping, but she ushered them inside.

Expensive art on the walls, a baby grand piano in the foyer and a sense of understated wealth and privilege jumped out at Sayeh, more so than she would've noticed when she was a kid.

All of this on a small-town cop's pension? Seemed unlikely, but she wasn't here to poke into Vera's background or how she might be acquiring her wealth.

Likely, the chief left her with a sizable life insurance policy.

Vera led them into a sitting room and primly took a seat, gesturing for Sayeh and Levi to join her on the opposite sofa. Everything in the room was delicate and refined, as if it belonged in the salon of an aristocratic lady and not the widow of a small-town police chief.

No wonder Nancy had thought Vera was a snot. Everything in this place was the opposite of her adoptive mother's vibe. Nancy had been sweet, kind, soft and round, always baking and showing her love through food. Kenna had inherited that trait from their adoptive mother. Not so much Sayeh or Luna—though they had grown to appreciate the value of a home-cooked meal even if neither particularly liked to cook.

Vera looked like she hadn't enjoyed a carb since 1975.

"I was so sorry to hear of your father's passing," she said, breaking the silence. "He was a kind, if not simple, man."

Was that a compliment? Sayeh wasn't sure, but she murmured, "Thank you, he's very much missed."

"Yes, I'm sure he is. Sadly, I wasn't able to attend the funeral. I was on a cruise in the Mediterranean and only found out about the unfortunate incident weeks after it'd all happened. Dreadful situation. I can only imagine what you girls went through. Cottonwood used to be such a nice town. Once Allen was no longer in charge, I fear, things went to pot."

Sayeh didn't want to talk about her dad's murder. She switched gears deftly. "I don't want to take too much of your time so I'll get straight to the reason I'm here."

Vera approved. "Excellent, dear. I do enjoy a straightforward conversation. At my age, it's best to get to the point."

Watching Sayeh in action gave Levi a thrill. She was like a shark, circling its prey, looking for the best chance to make her move. She didn't waste time and took her chances with what she got. Much different from his approach, which was far more methodical. He probably would've softened the old lady up first, taking the measure of her body language, left, done some research and then returned with a second set of questions. But Sayeh knew exactly what she wanted to ask, and she didn't dance around her intentions.

He appreciated how blunt she was, and yet there was a finesse to her style.

"I recently came upon some information that calls into question some of the late chief's actions, specifically, his reporting of certain events," Sayeh said.

Vera chuckled, plucking at an invisible string of lint. "Is that so? Fascinating."

"Yes, well, one case in particular you might remember."

"Which one would that be?"

"The night Chief Paul brought me and my sisters to Cottonwood."

"Darling, he was doing his job. He was a hero that night. If it weren't for my husband, you and your sisters wouldn't be here," she reminded Sayeh gently with the faintest reproach as if whatever Sayeh was implying was in poor taste. "And you acquired a lovely family in the process. While I recognize that it's not polite in today's world to point out that you and your sisters benefited from the tragedy of your parents' deaths, it doesn't make it any less true."

Levi felt Sayeh's temper rising, even though she remained calm. There was a test of wills happening between the two women. Levi wasn't sure if Vera was deliberately trying to bait Sayeh or she was genuinely an entitled woman who saw nothing wrong with her statement.

"Bill and Nancy were wonderful people," Sayeh agreed, but returned to, "However, as I said, I've recently come upon some information that calls into question the facts as they were reported the night my biological parents died."

Vera waved away Sayeh's statement. "Darling, it was ages ago. Some things are better left in the past."

"I don't agree," Sayeh returned coolly. "The chief lied

on the report. He said my parents died from a chemical explosion but I had the soil tested and there wasn't a single chemical marker left behind anywhere on that property."

Vera frowned faintly. "Wasn't there an explosion?"

"Yes. But it wasn't from drugs as Chief Paul said."

"They were drug addicts," Vera returned flatly. "Just because you didn't find a chemical trail as you call it, doesn't mean that their lifestyle didn't ultimately cost them their lives. I'm sorry, but the facts of your life before being adopted by the Griffin family are quite horrific."

Levi caught the subtle wince as Sayeh swallowed before saying, "Yes, I'm aware of my parents' past but I don't think everything is as it was presented. My mother, Mika, only had paraphernalia drug offenses, which could've been as simple as a marijuana pipe, and for all we know she could've used it medicinally but it was still illegal back then."

At the mention of Mika, Vera's eyes flashed with something almost akin to hatred, but she banked it quickly. She shrugged. "How will we ever know? My dear, your tenacity is admirable, but you're chasing ghosts. I don't have a reason why the trailer blew up aside from what was reported. I'm sorry."

But Sayeh stilled, pinning the woman with a look. "I never said it was a trailer. How'd you know?"

Vera swallowed, admitting with a forced chuckle, "Well, it's not every day your husband is the hero to three little orphaned Indian girls, now is it? I suppose I asked a few questions at the time but it was so long ago, I barely remember much beyond that."

"Did you know my mother?" Sayeh asked point-blank.

"As far as I'm concerned, your mother was Nancy Griffin."

"My mother was Mika Proudfoot—and something tells me…you knew exactly who she was. The question is… why?"

At that, Vera rose sharply, smoothing her linen pants. "I wish I could offer more to help but I simply don't have the information you seek. Whatever you think my husband did or didn't do, it doesn't matter because he's no longer here to explain. My advice to you, my dear, let the past remain in the past. You're the only one interested in chasing ghosts. The rest of us have moved on."

Moved on from what? Levi wanted to ask, but it wasn't his place. He was simply moral support for Sayeh. He looked to Sayeh for guidance as they both rose. Vera communicated effectively and without words that her hospitality had run its course.

Sayeh had no choice but to smile and thank Vera for her time.

"Of course, dear," Vera said as they walked to the door. A small hallway table showed two pictures—Vera and Allen in their younger years—and Levi did a double take.

Sayeh caught the direction of his gaze, but Vera moved in front of the table, her thin frame obscuring the view. "It was nice to meet you," she said to Levi.

"Likewise, ma'am," he said, following Sayeh out.

Vera closed the door behind them, practically catching the back of their heels as they crossed the threshold.

"What caught your eye?" Sayeh asked immediately.

Levi didn't know how to say it, but he had a bad feeling about why Vera reacted the way she did at the mention of Mika Proudfoot.

He asked Sayeh, "Have you ever done a DNA test?"

Sayeh stared in confusion. "No?"

"You should. And you should test your DNA against that woman's husband."

Sayeh's confusion grew. "Why?" she asked, baffled.

"Because the younger portrait of her husband...bore a strong resemblance...to you."

Chapter 18

Sayeh reeled, shooting a sharp look at Levi. "What do you mean?"

"I mean exactly what I said. The man in that portrait looked a lot like you…but as a man, of course, and I think his wife saw it, too."

Sayeh didn't know how to process this information. Her brain just shut down for a long moment, like a computer attacked by a virus. Total system failure. Her eyes watered for no good reason. Why did she feel like her world had just been crushed? "Are you sure?" she asked, almost desperately. "It was a quick look, maybe it was a trick of the eye."

"It was a quick look but it was long enough to feel punched in the gut for you. However, there's an easy way to erase all doubt."

"How so?"

"The department likely has the old chief's DNA stored. Have your sister submit a swab of your DNA and run it against the DNA of the chief's. Paternity will show up if I'm right."

Sayeh blinked at the simple but compelling logic. He was right. The answer could be easily discovered by running a scientific test, but she never in a million years would've suspected that Darryl wasn't her biological father. She'd been so intent on proving her parents hadn't died in a drug explosion she never considered the possibility that other secrets lurked in the background.

The fact that she'd always been lighter complected than her sisters now seemed more than just an odd quirk of genetics—it felt like a pointed finger that her father was someone other than Darryl Proudfoot.

"I have to talk to my sisters," she said abruptly. "Luna isn't at the office today but Kenna should be working at the vet clinic. Would you mind going with me?"

"I don't have any other plans," Levi said. "I'm here for as long as you need me…plus you drove, so I'm kinda stuck."

That last part was a joke, breaking through the frozen tundra in her head. She cracked a smile, appreciating his presence. He had a calming effect on her, which she sorely needed.

Her fingers shook as she texted Kenna to tell her they were coming. She replied saying that she would time it so she could take her break when they arrived.

Kenna stepped outside of the clinic, and immediately, her gaze flew straight to Levi with an appraising glance. "You must be Sayeh's new partner I've heard so much about," she said, shaking his hand in greeting, her smile warm.

"I hope it was good things," he said.

"Oh! Absolutely, all good," Kenna assured Levi quickly. Returning to Sayeh, she said, "Your text was a little cryptic. Is everything okay?"

"Everything is not okay," Sayeh said. "I… Well, it might be a false alarm but I'm going to run my DNA against that of old Chief Paul."

Kenna's face said it all. "Why would you do that?"

"Because we just had a nice little chat with his widow—"

Kenna grimaced. "Eww. Doubly why?"

"Because I'm trying to find out why her husband lied on the police report about our parents' deaths. I'm sure Luna's told you by now the soil sample came back as negative for chemical contamination."

"Yes, she mentioned it," Kenna said, "but I'm not sure what else you're hoping to find out. I want to be supportive, but I think digging all this up is going to poke at a lot of people."

"Probably, but I don't care. Maybe they need to be poked."

Kenna sighed, knowing there was no winning that argument, and Sayeh was glad she didn't try. She wouldn't be deterred, no matter what. "Okay, so did she have information that might be useful?"

"Not exactly but as we were leaving… Levi saw a portrait of a young Allen Paul…and he swore the resemblance between him and me was uncanny."

Kenna's expression faltered as the full implication set in. "Are you actually thinking that… Oh, no way, no. I can't believe that. Darryl Proudfoot was our father. Don't you think that if Mika had gotten pregnant by the Cottonwood police chief, the rumor mill would've outed that secret a long time ago?"

"Some secrets don't reveal themselves until much later," Sayeh countered. "Maybe she didn't even know until I popped out with blond hair and blue eyes."

Kenna wasn't convinced, warning, "I don't think we should jump to conclusions until we know more information. People can share a resemblance to one another and still be completely unrelated—and that kind of rumor can ruin lives."

"I've got a feeling in my gut, though," Sayeh said, shaking her head. "What if it's true?"

"We don't know enough about Mika to even guess if

that might be true. There are too many questions without a way to find answers. This is pure speculation right now."

"I know but I can't stop." There was something about not knowing her heritage that was burning a hole in her soul. She'd always felt apart from her family, and if it turned out that the chief was actually her father, that feeling would finally make sense.

Resigned, Kenna asked, "When are you planning to run this test?"

"As soon as possible. I have to talk to Luna when she gets back into town so probably within the week. It'll take at least two weeks to get the results, so I don't want to waste any more time."

"Don't you need to have his widow's consent to run that test?"

"Under normal circumstances, yes, but because there's probable cause to question the chief's report, I can treat it as a follow up to a crime scene."

"But it's not an official reopening of our parents' case," Kenna warned. "You could get in trouble. No one could legally stop you from taking soil samples and paying for an analysis, but running DNA? Feels like you're playing with fire and using your career as kindling."

Sayeh wouldn't budge. "Let me worry about that."

But Kenna persisted. "Don't you think once that old bird realizes you've been tinkering with her husband's DNA, she's going to squawk about it? Vera Paul is not known for her forgiving nature."

Sayeh didn't care. "Let her squawk. If she wants to make a big deal about this, we can go big. But something tells me she doesn't want a whole lot of publicity. I'm not looking to out him. I'm not looking to embrace him as my father, but if he is my father, I have a right to know."

Kenna softened. "If it were me, I would probably feel the same, but just know it doesn't matter what the results of that test turn out to be. You are still my sister, and that will never change."

Sayeh's eyes watered. "Thank you." She wiped at her leaking eyes, realizing, "Actually, it might not be a bad idea to run all of our DNA at the same time. There's no guarantee that Darryl was a father to any of us. It might be good to know."

Kenna sighed and reluctantly agreed. "I suppose so. Might as well rip the Band-Aid off and find out in one fell swoop."

"Do you think Luna will be willing to do it, too?"

Kenna shrugged. "I don't know, maybe. But Luna's not all that interested in dredging up the past. I don't want to speak for her, though. You'll have to ask her."

Sometimes Luna was hard to read. So far, she'd been supportive of Sayeh's need for answers. However, when it started poking into her actual life, Sayeh wasn't sure how readily she would jump on board. But then again, Luna might not care about the outcome of the test either way.

"I appreciate your support. It means a lot to me," Sayeh said, reaching for Kenna's hand. "How is that nephew of mine?"

At the mention of Ty, Kenna brightened. "He's doing amazing. I'm so proud of him. He's made so much progress. He's a different kid from that hooligan who was acting out and being a jerk to everyone."

"Well, I hope not too different because I love that little asshole."

Kenna snorted. "Well, then you can spend more time with him when he's being a pill and we'll see how much you appreciate his attitude."

"Hey, strong-willed people end up doing great things in life."

Kenna laughed. "Yeah? And who said that?"

"You did." Sayeh grinned.

"That's what I thought." Kenna checked her watch. "My break is just about up. Are you okay?"

Sayeh nodded. "I am. I think I was just in shock but I've got my head on straight now."

Kenna smiled, relieved. "Good." Then to Levi, she said, "You and Sayeh ought to come by for dinner sometime. I make a mean pasta salad."

Sayeh started to correct Kenna's assumption they were anything more than colleagues, but Kenna winked and disappeared into the clinic.

She turned to Levi, her cheeks red. "I'm sorry for that… My sister Kenna loves to play matchmaker. She's an unrelenting romantic and seems to think you're not complete unless you're attached to someone."

Levi chuckled. "Nothing wrong with being a romantic," he assured her, but he sobered to say, "No matter who fathered you, that strong female DNA is the same. Your biological mother must've been an incredible woman."

Sayeh didn't know why that struck her in the heart, but instant tears returned. Aggravated by the waterworks that seemed too close to the surface, she wiped her face, apologizing. "I don't know what is wrong with me, but I seem really emotional today. I'm not usually this weepy."

But Levi always seemed to know exactly what to say. "Cut yourself some slack," he said. "It's been an emotional day. You don't have to apologize for being human. We're going to find the answers you need—and in the meantime, lunch."

Sayeh laughed. "Always thinking with your stomach. How do you stay so fit when you do nothing but eat?"

He cut her a teasing look that she felt in her middle—and wisely left the answer up to her imagination.

Levi felt himself sliding closer to Sayeh, his feet slipping against the tilting landscape as he careened toward the enigmatic woman. She was mesmerizing to watch in action, but seeing her in a vulnerable moment was like catching a glimpse of something sacred.

He knew how she valued her privacy. That she allowed him into her personal space was an honor not lost on him.

They picked up sandwiches, and Sayeh took him to one of her favorite spots for an impromptu picnic.

The quiet park was idyllic and secluded. Giant ponderosa pines swayed in the gentle breeze as big puffy clouds scuttled across the sky, momentarily dimming the sun as they passed along.

"I used to come here when I was a kid and needed a breather from my family," she shared as they settled on the soft cushion of green grass. She unwrapped her sandwich and took a bite. "Growing up with two sisters could be a lot. Plus, my dad and I always seemed to be at odds with each other. I feel bad about that now. It's clichéd but you never know when you've shared your last goodbye. I wish I could take back all the times I'd been a jerk. Of course, if you were to ask either of my sisters, they might say I'd have no memories left."

Levi chuckled at her self-deprecating humor, recognizing the regret hidden beneath as he bit into his sandwich. "Sibling relationships are always complicated," he said. "But at the core, that's where the love remains."

Sayeh nodded, pausing to wipe something from his face. "Mustard," she explained.

That simple act made everything else fall away. The sunlight filtering through the canopy of trees caressed her face, casting a golden glow around Sayeh. She sensed the change between them, and her breath hitched. She met his gaze, following his lead.

He could pull back and end whatever this was or push forward and brush his lips across hers—effectively changing everything.

A cocoon of heat wrapped around them, locking out the world and any consequence. All that mattered at that moment was Sayeh and the proximity of her lips to his.

"This is probably," Sayeh started in a husky murmur, and he finished, "A bad idea."

Because they both knew it.

And neither had what it took to stop.

Chapter 19

The minute Levi's lips touched hers, Sayeh lost control of her ability to reason. She wasn't a kid—she knew infatuation could be deceiving—but she was swirling in a heated maelstrom that threatened to drown every ounce of logic in her brain.

He tasted faintly of the mustard from his sandwich, which should've cut through the sensual haze, but on Levi, it was perfect.

His tongue slowly tasted hers, igniting an electric spark that sizzled down her nerve endings. Suddenly, she was back in high school, making out with her boyfriend in this very same spot, lost in the moment, happy to forget about everything except the sun on her face and the intoxicating feel of another body pressing her into the soft cushion of the earth beneath. The crush of sweet grass under her back filled the air with an earthy fragrance that would forever remain lodged in her memory.

And now she'd come full circle. Once again she was here, in this place, losing herself with a man that ought to be off-limits.

But even as a dizzying sense of déjà vu stole her senses, there was one striking difference.

Kissing Levi felt natural as if she'd been kissing him

her whole adult life. Their rhythm matched, their wordless communication was seamless and being in his arms felt like coming home after a long absence.

Which made no sense—and it was that jarring realization that made her pull away. She needed to get her head straight and think this through before things spun out of control. Too much was riding on their shoulders to be careless.

The haze started to clear from their gazes, and Levi was the first to apologize, his cheeks flushing with guilt. "I'm sorry... I... That was inappropriate. I shouldn't have—"

"I was a willing participant." She stopped him, refusing to let him shoulder the responsibility for their actions. She reached for his hand and squeezed it tight as she looked into his eyes. "Levi, I wanted to kiss you and I'm not apologizing. I also don't feel bad for doing it. I just think we need to be smart about this and agree to certain things before we go any further."

"But I do feel bad," Levi said, pain in his gaze. "It feels wrong. Not just because we're colleagues."

"Because of Nadie?"

"Yeah," he admitted.

She didn't have an answer for that kind of pain. "You haven't dated since she died?"

"Not even once. I wasn't interested. Not until you. And even though a part of me wants nothing more than to feel you in my arms, there's another part of me that's calling me all sorts of names for betraying Nadie's memory."

"I can't tell you what the right decision is. Grief is personal. Only you know what that is."

"What if I don't know, either?" he returned with an edge of bitterness. "Hell, this is why I don't even bother with this 'moving on' bullshit. I can't seem to get it figured out and it's not fair to anyone else while I try." Sayeh chuckled, earning a sharp look from Levi. "Not sure what I said was funny."

"It's not but I get it," she said. "Here's how I see it. You need a rebound relationship to reorient yourself to life after Nadie and I need a man I can trust that won't try and tie me down. Seems like we might be perfect for each other."

"Most people don't like to think of themselves as the rebound relationship," he said, surprised. "And you'd be okay with that?"

"I'd probably prefer it. I'm not interested in getting married or moving in with someone, but I miss having a person to talk to at the end of a long day, cuddling and all the other adult privileges."

"I've never met anyone like you, Sayeh," he said.

"And you probably never will," she returned with a small smile as she climbed to her feet. Levi joined her. "Why don't you think about it and get back to me? If you decide that you want to give it a try, we'll talk about how. Until then, I guess we can just focus on the case."

Levi shook his head, reeling from her frank offer. She didn't begrudge him the need for time to think it through. She smiled and gathered up their trash. "Ready to go?"

"No," he growled, surprising her when he pulled her back into his arms. She melted against him, their mouths devouring each other as if the world was ending and this was their last chance to taste one another. "You deserve more than a rebound relationship," he murmured against her mouth.

"Don't tell me what I deserve," she returned, kissing him harshly.

He groaned against her lips, and his hands slid down her backside to grip each half of her behind. The possession in the curl of his palm on the flesh of her cheek took her breath away. This was a man who did nothing by halves. He was either all in or all out. That's why he struggled to let go of Nadie's memory—it was heartbreakingly honest and pure—a rarity in a man these days, and Sayeh felt herself falling a little more.

"If I take you into my bed tonight, it will change everything," he warned.

"Only as much as we let it," she promised in a husky murmur, fixating on the slick plumpness of his gorgeous lips. "Let's figure it out together."

"And the case?"

"The case is separate. We're adults, we can keep the lines drawn."

"Speaking from experience?"

She narrowed her gaze, admitting, "No. You'd be the first but I trust we can handle it."

A sardonic smile tugged at the corner of his mouth. "I guess we'll see if that's true." He slipped his hand into hers with a gruff, "Let's go," and Sayeh bit back her giddy smile as she followed him back to the car.

Levi couldn't get the desire for more out of his mouth. Sayeh was in his head and turning his willpower to mush. That shrill voice was still there, but it slowly faded into the ether as his hunger for Sayeh grew.

Was this how you moved on? You just obliterated your grief under a mountain of distractions until it suffocated from lack of oxygen?

He didn't want to forget Nadie or what she'd meant to him.

Landon's advice rang in his head. *Nadie would slap a knot on your head if she saw how you're acting like you ought to crawl into the grave with her*, and he shook his head, knowing Landon was right. Nadie had been more pragmatic about most things than he, which seemed impossible. Couples invariably play the what-if game with each other, and Nadie told him that if he died, she wouldn't stop living.

"What do you mean?" Levi had returned with a playful gasp and moral outrage. "I thought I was the love of your life?"

"You are," she said, crawling into his lap like a contented cat. "But I'm too young to stop living, silly man. If you were to go before me, I'd carry you in my heart but I wouldn't close my eyes to the beauty of the sunrise. Get what I mean?"

"You heartless she-beast. You better mourn me until you're gray and wrinkly," he growled, nuzzling her neck as she giggled, her laughter the light in his soul. They'd made love on the sofa that night, the conversation forgotten. Who thought of death when the promise of life stretched out like a glorious road to Heaven?

But death had come for Nadie way before they could've imagined.

And Levi had been left with the realization that it might be him that turned old and gray before he looked sidewise at another woman.

Until Sayeh.

"Having second thoughts?" Sayeh asked, breaking into his turbulent thoughts.

"No," he answered. "You?"

She chuckled. "Nope."

He smiled in spite of the mess in his head. Sayeh had an infectious laugh. It was deep and throaty, making him think of dark nights beneath warm blankets.

Before too long, he pulled into his driveway, pausing minutely when he realized no one but Nadie had been home with him, but he wouldn't back down now.

"Your house is cute," Sayeh said. "Rustic. I like it."

"If rustic is another word for fixer-upper, then yes," he chuckled ruefully. "We'd had grand plans to make all these improvements until we realized neither of us had the time to play DIYer. So, it remains as *rustic* as the day we bought it."

"I like it. It suits you," she said. "I'll take the grand tour, please."

He laughed at the idea of a walk-through of his small house, as anything aside from a blink would take you from room to room, but he appreciated Sayeh's enthusiasm.

Unlocking the front door, he made a grand gesture to the living room. "This is where I do almost everything most nights—eat, research and sometimes sleep, depending on the night—that couch has seen some things."

"Multipurpose. I like it," she murmured, her fingers lingering on the wood frame as she passed into the kitchen, exclaiming when she saw the old potbellied woodstove in the corner. "Are you kidding me right now? Do you even know how cool this is?"

He laughed with genuine amusement at her unfettered joy. Nadie had also loved that cumbersome thing. "The previous owners offered to throw it in for free, which was a blessing because I think Nadie was ready to throw down more cash than the asking price if they hadn't. She loved the smell of the woodstove in the morning. She said it always started her day off right. I was willing to do whatever it took to make her happy. Even if it meant starting that damn fire every day."

Sayeh stilled, casting a tender glance Levi's way. "You did it right," she murmured.

"What do you mean?"

She turned to face him, her back against the cold stove. "That saying, 'happy wife, happy life,' you had it figured out and you did it right. Reminds me of my dad. He was like that with my mom. Whatever she wanted, he made it happen. No matter what."

He didn't know why but Sayeh's soft praise made him swell up inside. "Well, I can't take all the credit. My dad taught us boys how it's supposed to be done. He'd tell us, *Boys, love, trust and respect are the holy trinity of any relationship. Don't mess with one or you unbalance the other.* And I took that to heart. But Nadie made it easy. She wasn't hard to please."

"I think I would've liked your Nadie," Sayeh said, pushing off the stove to walk toward him. He stilled, his body tensing with eager anticipation as she looped her arms around his neck. "I think it's time for you to show me the bedroom."

His groin tightened instantly, turning hard as a rock. "You sure?" he asked, maybe not only for her but for himself as well.

She nodded wordlessly, lifting to her toes to softly kiss his lips. That tender touch was all he needed to ignite the fire banked inside him.

Levi deepened the kiss briefly, then hoisted her into his arms, carrying her the short distance to his bed. Kicking the door shut with his booted foot, he symbolically shut out everything but him and Sayeh.

He shut down the voice in his head, worrying he was betraying his long-dead fiancée.

He ignored the anxiety that it'd been too long and he'd forgotten everything he thought he knew about making love to a woman.

He deliberately shut all that down to focus on the beauty in his arms.

Tomorrow would come soon enough—and with it, the emotional fallout.

Chapter 20

Sayeh awoke before Levi, which surprised her. She'd pegged him for an early riser but didn't mind rising first. She wandered into his bathroom, started the shower and stepped inside. Levi was a typical man—he had soap and shampoo that looked purchased from a gas station but no conditioner, so she piled her hair on her head and simply did a quick wash of her body.

She was nearly finished when Levi joined her. She caught her breath at his body. Built but not overly muscled, Levi had the kind of body that knew hard work but didn't begrudge himself a treat whenever he wanted. Faint scars laced his frame in places, which she traced with her finger in question.

One particularly jagged scar along his rib cage caught her attention. "How'd you get this?"

Levi chuckled. "Life on the ranch. Caught the sharp end of a bull's horns trying to get him into the chute. Son of a bitch caught me when I wasn't ready and nearly gored me to death. My dad thought for sure he'd just lost a son. He joked that's why he always wanted an *heir and a spare* because of situations just like that."

Sayeh cracked a grin. Levi's dad sounded like he'd been a hoot. "A sense of humor in the face of death is a good thing," she said. "Or highly inappropriate. I always get those mixed up."

"So did he," Levi returned dryly, reaching for the soap, realizing with chagrin he'd hardly been set up for visitors. "Sorry for the bachelor bathroom."

"Water and soap are fine enough," Sayeh assured him, sliding her hands over his soaped-up shoulders, marveling at the firm texture beneath her fingertips. "And this one?" she asked, tracing a smaller scar along his collarbone. "Another bull?"

"Nope, that was my brother, Landon. We were kids. Found two perfect walking sticks on the property and promptly turned them into swords. He got a lucky hit and scored my collarbone. My mom was pissed," he said, remembering. "Said I almost got a stick to the throat. Plus, my shirt was ruined."

She giggled, enjoying the story and the company. He pulled her close, the soap between them making their bodies slippery. "So how does this work?" he asked, his gaze roaming her skin as it glistened with suds. "I'm in foreign territory."

"Me, too, but I think I'll catch an Uber back to the office. You'll show up like you normally do. If anyone asks, I'll just say that I had too much to drink after work and didn't want to risk driving. Easy-peasy."

Levi pulled a subtle frown. "Sneaking around feels wrong."

"Yeah, well, the paperwork would be a complete headache and who needs that kind of drama in their life? This is easier." And no one got hurt if and when it ended, was what she didn't say. Aside from being her coworker, Levi was a big red flag flapping in her face. She'd be an idiot to let herself fall in love with a man still mourning his dead fiancée, but she also wasn't about to give up the chance to cuddle with him.

This was a win-win. Hopefully Levi felt the same.

They rinsed the soap off, and after a few more languid kisses beneath the spray, they finished and dressed. Sayeh snapped into professional mode almost as soon as her Uber arrived. She waved goodbye and left as if they hadn't spent the night together.

There were some things Sayeh could compartmentalize like a boss. Avoiding tricky emotional pitfalls was one of those things.

Luna would say she was simply avoiding dealing with her feelings but *potato-puhtahtoe.* Besides, Sayeh didn't have time to sort out that emotional mess.

The thing was Levi was intelligent, generous, kind and a sharp investigator. He was the kind of guy she *could* fall for—which was dangerous.

The Uber dropped her off at the office, and she went inside, passing Dakota in the hallway. Old Sayeh would've kept walking and put off the energy that she'd rather pound a nail in her foot than engage in idle chitchat, but she was trying new things, so she actually smiled and asked about her case. "Forensics come back on your cheating bar guy?"

Dakota laughed, holding up the file in her hand. "Actually, yeah, we're getting ready to serve an arrest warrant for the man's wife. Though I feel bad for her. I wish there was an out-clause in the law for when the vic totally deserved what he got."

Sayeh laughed. "If only. So it was the wife?"

"Yep. She was fed up with his bullshit and hit him in the back of the head with a wrench. Funny thing, that probably wouldn't have killed him if he hadn't fallen backward and hit his head on the counter edge on the way down."

"I'm guessing that's how the original cause of death was missed?"

Dakota nodded. "Yeah, it looked like he slipped on the wet floor and smashed his head on the counter at just the right angle."

"Damn, that's some crazy luck," Sayeh said. "Like one in a million, I'm guessing."

"Something like that, but the wife's luck ran out when we got our hands on some high-tech reconstructive imaging. We managed to borrow the FBI's imagery lab and they were able to reconstruct the victim's head and subsequent wounds so we were able to get a better visual."

Sayeh chuckled. The FBI and their toys. They didn't often get the chance to play with those high-tech gadgets in Narcotics, but Sayeh knew about them. "Glad to hear you're closing your case," she said.

"How about you?" Dakota asked.

"Not quite as cut-and-dried," she admitted. "But I think we're getting close to something. People are getting twitchy and that's always a good sign."

"True enough. Be careful out there. I don't have time for a funeral," Dakota said, waving as she headed on her way, and Sayeh continued to her office.

So, that wasn't terrible. Dakota seemed cool. Sayeh liked her sense of humor. She wasn't ready to pick out silverware together, but maybe being part of a team wasn't so bad.

Levi took his time getting to the office. A lot was happening in his head. The feeling that he'd done something wrong dogged his every step. Quickly stripping his sheets, he stuffed them in the laundry hamper and remade the bed with fresh linen. Nadie's smiling portrait on the bedside table made him feel like she was staring at him from beyond the grave.

Maybe it was too soon to start something casual or serious with anyone. It wasn't fair to the other person when his head was such a mess.

Plus, sneaking around only accentuated the feeling that he was doing something wrong. He got why Sayeh wanted to keep things private, but he wasn't the kind of guy who kept people on the down-low when he was involved.

Of course, he'd respect Sayeh's boundaries, but maybe he'd jumped the gun by allowing their feelings to cross the line.

But even as he tested the words in his mind, he knew he wasn't ready to give up Sayeh. There was something about her that he deeply craved, and letting her go just wasn't an option. Not yet. But wasn't that the biggest indicator that he needed to cut off whatever they were doing before things spiraled out of control?

Maybe so.

But not today.

Levi grabbed his keys and locked up, heading to the office. On the way, he detoured to get a tea for Sayeh and a coffee for himself.

When he walked into the office, he went straight to Sayeh and found her shutting down her computer. She brightened just as he walked in. "Perfect timing. I got an address for Christopher Roth. Ready to roll?"

"Where to?"

"He owns a construction company in Bozeman. I've already scheduled an appointment with his secretary. He's expecting us by noon. Let's hit the road." She accepted the tea with a gleeful smile and was already power walking out of the building.

Levi had no choice but to follow.

As soon as his butt hit the seat, Sayeh was already talking. "I pulled the trigger on the DNA analysis first thing this morning. I did a DNA swab of myself, packaged it up and sent it out with a request for analysis against Allen Paul's DNA. Now I guess the waiting game begins."

Levi was flabbergasted at how quickly Sayeh did things once she put her mind to it. The level of determination in Sayeh's personality could power a small country if science could find a way to bottle it. God, how could he not admire that in a woman? It was a damn sexy quality. "You ready for what the results might reveal?" he asked.

"I better be. There's no turning back now," Sayeh said with a brave grin.

He chuckled. "You got that right." *On many levels.* Back to the case. "I got to thinking about Daniel and how his disordered mind had mixed up the timeline of events but perhaps not the actual events. He'd said Echo's body was cold, freezing even. Something tells me Echo was already dead by the time she ended up in that creek. I think Daniel found her dead body, took the bracelet and in his mind thought he was holding on to it until Echo came back for it. He said he was *keeping her secrets.* I think that bracelet is important."

"If your theory is correct, that would mean Daniel didn't kill Echo," Sayeh said.

"I don't think he did," Levi said. "I'm leaning toward body dump and whoever did the dumping must not have known Daniel was in the area but found out when we started asking questions. The question is, how?"

"That's the million-dollar question, isn't it?" Sayeh returned grimly. "It has to be someone with access to the case in some way."

"With any luck, something will turn up with the Forensics on the bracelet," Levi said.

"Hopefully." Sayeh sighed and flicked on the radio, saying, "It's a long drive. Let's see how compatible we are with our musical interests."

Levi laughed. "I'm good with everything but jazz. The saxophone sets my teeth on edge."

"Same," Sayeh agreed with a shudder. "Classic rock it is."

They settled into a comfortable silence even though the inside of Levi's head was loud. A half-and-half mix of personal and professional thoughts, Levi bounced back and forth between topics, thankful for the distraction of music to keep him from saying something he shouldn't when it came to him and Sayeh.

For Sayeh's part, she seemed utterly unaffected by anything between them, humming to the music and bobbing her head to the tunes, pausing occasionally to sip her tea. What he wouldn't do for a peek into that head of hers.

Sayeh broke the silence, remembering suddenly, "Oh! First thing this morning I bumped into Dakota and they were serving an arrest warrant for the bar owner's wife. Seems she conked him on the head, which caused him to fall and crash into the counter. If it weren't for the FBI's high-tech imaging reconstruction of the wounds, they wouldn't have been able to see there were actually two injuries overlapping each other." She shot him a smile. "Seems you were right about the case being good to close."

It made him feel good that his instincts were spot-on. A win for Shilah and Dakota was a win for the task force in general. "Good. Now Isaac can relax a little. Gives us more breathing room to close our case."

"Has Isaac said something to you?" Sayeh asked, shooting him a sharp look, which made Levi realize that Isaac had only shared his concerns with him, not the entire team. He brushed off the importance, saying, "Only in passing. I just happened to be working late that night. Isaac's getting a lot of pressure from the brass for results—nothing we didn't know was going to happen, anyway."

"Yeah, I guess so," Sayeh said. "Just feels weird that he only mentioned it to you."

"I wouldn't make too much out of it."

"Easy for you to say," Sayeh said. "You weren't the one left out."

"Sayeh…it's not like that. Don't make problems where there aren't any."

"I'm going to put a pin in that for now because we have bigger fish to fry but don't think that I'm going to let that slide. You're the only man in our task force and our boss chose to speak to you about concerns he was having about our cases? You don't see an issue with that?"

Levi had to tread cautiously. "Maybe. I'm just saying, let's take a wait-and-see approach. It might be exactly as I'm saying it is and if it's not, we'll address it. In the meantime, we have a case to solve."

Sayeh couldn't argue that point. She conceded with a nod but was still a bit riled up. She was so passionate. He couldn't fault her for that quality because he found it sexy as hell.

Even if it made things a little stressful at times.

Chapter 21

Bozeman was a place money flocked to. In the winter it had the upscale feel of Sundance, Utah, without the celebrities milling around during the festival. Now in springtime, as the snowmelt ran through gutters and into open sewers, Bozeman felt like that five-star hotel you spent time in while attending some mogul's wedding.

The air smelled like freshly mowed grass and blossoming flowers. The city had an energy about it that made it seem as if anything could happen—and Sayeh was feeling the anticipation as she and Levi parked and entered the ritzy building.

Roth Construction's executive office on the fourth floor was appropriately appointed in a style that could only be described as "luxury rustic," reminding Sayeh of Logan's comment about the ranchettes in Cottonwood that didn't actually pull in any money but cost an arm and a leg to look like a working ranch. It was all about the aesthetic—and people paid out the nose to get it.

"BIA agents Sayeh Griffin and Levi Wyatt to see Mr. Roth," Sayeh said to the secretary, flashing her credentials.

The secretary, a dark-haired woman with high cheekbones and eyes dark as the depths of Flathead Lake, picked up the phone and rang her boss. She hung up and smiled. "Mr. Roth is expecting you. Go ahead on in."

Christopher Roth, a tall man with a full head of dark blond hair and an easy smile, rose as they walked in, eager to greet them. "Come in, come in, please have a seat. Can I get you anything? I know it's a long drive from Billings."

"Thank you, we're fine," Sayeh said. "We appreciate you seeing us on such short notice."

"No, I'm happy to help," Mr. Roth said, returning to his seat. "When you told me you were reopening Echo's case, I was really glad to hear it."

Sayeh wasn't expecting that response. Unlike Logan, he wasn't pretending not to know or remember Echo, which was interesting, but his eagerness to help was even more curious.

Levi also seemed to find Mr. Roth's helpfulness a shock, but he recovered quickly. "We appreciate your time, so we'll get straight to the point. It's come to our attention that you may have known Miss Jones. Can you elaborate as to the nature of your relationship?"

Mr. Roth looked as if he'd carried this weight on his shoulders for a long time and was ready to put it down. "We dated for a while back in high school."

Sayeh hadn't expected Roth to give up that information so quickly. "You dated? For how long?"

"I'm assuming you know my family left Cottonwood in the middle of my senior year. Echo and I broke up shortly before we left."

"Why?"

"We were kids, different backgrounds, you know how it is. I couldn't see myself in a long-distance relationship and we decided to end it."

"Amicably?" Levi asked.

"Mostly. I mean, neither of us were happy about breaking up but we both knew staying together was going to be next to impossible once I moved away from Cottonwood."

"How'd you meet?" Sayeh asked.

"At a party on the reservation. Me and a buddy of mine—"

"Logan Caldwell?" Sayeh supplied.

Roth nodded. "Yeah, I assume you've already made contact with Logan?"

"Yes, we've talked but he didn't remember Echo," Levi said, looking steadily at Roth. "Why is that?"

Roth chuckled as if he wasn't surprised. "Look, no shade against my buddy Logan, but his brain isn't what it used to be. We haven't talked in years, but he was heading down the wrong path for a long time. I wish him well, but I really wouldn't count on him for anything substantial. His brain is pickled."

Sayeh would agree with that assessment. "So, you and Logan didn't stay in contact?"

"Not really. Like I said, we went in different directions. I think our friendship just ran its course."

"He said that your parents didn't approve of your friendship because he was poor and you weren't," Sayeh shared. "Was that accurate?"

Roth shook his head, amused. "Logan always had a chip on his shoulder. Class warfare soldier-type. He always thought he was being judged because of his background, which wasn't the case. If anyone was judging him, it was because sometimes he acted like an asshole."

"And that's why your parents didn't care for the friendship?" Levi asked.

"Yeah, Logan had a thing against authority and he popped off to my dad one time. After that, he wasn't welcome and I didn't want to start a fight with my best friend at the time so I downplayed the situation and made excuses for why he couldn't come over."

Sayeh wanted to know more about his relationship with Echo, not his failed bro-romance. "Okay, so tell us more about your relationship with Echo."

"She was the most beautiful girl I'd ever seen," Roth said plainly. "That long dark hair, even darker eyes… She was all I could think about from the minute we met."

Sayeh looked to Levi, feeling the steam leave her sails. This guy was practically an open book. He wasn't trying to hide a damn thing, which didn't paint the picture of a guilty person. His eagerness to help was almost annoying.

Wouldn't it be nice if the guilty party stood up and admitted their involvement?

Of course, people like her would be out of a job.

Levi knew Sayeh wanted Roth to be guilty, but so far, he wasn't acting like someone with anything to hide.

"Why'd your family move from Cottonwood?"

"Had to go where the business was. My dad grew up there but when he realized that Cottonwood just didn't have the same kind of business opportunities he was going to need to build his business up, he pulled up stakes and went where the money was."

"Bozeman certainly has that," Levi agreed.

"And where is your dad now?" Sayeh asked.

"Sadly, my father passed away three years ago from cancer."

Sayeh and Levi both murmured condolences.

"Thank you. It was hard to go through but what are you going to do? One thing about cancer, it doesn't care if you're rich or poor. But I gotta tell you, if it weren't for my mom, I would've been lost. She's really the backbone of our family and I'm not ashamed to admit, a huge part of our family business success."

So far, Levi was having a hard time seeing Roth as anything other than what he seemed, which should've been a relief, but Levi had hoped they were onto a solid lead in this case. This guy was spilling his guts so fast that it was almost an overshare situation.

Sayeh pulled back to the main point of their visit. "You mentioned being happy that we were reopening Echo's case. Why is that?"

Roth sat up straighter, pinning them with his gaze. "When I heard about Echo's death, it broke me into a million pieces. I wanted justice for what'd been done to her. Even though we were broken up, I never wanted anything but good things for her. She was the kind of girl who could've had anything she wanted in this world because she had what it took to go after it. I wanted to see her fulfill her dreams. Finding out about her death…well, it changed me."

"Changed you? How?"

Roth admitted, "It made me want to be a better person."

Interesting. Levi hid the glimmer of hope that they were finally onto something. "Can you elaborate?"

"I was a spoiled kid," he answered simply. "Only child of well-off parents, used to getting what he wanted with little effort, you know the type—I was it. Echo was the only one who saw something different in me and made me want to live up to who she thought I could be."

It was almost tragically sweet and heartwarming, except for the part where the girl had to die to make the person change for the better.

Roth shook his head. "I know I'm probably making myself look like a suspect, but I'm just going to be honest with you. I never believed that stupid story about her dying of natural causes. There's no reason Echo would've been out there like that. Have you ever been to Yego Creek? It's in the middle of nowhere. I told anyone who would listen that it didn't make sense but no one was listening to me. By that point, my parents told me I needed to get on with my life. Nothing I could say or do would bring her back. So, that's what I did, but it never sat right with me and that's why I'm glad you're reopening her case."

Levi sighed, sharing a look with Sāyeh. Where to go from here? The man wasn't giving off any vibes aside from being an overprivileged white guy who suffered an attack of conscience to become a better person.

"Would you be willing to submit a DNA swab?" Sayeh asked suddenly.

Before Roth could answer, a tall, stately, attractive woman strode into the room. She graced them with a cold but efficient smile and apologized for being late. "My meetings went longer than expected." She looked to Roth. "We'll have to go over those Orchard Park Way plans again. The planning department is taking issue with the landscaping specs."

Roth brightened as he introduced the woman. "This is my mother, Olivia Roth, the true brains behind the brawn of this operation. Mother, these are the BIA agents I told you were coming, Sayeh Griffin and Levi Wyatt."

"Pleasure to meet you, ma'am," Levi said, ducking his head. Sayeh nodded with a brief, perfunctory smile.

"We were just talking with Mr. Roth about his relationship with Miss Echo Flying Owl Jones."

The woman's expression softened imperceptibly at the mention of Echo's name as she tsked mournfully. "Such a tragedy when a young life is lost." However, her expression turned befuddled as she said, "But I don't know how we would know anything about her case. We were in the process of moving when she died."

"We're just following leads that weren't explored at the time of the original investigation," Levi explained.

"Are you treating it as a murder investigation? I thought they concluded she died of natural causes?"

"We discovered due diligence wasn't applied to Miss Jones's case and we're doing what we can to do that now."

"I see—and how was my son's name dragged into this discussion?"

Roth seemed taken aback by his mother's tone and tried to settle her down. "Mother, they're just following protocol—and we're happy to help because we've got nothing to hide."

"Of course we don't. I just find it odd that they would come here when you barely knew the girl."

Sayeh paused, narrowing her gaze to inquire, "You didn't know your son and Miss Jones were dating?"

A shadow passed over her gaze, but she barked a short dismissive laugh. "Dating? Not to be rude, but I hardly consider what was happening between them as *dating*. It was a passing acquaintance."

Levi and Sayeh shared a look, no doubt thinking the same thing. It was clear Olivia wasn't aware of how close her son and Echo were at the time—either that or she didn't want to accept the facts as they were.

"Mother…" Roth warned, casting a sharp look her way. "You know we were more than that."

The woman snapped her mouth shut, twin spots of color rising to her cheeks as she jerked a short nod. "Well, either way, it's a tragedy what happened."

Was this plain ol' racism on the mother, or was it something else?

"Did you give her any jewelry?" Sayeh asked.

Roth took a minute to think, then slowly nodded as the recollection came to him. "A turquoise bracelet."

"Oh? You never told me," Olivia remarked, shifting with discomfort. "That was so sweet of you."

"I saw it and immediately knew Echo should have it. She loved turquoise."

"Well, I'm sure it looked lovely with her skin tone," Olivia murmured with a short smile before returning to Levi and Sayeh with a quick look at her watch. "Was there anything else you needed? We're expected at another meeting in a few minutes."

"Actually," Sayeh said, rising as she pulled a DNA swab kit from her bag, "would you mind giving us a DNA sample? It's real quick, I promise."

Roth started to answer, but his mother intervened. "I don't think so. I'm sure you can understand that a man in my son's position can't be called into question in an active murder investigation. Our company operates on a foundation of trust, integrity and unimpeachable moral fiber. Unless you have a warrant, there's no reason why my son would needlessly submit a DNA sample."

Levi watched as the two squared off. Roth was undoubtedly embarrassed that his mom was being difficult, but he wasn't going against her, either.

"We could get a warrant," Sayeh chirped brightly. "I have a judge on speed dial for this very thing but warrants are also public record so if you're hoping to keep this quiet... willingly giving a sample would prevent a nosy reporter from asking questions."

Roth shot his mother an irritated look and relented. "If it helps prove that I had nothing to do with Echo's death, I'm happy to cooperate. I want justice for Echo. You don't need a warrant, I'm willing to do it."

The woman looked mildly panicked. Was it because she feared a PR nightmare or because she worried her son might be guilty? But if her son was guilty, why would he willingly give up a DNA sample?

Levi supposed they'd find out soon enough.

Sayeh finished taking the swab and packaging it away for transport. They said their goodbyes with a promise to be in touch and then hit the road.

"I'd give my left kidney to be a fly on the wall for that conversation," Sayeh quipped.

"Yeah, I think junior might even get grounded."

Sayeh's snort of laughter made him grin. Maybe if they were lucky, something good was about to happen with this case.

Chapter 22

A few days later Sayeh received a curt letter from the Macawi Tribal Council requesting an audience regarding her investigation into the deaths of her parents. Sayeh checked to see if either of her sisters could come with her, but as luck would have it, both were busy with previous commitments.

She didn't want to ask Levi; stubborn independence was ingrained in her DNA, even though it was the bane of her existence, so she went alone.

As she walked into the Macawi Tribal Council chambers, she felt like she was walking into the lion's den against stacked odds for her survival, but she didn't let her trepidation show.

The room was empty save for one person—an older Native man with salt-and-pepper hair wound into two long braids on either side of his weathered face. He was probably in his midsixties, if she were to guess, but his gaze was sharp even if his smile appeared welcoming.

Surprised to see only one council member, she introduced herself.

"I'm Raymond Two Feathers but my friends call me Ray. I'm sorry for all this hoopla," he said, gesturing to the letter in her hand as she took a seat at the table opposite him, "but I've been asked to talk to you about your investigation."

Sayeh slid into the seat, prepared for this meeting to go one of two ways. Either they would be helpful or not, but she wouldn't stop until she had the answers she sought.

"What concerns does the council have with my investigation?" she asked, hoping for support.

Ray steepled his fingers in front of him, looking the part of the man forced to deliver bad news, and the tentative hope died in her chest. "You are Macawi—your ancestors are our ancestors. We are family. Losing members of our tribe always hurts and weakens our collective spirit but sometimes we have to take into consideration the collective good, too."

"I'm sorry but I'm not really great with metaphor. Can you be more to the point?" Sayeh asked.

Ray's lips firmed in reproach, saying, "You didn't follow protocol for your investigation. You took soil samples without permission on tribal land and now you're stirring a hornet's nest with all of your questions about the past."

"I had verbal permission," she said, kicking herself for not getting it in writing.

"By whom?"

"Sarah Williams."

Realization dawned, and Ray shared, "Well, this is embarrassing. Sarah is no longer on the council. She stepped down a few months ago—differences in tribal philosophy."

That made sense. Sarah had been sympathetic to Sayeh's cause and believed the truth was important. Sayeh hoped her departure wasn't directly caused by her investigation, but she wouldn't put it past the remaining council if they were anything like this old buzzard.

Sayeh drew a deep breath, trying for patience and diplomacy, even though she wasn't good at either. "I apologize for not getting the approval in writing—that's my mistake. However, I felt I was doing everything aboveboard. I used a licensed company that are experts in the field and I paid for the expense myself so that the tribe didn't suffer the financial responsibility. I'm sure you can appreciate how I'm just looking for answers."

"That's where we differ—the answers were already provided. The blast that killed your parents was determined to be chemical-related."

"Respectfully, that's where you're wrong—where the report is wrong. That explosion wasn't caused by the chemicals commonly used to manufacture methamphetamine. I would think knowing this information, the council would want answers, too."

Ray wasn't interested. "The council wants to move on from an ugly chapter in our history," Ray said. "It's not a secret that our people struggle with addictions. We can't get services fast enough to stop the spread of addiction overtaking our good people. It's a problem we're working to solve but there will always be those who take advantage of our weaknesses."

"Which is exactly why we shouldn't be covering up crimes," she returned, refusing to back down. "My parents, whatever their demons, weren't making methamphetamine. The soil reports show zero contamination. If they'd been blown to smithereens by a chemical blast, the site would've retained contamination in the soil."

"I knew Darryl Proudfoot," Ray said flatly. "He was a drug addict, a thief and a liar. You're defending a man who doesn't deserve your devotion."

Sayeh's eyes stung, but she blinked the tears away, mostly because she didn't understand why this man's judgment bothered her. Darryl Proudfoot was just a name on paper, but the truth mattered. "Be that as it may, he wasn't making methamphetamine as the report claims, which means my mother wasn't, either. Are you going to tell me that Mika was equally a shit person?"

Ray looked away, admitting, "No, I can't say that about Mika but she made poor choices, too."

"I don't care what their choices were—I want the truth of how they died. Someone manufactured a cover story about their deaths and I would think that the council would want that corrected. The old tribal chief and the Cottonwood police chief were working together—"

"Those are dangerous accusations," Ray broke in with a warning look. "I would be careful with what I say if I were you."

"Well, you're not me. I already know they were both corrupt as hell. The news reports already connected the dots between the Mexican mafia and the tribal police chief. He was getting paid to look the other way while they ran their operations through tribal land. What else might he have been paid to do? Perhaps get rid of a troublesome dealer? Darryl Proudfoot wasn't an angel, I get that, but justice is supposed to be blind."

"Maybe you're more interested in digging up hurts because you're a hurt little girl on the inside," Ray said.

Taken aback, Sayeh could only stare. "Meaning?"

"Your name is becoming synonymous with trouble on the reservation," Ray answered, narrowing his gaze. "First, you dig up trouble with your questions about a long-dead past and now you're poking at another case that only brings heartache to our people."

"What are you talking about?"

"Echo Flying Owl Jones," he said. "She died of natural causes but you can't accept that. You have to go poking at our pain, dredging up the past until there's nothing but unrest in your wake. How are you helping your people with these actions? Are you Macawi-loyal or not?"

"I don't know what you're asking," she returned stiffly. "If you're saying that I can't honor my heritage *and* demand justice for the victims of *two* separate crimes committed on tribal land, then we are at odds and are destined to stay that way."

Drawing himself up, he sighed, shaking his head. "I didn't want our conversation to end this way. It hurts my heart that a Macawi daughter is so blind to her people that she would rather chase ghosts than try to help heal the wounds from the past."

"Stop trying to emotionally manipulate me, it won't work," she said, irritated by the attempt. "I've worked with full-blown narcissists and what you're attempting is just embarrassing."

Ray's face flushed as he glared. "You have a nasty heart."

She rose, finished with the conversation. Ray followed her lead, his gaze hardening. "You leave us no choice. You're no longer welcome on tribal land."

Sayeh laughed at the audacity. "You don't have that authority." She fished her credentials out. "However, this right here gives me the right to go wherever I need to during the course of my investigation. I was hoping for your cooperation…but I don't really need it."

And then Sayeh let herself out, realizing as she stormed back to her car that her temper still had the power to land her ass in trouble.

Levi used the weekend to finally bite the bullet and meet up with his brother. The family ranch was a bit of a drive away from Billings, at least four hours; he left before dawn so he could get there in time to get a full day's worth of work in.

By the time he drove onto the ranch, Landon had already been up for hours with the cattle. Levi smiled, nostalgia flooding him as it always did when he came home.

He'd called ahead to let Landon know he was on his way. The minute he rolled onto the property and parked in the driveway, Landon was already dismounting from his horse and leading him to the barn so they could catch up.

"The prodigal son returns," Landon teased as he wrapped Levi in a bear hug, lifting him off his feet like he weighed nothing.

Landon was taller than him by a few inches—something Levi had always secretly envied of his big brother. He was a force of nature, and the height suited him.

"You better have coffee brewing," Levi groused in mock irritation as they walked into the main house. "Otherwise, I'm getting in my car and heading back where I came from."

"Shut your mouth, I got coffee, you big baby," Landon said. "You know where everything's at—I ain't serving you."

Levi grinned. He hadn't realized how much he'd missed the big jerk, but he'd been avoiding coming home since their dad passed, and unfortunately, that avoidance had bled onto his brother.

Landon looked the same, maybe a little grayer around the temples, a few more wrinkles from too much sun, but otherwise, he was the same guy Levi missed and loved.

"Man, I'm sorry it's taken so long to get back to the ranch," Levi started, settling in the old oak dining room chair. "Work's been... Well, it's been busy."

"Yeah, new jobs are hell. How's that going?"

"Good, good." He sipped his coffee, his thoughts immediately going to Sayeh. "Yeah, real good."

"Yeah? Is there more to that?"

"What is this, the Inquisition?" Levi said, half-joking, but his brother could tell he was chewing on something. He'd just keep needling him until he got it out of him, so he might as well get it over with. "Okay, look, I may have met someone who I click with, but it's all so new I don't even know if I want to talk about it."

Landon sobered, knowing how big this was. He poured himself a cup of coffee and sat opposite Levi. "When you're ready to talk about it, you know where to find me. In the meantime, we need to discuss Dad's things. I'm thinking we can donate his Western shirts and whatnot to the local Goodwill but I need you to go through his stuff and take what you want to keep—his rings, buckles…all that. The rest we'll just donate or throw out."

A lump rose in his throat, and his lungs felt squeezed of all air. This was what he'd been avoiding. The fact that Landon could speak so casually about it meant he'd already done the emotional work of preparing for this moment.

The urge to tell Landon to shut the door and think about it another day was almost as strong as his need to get it over with. "Right," he said gruffly, taking a minute to clear his throat. "Sounds good."

Landon understood how difficult this was and tried to lighten the moment with humor. "Remember that time Granny knit Dad that god-awful puke-green sweater and he insisted on wearing it to one of our back-to-school nights?"

Levi chuckled at the memory. "Oh, he knew it was ugly as sin but he liked embarrassing the shit out of us."

"I found that sweater in a box in his closet. Still had it

all these years later. I'm thinking we ought to keep it and hand it down to the next generation. It'll be Jack's legacy."

"Neither of us have kids," Levi reminded Landon.

"Yeah, well, it's about time you get started. You're not getting any younger."

Levi balked with fake outrage. "And what about you? You're getting grayer by the minute. You better find yourself a wife real quick before there's nothing left in your testicles but dust."

Landon guffawed at the ribald joke. "Yeah, well, you're right behind me, so tell me about this mystery girl that's got you all tangled up on the insides."

Levi sobered, realizing his brother was still too good at getting information out of him. If anyone should've gone into investigations, Landon missed his calling, but he never would've left their dad to wrangle the ranch alone.

Sighing, Levi said, "Her name is Sayeh Griffin...and she's my colleague. She's on the task force with me."

Landon whistled low with amusement. "Damn, brother, way to swing high. Aren't there rules against that kind of thing?"

"It's an HR paperwork nightmare but there's no specific rules against dating a colleague as long as you're not in a position of authority over the other. We're basically at the same level, so we're fine but technically we're supposed to disclose that we're dating."

"And have you?"

"Hell no. It's still really new—and Sayeh wants to keep it private."

"Are you sure she's not married? I've seen this kind of thing on that *Catfish* show. People pretending to be single but they're actually married with kids."

Levi wasn't sure what made him laugh harder—the idea

of Sayeh hiding a husband somewhere or his brother watching a sensational show like *Catfish*. "I can promise you she's not married," he finally managed to say. "She actually seems pretty allergic to making any kind of commitment."

Landon understood. "Ahh, well, you might want to cut bait on that one."

"Probably."

"But?"

"But… I don't know, there's just something about her that I can't seem to ignore. I like her. A lot."

Landon fell silent for a minute, and Levi knew what was coming next. "You feel guilty about Nadie?"

There was no point in denying it. "Yeah, and don't bother telling me that Nadie would've wanted me to move on—I know that, but it doesn't change my feelings."

"Fair enough." Landon rose and grabbed a muffin from a basket on the counter. He tore off a piece and stuffed it in his mouth. "Here's the thing, little brother, you already know what I'm going to say because it's true. Nadie was a good woman—the best—but she's gone and one thing she was real good at was talking straight. She'd never want you to waste your life pining for a woman that's gone and not coming back. If you like this Sayeh, see where it'll take you but don't be a wuss and blame your fear of being hurt again on Nadie. Her memory deserves better—and you know it."

"That's a low blow," Levi growled, but he knew Landon was right. He was being a wuss because he was afraid of being hurt. Recovering from the loss of Nadie had taken nearly everything he had. How could he chance going through that pain ever again?

Landon chewed methodically, adding, "Life is for the living, brother." He tossed a muffin to him before heading out, saying, "Boxes are in the hall closet. Take what you want, leave the rest for donation."

And then Landon left him to do what needed to be done.

Chapter 23

Sayeh was curious about where Levi went for the weekend, but when he didn't volunteer to tell her, she didn't ask. If she started pestering him about his private plans, that would go against her "let's keep it casual" suggestion, and hypocrisy was one thing she couldn't abide.

Especially not in herself.

But the curiosity was nearly burning a hole in her brain.

Well, that and her simmering anger over that blowhard Two Feathers having the gall to say she wasn't welcome on Macawi land anymore.

"Everything okay?" Levi asked when he passed her office and saw her staring off into space, having mental battles with every situation that seemed stacked against her. "You look ready to go to war."

Sayeh forced a smile. "Something like that," admitting, "I had a less-than-productive meeting with one of the Macawi Tribal Council members. Seems they're not happy with me poking around on either case—my parents' or Echo's."

Levi frowned. "You have less legal legs to stand on with your parents' investigation but as far as Echo's…you have the support of the BIA so there's not much the council can do about it."

"Yeah, I know, but I kinda lumped my parents' investigation in that support bracket. I may have overstated my authority a teensy bit on that score but if you could've heard the way he was talking to me, you would've been steamed under the collar, too."

Levi heaved a heavy sigh, shaking his head. "Sayeh, you have to stop letting your temper get the best of you. We can't afford to make waves with the Macawi Tribal Council when we're getting close to finding answers."

Sayeh glared. "If you're just here to lecture me, please feel free to keep walking."

"Not lecturing you, just reminding you of the big picture."

"Same difference."

Levi stepped inside and closed her door for privacy. He leaned across her desk and said, "Sayeh, I'm not the enemy. You've spent your entire career with a 'me against the world' attitude, and that might've been necessary in your previous post, but it's not here. We're a team. We need to work together, but that means doing things by the book, not going all rogue when you get a wild hair up your ass."

Old habits were hard to break and made worse by the fact that her feelings were bruised by Levi's reproach. It didn't matter that he was right. She stiffened, retorting coolly, "Thank you for that rousing and inspirational speech. You should have T-shirts made. If there's nothing else you have to share, the door—" she pointed "—is that way."

Levi, realizing she wasn't going to budge, gave up. "Sayeh, you can keep pushing away everyone who's good in your life but all that's going to do is leave you alone when you need someone the most."

"Fascinating," she said flatly as she returned to her paperwork.

But as Levi left her alone, tears stung her eyes. What

Levi thought of her mattered, and it hurt that he hadn't immediately taken her side. Luna would call her reaction immature, and maybe it was, but damn, she wasn't prepared for how much it hurt that she felt as if she'd let him down.

"Get a grip," she muttered, wiping at her eyes. "He's a fun bed partner at best and just a colleague at worst... Don't get attached."

It was solid advice, but it felt hollow and dissatisfying.

She expelled a sigh and leaned back in her swivel chair to stare at the gray drop ceiling that looked like it'd been installed in the 1960s, wondering if all federal buildings built in the same era had gotten a discount.

Why was she the way she was?

Why did she have a perpetual chip on her shoulder?

Neither Luna nor Kenna had this problem—only her.

Maybe her bad attitude was the biggest indication that she had a different set of DNA than her sisters.

She checked her email to see if the DNA analysis for paternity had come back yet, but nothing popped up.

"A watched pot never boils," she reminded herself under her breath, returning to the case files. She spent the entire day cloistered in her office, privately hoping Levi would pass by again so she could apologize for being a pill, but he didn't, and by the end of the day she was left alone at the office.

He hadn't even said goodbye.

I guess that means no cuddling tonight, she thought morosely. *Way to go, Sayeh.*

She spent another hour on the case, researching Roth Construction—and finding nothing remotely resembling a red flag—then shut everything down. It was dark outside, and her stomach was grumbling. She'd forgotten to eat lunch, and now her stomach was demanding some kind of sustenance before complete system shutdown.

She locked up and headed for her car. Maybe she'd grab a pizza and show up at Levi's place, offering the pie as a peace offering, along with her sincerest apology for being a jerk. Maybe even admitting that she'd been in the wrong. That ought to go a long way, right?

Just as she clicked her car fob, something sharp and hard smashed into the back of her head, sending stars to burst behind her eyeballs as she crashed to the pavement of the empty parking lot. A booted foot caught her chin as she writhed on the ground, unable to catch her breath.

Excruciating pain, unlike anything she'd ever known, stole the air from her lungs as her assailant continued to kick the shit out of her until all she could do was curl in a ball and try to protect her head the best she could.

One good kick to the temple could kill a person.

I can't die like this, she thought in a pained daze. Of all the ways she could've clocked out in this life, getting mauled in the parking lot of her own damn building wasn't going to be it.

Suddenly the cruel grip of a hand wrenched her head back so violently that she could feel her hair being pulled from its roots. A deadly voice hissed in her ear. "Anyone can get to you. Remember that, bitch." He twisted her neck farther with each word until she feared he would rip her head off.

Then he released her, but he lunged forward before she could catch her breath, delivering a final blow that knocked her out cold.

Levi's cell rang, and he answered, hoping it was Sayeh, but it was Isaac.

"Hey, Isaac, everything okay?"

"No, Sayeh's in the hospital," he said. "She's been attacked."

Levi felt the floor drop out from beneath him. "What happened?"

"We're not sure. An anonymous 9-1-1 call came in. Someone saw a man dressed in all black attacking a woman in our parking lot after hours. By the time first responders showed up, the assailant was gone and Sayeh was unconscious. Whoever it was beat her up pretty bad. I'm going to the hospital now."

"I'll meet you there."

"They took her to St. Vincent's."

Levi clicked off, sprinted out the door and jumped in his car, his thoughts racing as fast as the tires. How the hell had someone gotten the jump on Sayeh? And why? It had to be related to something she was investigating...but which one? Was it related to her parents' investigation or Echo's?

Seeing as someone had already gone to great lengths to kill their one and only lead, he was leaning toward Echo's case, but then, that nasty reception from the tribal council member wasn't a good sign, either.

Either way, someone wanted Sayeh down and out.

Levi cursed himself for leaving her alone at the office. This case was already getting dangerous. He should've known better. If Sayeh didn't pull out of this, he'd never forgive himself.

He screeched into a parking spot and ran into the emergency room, barely waiting for the double automatic doors to slide open.

Levi showed his credentials to the front desk and gave Sayeh's name. They let him through, and he found Isaac talking to the doctor.

"How is she?" Levi asked anxiously. "Is she going to be all right?"

"She's a tough cookie," the doctor said, shaking his head. "She protected her face as best she could and avoided breaking any of her facial bones, but her wrist is fractured from taking the brunt of the blow. She also has a mild skull fracture that we're going to want to keep an eye on to make sure she doesn't start a brain bleed, but overall, she's one lucky woman. I've seen these things go the opposite direction too many times."

"Can we see her?"

The doctor looked to Isaac. "Per your instructions, she's been given a private room to recover in."

"I want security posted at all times," Levi said. "And I'm not leaving her side."

To the doctor, Isaac said, "Aside from medical personnel, if they don't have credentials like this—" he flashed his badge "—no one is allowed in her room."

The doctor nodded and went to inform the front desk, leaving Isaac and Levi to talk. "Any idea who might've done this?" Isaac asked in a low tone.

Frustration laced Levi's voice as he admitted, "No, not really. This case has us going in all sorts of directions. It could've also been related to something private Sayeh's been running down about her biological family."

"You need to find out."

"I absolutely will. Where's the investigating officer?" he asked.

"He's already left."

"I want the forensics sent to our team. We can put a rush on anything she might've picked up during the attack. With any luck, we'll be able to find who did this to her."

"I'll authorize whatever you need. I have the IT team

pulling the front camera footage. One way or another, we'll find who did this."

Isaac left, and Levi went to find Sayeh in her recovery room. As he walked in, nurses were checking her vitals and double-checking her IV. Instantly, his knees locked as rage followed at the sight of the devastation to Sayeh's face. Mottled black and blue spread across her swollen face, and her lip was split.

If he ever got his hands on whoever did this to her, there would be nothing to prosecute because the man would be dead.

Nadie had died instantly in the wreck, and the damage had been so horrific the family had held a closed-casket funeral. Seeing Sayeh so broken made him realize that not seeing Nadie in her final moments had been a blessing because he couldn't imagine his last memories of Nadie to be like this.

He shook with impotent rage as he pulled a chair to sit by her side.

One eye dragged open and focused blearily on Levi. "Y-you should see the other g-guy," she said through cracked lips in a raspy whisper, though pain radiated from her gaze.

Good God, Sayeh. "What happened?" he asked softly, gently stroking her hair, immediately feeling the matted blood beneath his fingertips.

She swallowed with difficulty, taking a minute before she could answer. "J-jumped me from behind. Must've b-been waiting for me. N-never saw him."

"We're going to have our forensic team process any DNA evidence collected," he reassured her. "I want to make sure it's done right and Isaac's already given the green light to rush everything. We're going to find who did this."

Sayeh nodded and closed her good eye, drifting off

again. The slight but mighty nurse looked at him. "She's on heavy painkillers and needs to rest now. You can stay but only if you're quiet."

The nurse looked like she wasn't going to take anything but cooperation when it came to caring for her patient. Levi liked that quality in a nurse. Especially when Sayeh was the one needing care. He nodded and settled in for a quiet but watchful night.

Chapter 24

Sayeh didn't know how much time had passed between that horrible moment when someone tried to cave in her skull and now, but she assumed it'd been more than a few hours because Levi looked like he'd been sleeping in that chair for weeks.

"You look like hell," she croaked, shocked at how dusty her vocal cords sounded. "What time is it?"

Levi awoke with a start and immediately scrubbed the sleep from his face, surprised by her waking. "Hey, sleepyhead, how do you feel?"

"Thirsty," she groused, struggling to sit up, but Levi was on her in a second, treating her like she would break if she lifted a finger. He helped hold a paper cup to her lips, and she sipped at the cold liquid, wincing as her throat protested. "How long have I been out?"

"Three days," he answered.

"Three days! Are you joking?" she exclaimed, which was a mistake because her head throbbed like a son of a bitch. "I need out of this bed."

"No, you need to rest. You nearly died, Sayeh."

She stilled, trying to remember the details of what happened. "What do you mean, died?"

"You suffered a skull fracture. At first, the doc thought

it was mild and should be fine with rest but then you spiked a fever and they realized you suffered a brain bleed. They rushed you to surgery, drained the bleed and patched you back up, but you've been out since then. Doc said the trauma to your brain was more severe than they thought."

Sayeh gingerly touched the back of her head and gasped when she felt a buzzed spot. "Am I bald?"

He chuckled wearily, shaking his head. "No, just a small square where they inserted the shunt. Your sister Luna suggested the doc shave your entire head as payback for the time you cut her hair in her sleep."

"She needs to let that go. I was five," she said in a raspy voice. "My sisters know what happened?"

He nodded. "We've been taking shifts. Kenna and Luna went down to the cafeteria to grab a bite to eat. They should be back in a few minutes."

For some reason, knowing her sisters were there made tears spring to her eyes, which only made her nose throb violently.

Levi dabbed the corners of her eyes with a soft tissue. "You scared us. It was touch and go for a bit."

Sayeh didn't like to know that. She shifted with discomfort at the knowledge that someone had gotten the jump on her. How could she have let that happen with all her training? She'd gotten sloppy. "Any word from Forensics?" she asked, trying not to focus on the urge to cry.

"Not yet. I expect something soon."

"When can I be released?"

Levi barked a short laugh as if her question was ludicrous. "You're not going anywhere. Your damn skull was cracked open like an egg."

"Yeah, that's what you said. My question stands. I hate hospitals."

Levi gestured to the sterile accommodations with a grin. "What? This is five-star luxury right here. Room service at the press of a button, full-time security watching to make sure no one enters without clearance, and me, your handsome concierge/bodyguard/lover, to make sure your every need is looked after."

Sayeh blushed, the warmth of foreign emotion flustering her as she tried to shift to a more comfortable position. "I think I could recover fine from home."

"Not until the doctor says you can," Levi returned without hesitation. Before she could further argue her point, Kenna and Luna walked in, rushing to her side when they realized she was conscious.

"Oh, my God! You're awake!" Kenna exclaimed, gently squeezing the hand that didn't have an IV attached. "Don't you ever scare us like that again. I've been texting Ty every day to give him updates, and he told me to tell you that his favorite auntie is not allowed to die. So, don't even think about it."

"I won't take offense to the *favorite auntie* but only because Sayeh is lying in a hospital bed," Luna said dryly, focusing on Sayeh. "How are you feeling?"

"Like a bag of dog doo that's been kicked from here to creation," Sayeh answered. "But alive, which is something."

"Damn right it is," Luna agreed. "We were so scared that you weren't going to pull through."

"I'm too stubborn to die," Sayeh said in a hoarse tone, which coaxed smiles from her sisters as they grudgingly agreed. She tried to smile, but it hurt her bruised lip. "Ouch. I swear if I get my hands on the asshole who did this—"

"You'll have to wait in line because I'm getting first swing," Levi said.

Sayeh met Levi's gaze, and something shifted between

them. She saw the truth in his eyes—he meant every word. A shiver passed through her. She saw more than a colleague expressing concern for a coworker, which humbled her. "I was going to bring you a pizza," she remembered. "To apologize."

Luna and Kenna exchanged glances and, after pressing soft kisses on her forehead, made excuses to leave Levi and Sayeh alone for a minute.

Sayeh appreciated her sisters' intuition. "I'm sorry for being such a stubborn jerk," she said in a low tone. "You were right that day."

"I shouldn't have left you alone at the office," he said, brushing a tender kiss across her abused lips. "I was trying to give you space and not be clingy. I should've known better."

"You had no way of knowing that someone was going to ambush me," she said, trying to relieve him of that burden. "For that matter, I should've known to be more aware of my surroundings. It's embarrassing how easy he got the jump on me. Head on a swivel was practically ingrained in me from day one of training. I got sloppy."

"What you're not going to do is blame yourself for some sick asshole's actions, got it?" Levi said sternly. "We're going to catch whoever did this and then we're going to nail his ass to the wall. Period."

Sayeh didn't argue. "Kiss me again," she murmured, holding his gaze.

"With pleasure," he said, gently brushing his lips across hers. "When this is all over, we need to talk."

"That sounds ominous," Sayeh said, but she knew what he wanted to discuss. "Fine. But until then, help me get out of this bed. I feel bedsores happening."

"Whoa there." Alarmed, Levi gently prevented her from

rising. "You're not going anywhere until the doctor gives you the all clear. I know you think you're invincible but that knock on your head says otherwise."

Sayeh exhaled a long sigh but didn't argue. Instead, she acquiesced with a grumble. "Fine. If I can't leave, you need to bring the office to me. I need my laptop. I have work to do."

Levi shouldn't be surprised that the minute Sayeh's head wasn't full of cotton, she'd want to hit the ground running, but he wished she'd at least take another day or two to recuperate.

Still, he brought her laptop and his own, setting up a mobile office amid the machines and tubes, nurses and doctors coming and going.

Luna and Kenna went home, leaving Levi to watch after Sayeh but with strict instructions to call if anything changed.

"We got a hit on the forensics collected at the scene. You managed to get some skin beneath your fingernails. We ran it through the system and a name popped up."

Sayeh was all ears. "Yeah? Who?"

"Garrett Coleson," Levi answered, checking his watch. "We've got local PD picking him up now. I'm going to meet them down at the station for questioning."

Sayeh tried to climb from the bed. "I can be ready in ten minutes if you can help get these tubes out of me," she said as if that were actually going to happen.

"Get your ass back in bed. You're in no position to leave this bed much less head to a police station to interrogate a suspect."

Frustration made her snappy. "And I'm just supposed to sit here like a toad on a lily pad waiting for a juicy fly to land in my mouth?"

"Yep."

Sayeh growled and glared, but he wasn't going to budge. "Doc says you're not cleared to leave yet so you're going to sit right here. I have a security guard posted at your door. You'll be safe until I return. Hopefully, with some answers."

Sayeh settled back into her bed with an unhappy sigh. "Fine but I want to know what's going on at all times. Text me updates or I'll find a way to sneak out of this hospital, hijack a car and meet you down at the station."

Levi didn't want to laugh, but as absurd as Sayeh's assertion was, he could see her doing it. "I promise to update you. Now, eat your pudding like a good little frog and I'll be back as soon as I can."

"I hate pudding," she muttered, folding her arms. Levi chuckled, kissed her forehead and left for the station.

Within minutes he was at the Billings Police Station and conferring with the investigative officer. They weren't exactly happy about a federal agency stepping into their investigation, but the local brass didn't want to press the issue with the feds, so they grudgingly acquiesced.

Levi took a minute to calm his heart rate so he didn't walk into interrogation and immediately start pummeling the guy.

Garrett Coleson was a lean, muscled type with a dark-haired mullet that looked greasy and unkempt. He slouched in the metal chair, trying to appear annoyed but unworried as Levi sat opposite him.

"Garrett Coleson, thirty-six, of Kettleman City..." Levi made a show of reading his file. "You're a long way from home."

"Is that a crime? I travel for work, so what?" Garrett asked, shifting against the shackles holding him to the metal desk. "What's this all about?"

"Think real hard."

"Man, I don't know what the hell you're talking about. This is harassment."

"No, this is forensic science at work."

"Huh?"

"Funny thing about science…it's super techy these days. Not only do we have you on CCTV assaulting a federal BIA agent, we have your DNA collected from her fingernails as she tried to protect herself from the steel-toe boots you were wearing. The mistake you made was when you pulled her hair, she reached up and scratched your neck, getting a nice big clump of your DNA under her fingernails."

Garrett lost his bravado, licking his lips like a nervous dog as Levi slid him the grainy black-and-white photos of the night in question.

"You thought that by wearing a ski mask and all black clothing no one would be able to identify you, but you also drove away in your beat-up old Ford, and your license plate was in full view. I guess it's a good thing you're not what we'd call a criminal mastermind, but you are a goddamn coward that's for sure, and I'm going to love sending you to prison."

"I—I…hold up!" Garrett protested as Levi made a show of leaving. "I have information! I'll talk for immunity."

That's not how these things worked, but Levi was willing to lie. "Tell me what you've got and I'll decide whether or not it's worth making a deal." He leaned toward Garrett, delivering in a hard tone, "Who hired you to assault Sayeh Griffin?"

"They never said nothing about it being a federal officer, I swear it," he said, trying to make points. "All they said was some uppity bitch making trouble needed to be taught a lesson and I figured I'd just rough her up a little bit. I didn't mean for it to go that far. I swear it!"

"You fractured her skull and broke her wrist," Levi said, barely able to say the words without snarling. "You almost killed her."

"I swear I didn't mean to hurt her that bad. I just got a little carried away, is all. You know how it is, a woman starts mouthing off and then, it just happens."

Yeah, Garrett liked to hit women, that was all over his criminal record—plenty of domestic violence charges—and whoever had hired him had known it wouldn't take much to get him to press that button.

"Who hired you?"

"I never got a name. I was texted the address from a burner phone, told to wait until night and then clean her clock. It was just supposed to scare her a little."

"How much they offer you?"

"Two grand. Half up front and half once the job was done."

"Are you in the habit of taking odd jobs of beating up innocent people?" Levi asked with deceptive calm. "Is this your regular side gig?"

"No, man, this is my first time," he said earnestly as if that would make a difference. "I swear it."

"I believe you, Garrett. You're too damn stupid to make a career out of being a criminal."

Garrett's face flushed with shame. "Please, man, I made a mistake. I won't do it again."

"I know you won't because you're going to prison for assaulting a federal agent."

Garrett paled. "But you said—"

"No, I didn't," Levi cut in, closing the file. "You assumed. I never offered you shit."

"I got kids," Garrett pleaded.

"And they'll be better off without you as their father figure," Levi said, going to the door. Something made him pause and ask, "Where do you work?"

"Roth Construction," Garrett answered dully, refusing to meet Levi's gaze. "I'm not answering anything more until my lawyer gets here."

"Fine by me. I got what I need. Enjoy prison."

Chapter 25

Sayeh was released a week later, but it felt like an eternity. Even though her doctor wanted another week of bed rest, if she had to spend one more day in that sterile hospital room, she'd lose her ever-loving mind, and he reluctantly signed off.

"I appreciate you driving me to my place," she said to Levi, happy to be free of that hospital room. There was only so much she could accomplish from her bed. The doctor grudgingly released her on the condition that she'd be on light duty, and aside from the cast on her arm, she felt ready to get back into the swing of things. "I mean, I could've just asked one of my sisters, though."

Levi shot her a possessive look that was as sexy as it was surprising, and Sayeh had to remind herself that sex was off the table for at least another two weeks. Patients with a "traumatic brain injury" had a serious set of rules to follow. "I'm taking you home and I'm also going to stay with you while you recover," he told her.

"Is that so?" Sayeh shot back with a grin. "That's a sneaky way of saying you want to move in with me."

He laughed, shaking his head. "Something tells me you're a terrible roommate."

"Oh, I definitely am, but I'm an awesome snuggler, so there's that."

Sayeh was making light of his announcement, but she sensed something changing between them, possibly even more deeply than either were ready but couldn't stop. Almost dying had a way of changing perspective. Her feelings for Levi were more powerful than she could've ever planned for—but that didn't change their situation. She wasn't ready to proclaim anything official, and it would be hard to get around that if he was sleeping over every night.

"You okay?" Levi asked at her sudden silence. "Head hurt? I have your medication in that bag behind the seat."

Yes, her head hurt, but it was manageable. She refused to fall down that rabbit hole of prescribed addiction when the addiction gene ran in her family. "I'm fine. I was just thinking, it's probably not a good idea for you to stay over. As much as I would love to cuddle with you at night, someone is going to notice and the last thing either of us need is the HR paperwork. I'll be fine. I promise."

"No."

He wasn't even willing to discuss it. The set of his jaw wasn't conducive to negotiation, but she wasn't one to accept being bossed around—not even when it was in her best interests. "Levi," she warned, not wanting to fight. "Be reasonable. You know I'm right. Besides, we both agreed—"

"No, *you* be reasonable. You damn near died and we still don't know who hired Garrett Coleson to kick the shit out of you. Don't ask me to drop you off at the curb like nothing happened. It ain't happening."

Whenever Levi got riled up, the country boy came out in him. Under most circumstances, Sayeh found it incredibly cute and usually teased him about it, but she knew it wasn't a good idea this time.

She fell silent. One night wouldn't cause too much of a stir. Maybe dropping it for tonight and revisiting the conversation tomorrow was better. She nodded and settled against the seat. Levi, sensing she'd backed down, relaxed, immediately apologizing for being terse. "Seeing you in that hospital bed, watching you fight to stay alive…it was too much. I won't let it happen again. Not on my watch. Okay?"

Sayeh heard what he wasn't saying, and it humbled her. There were worse things than to be loved by a man like Levi Wyatt.

But could there be anything worse for Levi than to be loved by Sayeh Griffin?

She wasn't cut out for the "happy family, white picket fence" life.

Even if a part of her wished she were.

Still, that was a conversation for later. Everyone was still raw from what went down. Better to focus on the case—at least there, they didn't have any conflict.

Sayeh's cell rang, and she picked up, expecting one of her sisters. It was an unknown number. Immediately tensing, she answered, "Sayeh Griffin, Bureau of Indian Affairs," and held her breath.

"Miss Griffin? I may have information you might want about Echo Jones. Can you meet me right now?"

Sayeh's eyes widened as she gestured madly for Levi to find her something to write an address down. "Yeah, yeah, of course. Where should we meet?"

Levi's lips firmed as he shook his head, but he could tell she wouldn't back down.

"And who am I speaking with?" Sayeh asked.

"My name is Gretchen Yaley. I was a nurse on shift the day Echo came into the clinic."

Sayeh's jaw couldn't drop any farther. She wrote down the address and said, "We'll meet you in thirty minutes," clicking off.

"What was that and why do I get the impression we're not heading to your place so you can rest?"

Sayeh was so excited she forgot about her aching head. "That was a nurse who claimed to be working the shift the night Echo came into the clinic. She has information that might be useful. We're going to meet her at a small diner on Evergreen Avenue called The Rusty Spoon."

"Why don't I take you home and I'll meet this mystery woman," Levi suggested, but Sayeh cast a sharp look, cutting off whatever nonsense he was about to tack on. He sighed. "Fine, but we're going in together."

"That's fine by me." Sayeh grinned, too happy to be working on the case again.

The diner was an old place that'd seen better days and probably served salmonella along with the special of the day, but it was away from downtown, and the patrons were less likely to be noticed but more likely to be murdered.

"I don't like this," Levi murmured as they parked. He tucked his gun behind him and under his shirt. Unfortunately Sayeh was unarmed. She'd have to rely on her cutting sarcasm and sharp wit to save her ass if it came down to an altercation at the ol' Rusty Spoon.

Old creaking fans caked in grime that looked as if they hadn't been cleaned since the 1970s circulated the air as efficiently as a blind man serving as a lifeguard in a crowded community pool.

"Nice place," Sayeh said under her breath. "Remind me to douse myself in hand sanitizer when we leave."

A lone woman sat in a corner booth, anxiously biting her nails, furtively watching the front door. She made eye contact and waved them over.

Sayeh followed Levi, and they slid into the booth opposite the woman.

"Gretchen Yaley?" Sayeh supposed. At the woman's nod, she said, "You said you had information regarding Echo Jones?"

Gretchen bobbed a quick nod. "Thanks for meeting me on such short notice. Honestly, I knew I had to do it right now before I lost my nerve. As it is, I feel like my guts are filled with rocks. I have a nervous stomach," she explained.

Sayeh gave Gretchen an understanding smile for that overshare and waited for her to continue.

"It was my last day at the clinic. I was at the end of my shift and shift changes are always chaotic. Especially for a clinic that's understaffed and overworked. I remember she came in, bruised and bloodied like she'd been in a fight. She was so young. I felt bad for her but I also wanted to get home. My boyfriend at the time, a real loser as he turned out to be, had a temper so I didn't want to be late. We were moving the next day and the movers were coming first thing in the morning but I still had a lot of packing to do so I was anxious to leave. Well, the doc had ordered X-rays on account she was pretty banged up. It's standard to give women a pregnancy test before X-rays just to make sure they're not pregnant. I think she was too upset over whatever had happened to her that she didn't fight me on the sample. I didn't think nothing of it because it was more of a precaution than anything else. But then the test came back positive and I don't think she expected that."

"Echo was pregnant?" Sayeh couldn't calm her excitement. "Are you sure? It's not in her medical file and it's not in the autopsy report, either."

The woman looked shamefully embarrassed. "It's my fault. I didn't write it down. I got distracted by the fact that my boyfriend was blowing up my phone and I still hadn't finished writing up my notes for the next shift. After I told her the news, I left to get the doctor but he wasn't available. I went back to the room to tell her the doctor would be with her in a few more minutes and another nurse would help her after the shift change but she was gone. The room was empty."

"So she left *after* you told her she was pregnant?" Levi clarified.

Gretchen nodded. "I never expected to hear about the poor girl dying two weeks later but by then I couldn't tell anyone that I'd forgotten to write down the pregnancy test results in her chart, and I figured the autopsy would've shown that she was pregnant. I didn't want to risk seeming incompetent at my new job so I never said anything but now I wish I had. You think someone killed that poor girl?"

"That's what we're trying to find out," Sayeh said. "Do you remember her mentioning who the father might be?"

"No, I didn't get the chance to ask. She seemed real shook up, though. I mean, she was sixteen so I'm sure it wasn't the news she was hoping for."

Levi asked, curious, "How'd you hear about the case?"

Gretchen admitted, "That old boyfriend I had? Well, he had family on the reservation that I stayed close with even though I dumped him. They were talking about the BIA reopening the case. I guess it's all the talk around the Rez right now. That's how I knew I had to come clean. I don't know if it helps you or not but I figured you ought to know."

"Thank you for coming forward," Sayeh said. "We appreciate the information. One question, though, why did you want to meet at this dump?"

"I just don't want no one asking why I was meeting with two BIA agents. I live a quiet life and I like it that way. Maybe I'm being overcautious but I don't need that kind of drama. I'm starting over on my own and trying to make amends for some of the shitty things I've done in the past. I became a nurse because I wanted to help people but then somehow I ended up with people who did nothing but hurt me and twist my original purpose. I'm done with that, but that also means I need to stop holding on to secrets that aren't mine to keep. Anyway, I hope that helps."

Gretchen scooted from the booth and hustled out of the diner. Levi and Sayeh followed, climbing into their car. Sayeh's head was spinning. "If there's blood on Echo's clothing still in evidence, we can test the maternal DNA for any fetal cells—and then we can test that against the DNA sample we collected from Christopher Roth."

"Do you think he's the father?"

"I'm willing to bet my pension he is, which would make him our number one suspect."

Levi mused, saying, "Yeah, but he seemed real eager and ready to submit to whatever we asked for—guilty people aren't usually so accommodating."

Sayeh shrugged. "Maybe he wants to be caught. Guilt can do strange things to people."

"No argument there but it just seems too easy. I feel we're missing a puzzle piece somewhere."

"Well, let's see how the puzzle pieces we have fit together and then we'll go from there."

Sayeh pulled her laptop free from her travel bag and started the requisition from evidence to have Echo's clothing tested and compared against Christopher Roth's DNA sample.

She smiled, almost giddy. "This feels like we're finally onto a true lead. This could blow our case up."

"Here's hoping. We could use a twist of good luck."

Sayeh brightened, suddenly remembering she'd had nothing but hospital food for the last two weeks. "Can we grab a pizza? I'm dying for something that's not nutritionally balanced by a dietician who doesn't care about flavor or texture—and if I see another pudding cup in my life, I'll vomit."

Levi chuckled. "One pie coming up, but after that, no more detours. You need to rest, you lunatic."

Sayeh smiled, leaning over to kiss him on the neck. "You're the best. I'll even let you pick the toppings."

Maybe things were actually starting to go their way. It only took nearly dying to catch a break.

Chapter 26

Sayeh was back at the office, under the watchful eye of everyone it seemed—even Shilah was warming up to her—but she was so anxious to get the results back from the DNA analysis on Echo's clothes that she didn't mind being stared at.

These things took time, but Sayeh was out of patience. She felt antsy like the metaphoric shoe was about to drop. Levi assured her it was residual anxiety from her attack, which only reminded her that she was required to book a therapy appointment per HR.

Isaac dropped by her office on her first official day back. "Glad to see you back. Just a reminder, HR is requiring a mental health check. Standard requirement after a traumatic event on the job. Insurance and all that," he said, jabbing a finger her way. "Book that appointment."

She gave him a thumbs-up, even though she was putting that way at the bottom of her priority list. If her sister couldn't get her into therapy, a near-death experience wouldn't do it, either.

Not that she didn't need it. Hell, she was probably the poster child for someone who desperately needed therapy, but who had time to get mentally adjusted to their trauma? *Not this girl.*

She opened her email and grabbed her tea but stopped mid-sip when she saw the innocuous sender in her inbox.

The spit dried up in her mouth. Her *personal* DNA results were in. She glanced around, suddenly apprehensive about finally knowing the truth. What if finding out that Darryl Proudfoot wasn't her biological father threw her into an emotional tailspin? She didn't have time for that nonsense in her life, either. Or maybe she was worrying about nothing because the test revealed that Darryl *was* her father. She stared at the unopened email, paralyzed.

Just rip the bandage off, she groused to herself; *whatever it says, it is what it is.*

Drawing a deep breath, she clicked Open, revealing the results.

Paternity Testing Results for Sayeh Gemini Griffin (Proudfoot)

I am writing to provide the paternity testing results conducted by DNA Verify to establish paternity in the case involving Mr. Allen Paul. The testing was performed in accordance with established protocols and guidelines, and the results are as follows:

Alleged Father: Allen Charles Paul (deceased)
Mother: Mika Crow (deceased)
Child: Sayeh Gemini Griffin (Proudfoot)
Case Number: 1916218

Testing Methodology:
The paternity testing was conducted using DNA Verify, a scientifically validated and widely accepted method for

establishing biological relationships. DNA samples were collected from Mr. Allen Paul and the child in question.

Results:
The analysis of the DNA samples reveals a 98% probability of paternity between Mr. Allen Paul and the child, Sayeh Gemini Griffin (Proudfoot). This percentage exceeds the threshold typically considered conclusive for establishing biological paternity.

Conclusion:
The results obtained from the paternity testing conducted by DNA Verify provide strong evidence supporting the biological relationship between Mr. Allen Paul and the child, Sayeh Gemini Griffin (Proudfoot). These results can be utilized as crucial evidence in legal proceedings pertaining to the establishment of paternity in a court of law.

We certify that the testing followed strict quality control measures to ensure accurate and reliable results. The DNA samples were handled and analyzed by trained professionals using state-of-the-art equipment and techniques.

Tears welled in Sayeh's eyes, and she leaned back in her chair and processed that she'd been lied to her entire life, and if it hadn't been for Levi's keen sense of observation, she never would've known.

What was she supposed to do now? Aside from curling in a ball and crying her eyes out?

No, that had never been her style, and she wasn't about to start.

She snapped into action, knowing exactly what she

needed to do. Clocking out, she took a personal day, popping into Levi's office to let him know.

"It's a girl," she half laughed, half cried. "My father's paternity results came in. The old corrupt police chief was my actual father and I don't know if I should cry, puke or go get drunk. Maybe all three, but before I do all that, I'm going to Cottonwood to have a word with *Daddy's* old battle-ax of a wife."

Levi didn't hesitate, grabbing his keys and shutting down his computer. "Let's go."

Lord love him but... "I should do this alone."

"The hell you are."

"Levi..."

He grasped her by the shoulders, looking into her eyes. "I'll drive and sit in the car but you're not going alone. Period. Got it?"

"You're starting to be a real pain in my ass," she grumbled, but secretly, she was grateful for his company. Even though this wasn't something she wanted an audience for, she wanted Levi with her—as long as he stayed in the car like he offered.

They made the drive to Cottonwood in silence. Levi must've sensed that she needed to get her head straight before storming into the old bat's perfectly ordered house and destroying her world with the news.

But as they parked in the driveway, Sayeh hesitated. What if she found out more than she was prepared to know? Maybe one devastating revelation per day was enough. No, she was here; time to get it over with. Otherwise she might remain stuck in this driveway until the end of time, locked in a personal hellscape with no end in sight.

"Wish me luck," she muttered, exiting the car like she was on fire.

Sayeh walked up the sidewalk, stopped at the door, drew a deep breath and knocked.

After a minute or two, Vera appeared, looking much the same as the last time, prim, proper and always wearing an expression of faint disdain for those she believed beneath her. "You again," she said, not bothering to hide her distaste, even as her gaze narrowed slightly at the sight of Sayeh's facial bruising. "How can I help you this time?"

Sayeh opened her mouth to blast her, but then it occurred to her that maybe Vera was also a victim of her husband's actions. She swallowed the bile she'd been prepared to spew at the woman and tried a different tactic. "May I speak with you, please, Mrs. Paul?"

Perhaps it was the somber earnestness in her tone, but Vera reluctantly relented, stepping back to allow entrance, though she didn't lead Sayeh into the sitting room as before, communicating wordlessly that her hospitality would be brief. "Please make it quick, I have a full afternoon scheduled."

Sayeh licked her lips, which were suddenly dry. "I don't know how to say this in a way that isn't upsetting to both of us so I'm going to put it out there and let the chips fall where they may."

"Get on with it, then."

Sayeh paused, her gaze drifting to the portrait on the hallway table. She pointed, saying, "There's a reason why my friend did a double take when he saw that picture of Chief Paul the other day."

"Which is?"

"I think you know why."

The older woman stiffened, but her bottom lip started to quiver. "I don't know what you're talking about."

"Yes, you do. I think you've known for a while. Perhaps

the first time you saw me back in town after a long while. You saw the resemblance and you knew. Chief Paul…was my biological father."

Vera seemed to wilt like a flower without a drop of rain, and Sayeh worried she would have a fainting old lady on her hands. If she had to catch Vera Paul… *Good God, could this day get much worse?*

Levi could only imagine the conversation between the two women in that house. He hoped it was civil, but he knew that sometimes killing the messenger was the easiest way to soothe a broken heart.

His cell chirped, and he saw the arrest warrant had come in for Christopher Roth. *Good.* Whatever was happening in that house, this news ought to cheer Sayeh up.

He quickly phoned Roth Construction. The secretary answered.

"This is Levi Wyatt with the BIA. We need to schedule an appointment with Mr. Roth ASAP."

"Oh, Mr. Wyatt, I've been instructed to transfer you to Mrs. Roth. Hold, please."

Not surprised, Levi waited on the line.

Seconds later Mrs. Roth picked up the line. "What's this about?" she inquired sharply. "My son is a busy man. I find it appalling how my son has been treated by the BIA when he's been nothing but accommodating to your investigation."

"Ma'am, we just wanted to follow up with some questions," he lied. He didn't want the Roths to have a reason to run off to another country. They had the money and resources to be a flight risk. "It's pretty much routine. We appreciate how forthcoming Mr. Roth has been."

"Perhaps our attorney should be present," Mrs. Roth

said. "I don't trust you or your partner. In my experience, women like your partner will do just about anything to achieve their agenda."

Women like your partner? "I assure you, Agent Griffin is as professional as they come. When can we meet up?"

"He's very busy," Mrs. Roth returned as if that was an acceptable answer.

"Ma'am, I hate to be the bearer of bad news but we're extending a courtesy that we aren't required to. We will have our audience, one way or another. Don't make this harder than it needs to be."

"Very well. Tomorrow, then. Ten a.m. sharp."

"Tha—" he started, but Mrs. Roth had hung up already "—nk you." *Miserable, racist woman.* "Can't wait."

He would personally love a reason to put that woman in silver bracelets. If only it were possible to arrest someone for being a raging asshole.

Levi called Isaac to keep him in the loop. "We got the warrant for Roth. We're serving it tomorrow. So we'll be heading to Bozeman early."

"Call the local PD for backup," he advised.

But Levi didn't think they'd need it. "It's just the old lady and her son. I doubt either of them will be a problem. I still don't quite get why Christopher Roth is being so accommodating. If anything, it's his mother that's digging her heels in. Doesn't make sense. I guess we'll find out tomorrow what the real deal is. Sayeh thinks it might be guilt. Maybe he's relieved to finally spill the beans."

"Maybe so. Keep me apprised of the situation."

"Will do."

Sayeh finally exited the house, wiping her eyes as she returned to the car. He was afraid to ask, so he waited for her to share first.

"She knew." Sayeh looked heartbroken. He wanted to hold her so tight all her broken pieces mended together like magic. "She said she always suspected but hoped she was wrong. When I returned to town after all these years, she saw me and immediately saw the resemblance."

"Are you okay?" Levi asked, gently wiping a tear away.

She sniffed. "Not yet. But I will be. I know this is crazy but for a second I thought, maybe, she was just as broken by this news as I was. I saw a flash of pain in her eyes that I can only imagine was a wife who'd realized the depth of her husband's betrayal. But then she basically tossed me out of her house and told me that she never wanted to see my face again or she'd have me arrested for trespassing."

"I'm sorry, babe," Levi said, ready to put some distance between this pain for Sayeh. "Let's get out of here."

"I need to talk to my sisters. Luna should be home today and Kenna has the day off. I need to tell them."

"Whatever you want to do," he said, pulling out of the driveway and hitting the road to Luna's house. He could tell her about the warrant later. Right now, she needed to focus on her family stuff.

As they drove, Sayeh silently cried. Tears dribbled down her face, but she stoically held in any sound as she texted her sisters, letting them know she was heading to the house. When they got to the house, she turned to him with a question, and he knew. "I'll be right here," he assured her.

"Thank you," she whispered, reaching over to kiss him soundly, the taste of her tears breaking his heart.

Then she disappeared into the house. He figured he'd be out here for a while, so he closed his eyes and prepared to take a nap, knowing if anyone could help heal her heart, it would be the women inside that house.

Chapter 27

There was a time for grief and a time for focus—and focus was the order for the day as they prepared to bring Christopher Roth in for questioning.

Sayeh's cast was a cumbersome irritation as she tried to find a comfortable position in the passenger seat. "I feel like the tin man, except I'm wrapped in plaster. I can't wait for this thing to come off."

"I think we should just be thankful you escaped your attack with a fractured wrist and skull when most people wouldn't have walked away from that experience."

"That's me, the Unsinkable Molly Brown," she quipped, though Levi was right. She ought to stop complaining when she was fortunate to be alive. "At least it wasn't my dominant hand," she grinned. "I went to the range the other day and can still hit the target with only one hand." She swiveled an air pistol and blew away the imaginary smoke. "I felt like Billy the Kid—and impressed the range master. Win-win in my book."

Levi laughed, shaking his head. "You got signed off to have your sidearm with only one functioning hand?"

"Well, you probably don't know this but I placed top of my class in marksmanship. I only need one hand to be a badass."

"Thankfully, I doubt we'll need your Billy-Badass skills today. Christopher Roth doesn't seem the type to get squirrelly. He'll likely have his lawyer and mother there squawking but other than that, it should be pretty low-key."

"I'm just happy to have forward movement," Sayeh said, smiling.

Yesterday was awful, but today was a new day—and arrest warrants always cheered her up. It was the one thing she missed about working Narcotics. The drug busts were always epic and exciting.

"One time when I was working Narcotics, we busted a drug deal in an abandoned warehouse and the only shot was an impossible angle that no one was willing to take, but I saw the situation escalating and took the shot. Let's just say, I saved the day. We got the arrest and managed to take $3.2 million in cocaine off the streets. Overall, it was a good day—but then their lawyer got them off on a technicality and we had to start all over. Defense lawyers for bad guys are the true cockroaches of the legal system."

"Some defense attorneys are good people. Remember, justice is supposed to be blind," he teased.

Sayeh grinned with a shrug. "Whatever."

The BIA was a bit more low-key than working Narcotics. *Yeah? Tell that to my broken skull.* Okay, so *most* of their work had been low-key in comparison. *And what about the dead homeless guy?* He might not consider their casework low-key. *By the way...* "Has there been any movement on the forensics from the Daniel Irontail case yet?"

Levi remembered, "Oh, yeah, I saw something in my inbox before we left this morning. I figured I'd open it up after processing the warrant. Go ahead and check for me." He handed her his cell, and Sayeh opened his work email.

She clicked the message, frowning as she read. "The

DNA found on the bracelet matched Echo's, which confirms it belonged to her, but there was also an unknown DNA contributor. Analysis excluded Daniel Irontail's DNA. No match in CODIS, either."

Sayeh typed in a response. Cross-reference against DNA collected from Christopher Roth ASAP.

"If Christopher Roth's DNA is on that bracelet, that's pretty good circumstantial evidence that he was with Echo the night she died."

"A confession would pair nicely with that circumstantial evidence," Levi said. "Maybe we can get him to spill his guts with a little prodding."

"Might be fun," Sayeh said with a grin.

"Might be," he agreed.

Just as they approached the Bozeman city limits, a text from an unknown number came to Levi's phone.

Sayeh frowned, sharing, "Change of plan. You just got a text from Roth's secretary with a new address. She says that Olivia and Christopher Roth would like you to meet them at their winter cabin. The address is 1422 Walker Road, Thalía…" She plugged the address into the GPS. "Looks like it's a bit out of town, up the mountainside."

"At least the view will be pretty," Levi said.

"Yeah, but why the change?" Sayeh asked, disliking sudden switches. Nothing good came from changes out of the blue. "Maybe we ought to call for backup."

But Levi wasn't worried. "Mrs. Roth is a stuck-up old biddy who cares more about appearances than anything else. She probably just wants to make sure there isn't an audience for what's coming. An out-of-the-way place is preferable to one in the middle of downtown where anyone could see law enforcement showing up on the property. She wasn't exactly welcoming the first time we visited."

That made sense, but Sayeh still didn't like it. Her good mood was slowly evaporating. The last time something like this happened in her career, her informant died. Memories like that were hard to shake.

As they detoured out of the city and headed up the mountain, the scenery was breathtaking—and the homes were so outside of her tax bracket they might as well be on the moon. "Must be nice to be filthy rich," she mused. "Ever wonder how people afford these places? Like what kind of job does one have to have to afford stuff like multimillion-dollar homes?"

"My brother runs a multimillion-dollar cattle ranch but all the money goes right back into the business. He's what's known as *cash poor* and *land rich*."

"Yeah, well, something tells me the people footing the bill for these—" she gestured to the passing billionaire rustic playground "—aren't cash poor."

Levi laughed, agreeing, "Yeah, definitely not."

The driveway leading up to the Roth cabin was smooth pavement lined with ash trees on both sides. The property screamed luxury that only the truly wealthy could afford. It was secluded, private and gorgeous—but Sayeh didn't like it.

They exited the car, and Sayeh took a minute to adjust her gun, tucked in the back of her waistband.

The cabin—if you could call it that—was a vast, rambling five-bedroom log-cabin luxury style surrounded by forested trees and majestic mountaintops. Sayeh could fit her entire apartment in one room of this rich man's version of country living.

Levi knocked soundly on the front door and waited for a response. Birds screeched in the distance; otherwise, it was silent as the grave. Levi stepped back to peer around the corner. "I don't see any vehicles. Think we've been set up?"

"Maybe they're parked in the garage?"

Just as Levi moved to knock again, the door opened, and Mrs. Roth appeared wearing a chilly smile. "I see you had no trouble finding the cabin," she said.

"GPS is usually pretty solid," Levi said. "May we come in?"

"Please do," Mrs. Roth said, stepping aside and closing the door behind them. "Follow me."

Their feet on the polished hardwood was the only sound as the woman led them onto the back porch, which seemed to be in the process of a remodel, though the porch area itself remained intact. "Pardon the mess, we're changing a few things," she said with a short smile as she moved to the outside bar. "Would you care for a beverage?"

"No, thank you," Levi said, glancing around. "Is Mr. Roth joining us soon?"

Mrs. Roth smiled as she mixed a drink, ignoring Levi's question. "We bought this place as part of our new beginning after leaving Cottonwood. The minute we saw the place, we fell in love. The green trees, the swaying meadow grass, the shadow of the mountains behind us… It just spoke to a beautiful fresh start."

Sayeh didn't like the story hour. She was stalling. Why? "Money buys beautiful places, that's for sure. Is Christopher on his way?"

"No, he's not."

Levi sighed at the game the woman was playing. "What's going on?"

"I told you he was a busy man. He's at a conference in Boise, Idaho. You can't expect him to drop everything at your whim."

"You've just made this a whole helluva lot harder for him by pulling this stunt," Levi growled, pulling out his cell phone, but the woman moved faster than Sayeh would've imagined possible for a woman her age. A shot rang out, and Levi crumpled to the mahogany hardwood, blood spreading quickly beneath him in a pool. Sayeh tried to reach for her own gun, but the woman had the gun trained on her. "Don't try to be a hero. Your story ends here, my dear." She gestured. "Now, if you would kindly— and slowly—remove your gun and toss it over there, that would be lovely."

Levi couldn't breathe around the excruciating pain radiating throughout his entire body as the blood from his veins emptied faster than a bucket with a hole in it. If he didn't get medical attention quickly, his story would end here, too.

But even as his breathing became more shallow, his only thought was of Sayeh. His mouth worked, but no sound came out. He could hear everything but could do nothing.

"What are you going to do? Kill two BIA agents in cold blood?" Sayeh asked, moving closer to Levi. "Prison won't be a good look for you. There's still time to fix this. Put the gun down and let's talk it out."

"I'm not going to prison, you stupid bitch," Olivia Roth said with cold amusement. "I'm going to bury your bodies so far up the mountain that no one will ever find your bones and then I'm going to go on with my life and finally put an end to this unpleasant chapter."

Levi caught the subtle movement of Sayeh pressing the emergency button on her smartwatch, silently activating emergency services to their location. *That's my girl*, he thought with pride even as his vision clouded.

"Echo was pregnant," Sayeh said. "That's why he killed her, isn't it?"

Olivia snorted, narrowing her gaze at Sayeh in warning. "Move another muscle and I'll blow your head off."

"Something tells me you're going to do that anyway," Sayeh countered. "What's with the story hour?"

"So ready to meet your maker?" Olivia asked, shaking her head, sighing as she admitted, "You are like a cockroach with an inexplicable ability to skirt death, but I should've known, never send a man to do a woman's job."

"You hired Garrett Coleson," Sayeh surmised, and when Olivia grinned, Sayeh lifted her casted arm to caustically add, "Thank you for this. Lots of fun."

"You could've just had the good grace to die and maybe your partner wouldn't be bleeding out on my porch. Good thing I'm planning to rip it up and replace it. Blood is so hard to remove."

"And so easy for Forensics to find," Sayeh said. "Speaking of DNA, how's it feel to know you're covering up a murder for your son?"

"My son had nothing to do with that girl's death. He felt guilty for slapping her around a bit on the night she died but he didn't kill her," Olivia said, grabbing her glass, still holding the gun on Sayeh. "And if he'd known about that abomination in her belly, he would've wanted to do something stupid like marry her, which wasn't going to happen."

"Because she was Macawi?" Sayeh asked, incredulous.

"No, you idiot, because she was his half sister," Olivia hissed.

Sayeh sucked in a wild breath, shocked.

"The little slut was just like her mother. How much more was I expected to endure at the hands of that family? They just wouldn't leave us alone! She showed up at the house, making a ruckus, demanding to talk to Christopher, but Christopher and his father had already left for the airport. Christopher had a college tour scheduled in Colorado. That's when she told me about being pregnant. I tried to encourage her to get an abortion—I even offered to pay for it—but she refused. I thought if I told her the truth…she'd finally see reason and want the abortion. But she ran out of the house into the storm. At first I thought maybe the weather would take care of the problem. It was certainly cold enough, snow would come. But I couldn't take that chance. I followed her."

Levi tried to suck air into his aggrieved lungs, but it was like sucking on a straw stuck in mud. He was running out of time. By the time emergency services arrived…he might already be gone.

Hell, was this how it ended? He should've listened to Sayeh. Her instincts had been spot-on.

Too bad he might never get the chance to tell her that.

Chapter 28

Sayeh needed to keep Olivia talking, but Levi didn't look so good. The color had leached from his face, and his breathing was painfully shallow. If Sayeh was willing to guess, his lungs were filling with blood and slowly suffocating him.

Panic wasn't her style. A funny thing happened when everything was falling to crap—Sayeh's focus became razor-sharp. She saw things most people missed; time seemed to slow to a crawl as she assessed every angle.

Levi was dying.

Olivia was a killer in a designer suit who'd planned out her next two murders with cold efficiency. Sayeh held no illusions that Olivia would let her walk away from this. Olivia was also toying with her, feeding her details only because she knew nothing would come of it.

A malignant narcissist with psychopathic tendencies, perhaps? Or maybe she was just a woman pushed to her limit by circumstance and a nonexistent ability to empathize—Sayeh didn't care; she needed to get that gun off her, so she took a chance.

"How'd you do it?" Sayeh asked.

"Strangled her," Olivia answered without an ounce of remorse. "She was a tiny thing. Easy to stuff in my trunk and take her someplace while I thought of a plan."

"She was carrying your grandchild," Sayeh said, marveling at the woman's callous disregard for human life.

Olivia snarled. "That *thing* should've never happened. I was just correcting a horrible mistake. The stupid girl brought it on herself." She shrugged, saying, "Anyway, glad to be finally done with this horrid chapter. Now maybe with you gone, this case will die with you."

This was her last chance to make something happen. Olivia took her attention away from Sayeh for a heartbeat to drain her glass, and Sayeh sprang into action, using her cast as a weapon. She reared back and cracked Olivia across the face with the hard plaster, splintering the older woman's facial bones like brittle kindling and sending her gun flying.

Blood sprayed from Olivia's broken nose, but she still had a surprising amount of fight. Sayeh had just enough time to roll to the dropped gun, pick it up and fire a shot, knocking the woman through the plate glass window behind her. Sayeh shielded her face as glass shattered everywhere, but she quickly scrambled to her feet to ensure Olivia Roth wasn't moving.

The older woman groaned as Sayeh quickly tucked her gun in her waistband, awkwardly handcuffed the woman so she wasn't a threat, and hurriedly returned to Levi. "Hold on," she whispered, fear flooding her at the realization that he wouldn't make it if EMS didn't arrive soon.

As if angels heard her silent plea, an ambulance siren splitting the air echoed off the mountain, and tears dared to crowd her eyes. "Help is coming," she promised, stroking his hair and making promises to God that she swore she'd keep if Levi survived.

There'd been too much death in her life. She couldn't take another.

Not Levi.

He meant more to her than she'd been ready to admit. He was the first person to make her want to be a better woman, partner and version of herself—and she didn't think she could do it without him.

He was the cool, calm head—the voice of reason in the center of her chaos—and she needed him in her life.

She'd even be willing to try the white picket fence and real boyfriend-girlfriend gig with him, but she didn't know how to recover if he didn't.

"You'd better not die, Levi Wyatt," she said, fighting tears. "I will never forgive you if you clock out right now. We're supposed to have a lifetime together and you're not going to cheat me of that experience. Do you hear me? Levi? Levi?" Her voice took on a shrill note as paramedics burst through the door and found them. "Levi!"

Everything after that took on a surreal quality.

Paramedics started working on Levi immediately, rolling him over on his side and puncturing the pleural space to drain the blood suffocating his lungs, but just as the blood gushed from the puncture needle, his heart stopped, and they had to shock him back into rhythm.

Another team worked on Olivia Roth, but Sayeh had nothing but cold contempt for that woman. The only reason she didn't want her to die was so she could look her in the eye when she testified against her in court.

Olivia moaned as they hoisted her onto the gurney, and the investigating Bozeman police exclaimed, "This is Olivia Roth! Careful with her!"

And Sayeh snarled in response. "She's the one who put a bullet in my partner and was about to do the same to me. She's not the victim. I don't care if you drag her behind the wagon as long as she gets there alive to face prosecution."

The man stiffened. "I've known Olivia Roth for years. She's a pillar of the community."

"She's a killer," Sayeh returned bluntly. "So don't count on her for your next community fundraiser."

Sayeh didn't trust anyone but herself to bag the evidence. She carefully picked up Olivia's gun and dropped it into an evidence bag, sealing it tight. She called Isaac to let him know what'd happened, and then she followed the ambulance to the hospital.

Now it was her turn to hope and pray by a hospital bed.

Levi heard far-off voices that sounded like gibberish, and he wondered if this was how it felt in your final moments.

Memories of Nadie floated through his head, her laughter echoing in his mind. Then he saw Sayeh—proud, strong and beautiful Sayeh in all her stubborn glory—and knew he wasn't ready for his story to end.

Not when the best part had yet to be written.

Fight, Levi.

He wanted to live. He wanted to build a life with Sayeh—whatever that may look like. He wanted to be by her side as she navigated the emotional ups and downs of her family discovery. He never wanted her to feel alone ever again.

But he couldn't do that if he died right now.

Colors swirled around him as he drifted into a cold space only to be sucked downward, and fresh pain exploded through his nerve endings.

Surviving that bullet wound was going to hurt, he realized.

But the pain would be worth it; he knew that in his soul.

Anything he had to endure to return to Sayeh would be worth it.

Hold on to that belief—you're going to need it.

* * *

Sayeh lost track of how long she sat by Levi's bedside, waiting for him to wake up, but her eyes snapped open the second she heard him groan.

"I feel like dog crap," he said in a hoarse voice, his vocal cords ravaged by the trach tube from surgery. "What happened? I think...I was shot."

A bubble of near-hysterical laughter threatened to pop from her mouth in sheer relief. The surgeons had assured her he'd come through surgery with flying colors, but she wouldn't assume anything until he opened his eyes and started talking.

"You were definitely shot," she confirmed with a watery chuckle, rising to press a kiss on his forehead. "And you did die, for about a minute, but then they got your ticker going again. You officially win the 'Best Injury on the Job' competition around the office but we all agree that's a dubious honor."

Levi chuckled weakly, then winced. "Don't make me laugh. Hurts."

"Sorry, I'll try to keep my witty banter to a minimum."

She sobered, gently smoothing his hair away from his eyes. "You really scared the shit out of me. Had me praying to God, and I never do that. Now I have a whole lot of promises to live up to and I blame you."

"Sorry," he said, his voice still weak. "I'll try not to eat a bullet next time."

"That would be great. Thank you."

"What happened?"

Sayeh drew a deep breath and exhaled before sharing the good news. "Olivia Roth was taken into custody, denied bail, and she's still sitting in jail awaiting her arraignment. Honestly, if I hadn't been so worried about leaving your side, I would've paid good money to see her in a prisoner jumpsuit. I wanted to kill her. It took everything in me not to finish the job," she admitted quietly. "The only thing that stopped me was your voice in my head reminding me that we needed her alive for a conviction."

Levi's tiny approving smile as he said, "Good job," filled her heart with joy. "She's angling for a plea bargain. She's agreed to give a full confession in return for lenient sentencing on account of her age."

"I'm never going to live it down that I was bested by an old lady, am I?"

"Well, I didn't want to say anything just yet, but yeah. It's going to be a while before we can let that go."

Levi chuckled again. "Hey, at least I'm alive to take it on the chin."

"I also want to go on record to say that my Billy-Badass skills, as you called them, took that crazy rich bitch out. Shot her through a plate glass window. It was epic. Of course, I couldn't fully appreciate the moment because of you almost dying and all, but trust me, it was damn impressive."

Levi held her gaze. "You were right."

"Well, of course I was…but could you clarify?"

"Your instincts were right. We should've radioed for backup the minute the meeting place was changed. You knew something was up and I ignored your judgment. I won't do that again."

Sayeh blinked back sudden tears. She'd spent her entire career in the FBI being second-guessed by her peers and superiors, fighting for every win, but having Levi admit he was wrong meant a lot to her. But it also made her realize it was time to let go of the past, which meant letting go of old hurts and biases. She wanted a fresh start with Levi and everything that came with it.

Levi reached up to caress her cheek. She wiped her leaking eyes, saying, "Don't you ever pull a stunt like that again. If you ever try to die on me a second time, I will kill you myself."

"Threatening to kill someone is a felony," he reminded her with a grin. "But if that's your way of asking me to be your official boyfriend... I accept."

Sayeh laughed and gingerly placed a gentle kiss on his cracked lips. "Yeah, I guess that's what I'm asking."

Levi wound his arms around Sayeh, pulling her as close as he could without aggravating his stitches, and Sayeh knew her future, no matter what it looked like, would always include Levi.

All she knew was that building a life with Levi Wyatt was all she wanted—even if it meant retiring her "lone wolf" persona and contacting HR to declare their official status.

Some things were worth the paperwork.

Chapter 29

Following Levi's release from the hospital, Sayeh took great pleasure in serving an arrest warrant for Raymond Two Feathers, and she made sure to serve the warrant when it would embarrass the man the most.

Dragging him out of a tribal council meeting, Sayeh had Raymond arrested on multiple charges—most notably obstruction of justice, accessory after the fact and the murder of Daniel Irontail.

In addition to her testimony and confession, Olivia Roth admitted to a long-standing affair with Raymond Two Feathers that extended to a lucrative business relationship with Roth Construction over the years. When Roth strangled Echo, she went straight to Raymond for help. He put Echo's body in a freezer until two weeks later and dumped her body in a panic in Yego Creek, believing the animals would take care of the corpse.

Once that detail was uncovered, Daniel's statement of Echo's body being "frozen" was actually literal, and her "secret" was her love for Christopher Roth, who, at the time, had been a self-important, entitled little prick and one who Echo had known her aunt Charlene would disapprove of.

As it turned out, the mole leaking information was an inadvertent accomplice. Russell Hawkins was sharing information with Raymond, his uncle and tribal council member, completely unaware that he'd been feeding information to the wrong person.

Russell felt terrible but learned a valuable lesson about keeping his mouth shut about any investigation, no matter who asked the questions.

Raymond couldn't take the risk that Daniel had seen him dumping the body that night and, using a long-range hunting rifle, killed Daniel the night before Sayeh and Levi were supposed to talk to him.

Christopher Roth returned from his business trip to face his mother's horrific actions and that he and Echo had been half siblings; he checked himself into a mental hospital for a near breakdown.

Sayeh actually felt sorry for the guy and hoped he found peace. The fact that he'd been innocent of Echo's murder still left her head spinning. It showed that assumptions would tank a case if you didn't follow the evidence.

The last thing Christopher said to Sayeh before checking into a mental facility, "I actually loved her," hurt her heart. Theirs was a tragic love story from start to finish with no hope of a happy ending.

Although Charlene and Luna had hit it off, Charlene was happy to return to the reservation, finally able to put Echo to rest. Once Raymond was gone from the tribal council, Sarah returned, and together they scattered Daniel's ashes in his beloved Yego Creek so he could spend eternity enjoying his happy place where he'd always felt the safest.

Solving Echo's murder was a big win for the task force, hitting the national news, gaining the momentum in the press they were hoping for and allowing Isaac to lay off the antacids briefly as the pressure subsided from the upper brass.

All that was left was the mystery of how and why Darryl and Mika Proudfoot were killed.

And that answer came unexpectedly one day via an actual letter.

Dear Sayeh,

Since our last meeting, I've had time to think, and I realize the time has come to release secrets that were never mine to keep. I've allowed my personal pain to cloud my judgment, and as I've come to the twilight of my life, I no longer have the stamina to fight a battle not worth fighting.

You see, Allen and I tried for many years for our own family. When it became apparent that conceiving wouldn't happen, bitterness became my constant companion. I envied how easily other women seemed to conceive, and it became a harsh reminder of how I'd failed as a woman.

But that was just a smoke screen for the epicenter of my unhappiness.

My marriage was a terrible thing, held together by circumstance and expectation. Divorce wasn't acceptable in my family, and Allen never would've allowed such a humiliation.

So, I persevered in the only way I knew how.

I looked the other way; I turned a blind eye.

And in return, he provided a lavish lifestyle that soothed my broken, disillusioned heart.

I can attest that the deepest cynic was once a starry-eyed romantic.

But then he showed up one night with three little girls, and even then, somehow, I knew you were his, but I didn't dare say anything. It was a figment of my overactive imagination if I didn't ask.

Then he practically gifted you and your sisters to his best friend, Bill Griffin, and I knew…he wanted his only child close enough to him that he could watch you grow without admitting he was your father.

Silently, I raged at how eager he was to bend the rules so that you and your sisters could be raised in Cottonwood. In my own way, I tried to circumvent his will, but he was far more influential than me and, ultimately, got his way.

I think he loved you in his way, and that hurt me even more deeply than I could've imagined.

The worst part is that I think he was obsessed with your mother. Mika was a beautiful woman, and you are her spitting image. I don't think she was supposed to be at the trailer that night. I don't know why she was there. All I know is that Allen left in the middle of the night like the devil was on his heels, and when he returned, he had you girls.

I don't believe Allen had a part in your parents' deaths, but I think he always knew it wasn't drug-related like the report claimed, but by that point it was too late, and an investigation would've drawn undue attention to the things he had going on the side with the tribal police chief at the time. As I said, I don't know all the details because I purposefully didn't ask.

It's unlikely anyone would know the true details at this point, but I've shared what I can. I hope it helps settle some of the mysteries left in Allen's wake.

I realize I owe you that much.

I wish I would've had the strength to walk away from Allen when I should've. To admit that our marriage was toxic, but I was in too deep, and my ego wouldn't allow such a defeat. Maybe if I'd been stronger, I could've been the one to raise you and your sisters, but I couldn't see past my own pain to embrace motherhood in a way different than I'd imagined.

In the end, Nancy was the mother you girls needed, and I was left to nurse my anger.

And here we are today.

The truth is known, and it's just a matter of time before the whole town realizes the extent of my husband's betrayal, and that's a cut I cannot bear.

By the time this letter reaches you, I'll have left Cottonwood.

However, as Allen's only child, I've left the house in your name.

I want nothing to remind me of the life I'm leaving behind.

Do with the house what you choose—live there, sell it, raze it to the ground—I no longer care.

Regards,
Vera Paul

For a long while Sayeh sat with the letter in her hand, crying for reasons she didn't understand, but by the end she felt emptied of a heavy weight she hadn't realized she'd been carrying.

It was over.

It was likely the old tribal police chief had killed Darryl and Mika for his own criminal reasons, and seeing as he and Allen Paul were both dead, no one would answer for that crime.

But knowing the answer soothed the fever that'd been burning inside her for longer than she knew.

It also felt good to know who she truly was, but her sisters put it in perfect perspective.

Luna, holding her hand and staring into her eyes with all of the intense love a big sister was capable of, reminded Sayeh of the only thing that mattered. "You are Sayeh Gemini Griffin. It doesn't matter what that piece of paper says. You're still the same baby girl that crawled into bed beside me during lightning storms yet stared down boys twice your size when you caught someone being bullied. You are our fierce, smart, badass baby sister and nothing will ever change that. Do you hear me?"

Kenna joined in, caressing Sayeh's cheek the way she used to when they were small. "Absolutely nothing could ever change that."

Sayeh understood at that moment that whatever that elusive thing she'd been searching for had been right in front of her the entire time—it just took nearly dying and then the love of her life *actually* dying and returning from the dead for her to see it.

She might be a slow learner, but it was lodged in stone once she got the lesson.

With her demons put to rest, she was ready to embrace a new life with a man worth loving and sisters anyone would be lucky to call their family.

As Nancy used to say, some blessings came disguised as rain but ended up as rainbows—and Sayeh finally understood that to be true.

* * * * *